CONCEALED

CONCEALED

CHRISTINA DIAZ GONZALEZ

SCHOLASTIC INC.

This book was originally published in hardcover by Scholastic Press in 2021.

ISBN 978-1-338-64722-8

10 9 8 7 6 5 4 3 2 1   21 22 23 24 25

Printed in the U.S.A. 40
This edition first printing 2021

Book design by Baily Crawford

FOR MY BROSKI DAVID

CHAPTER 1

THE NAME GAME

"YOUR NAME?" THE BARISTA asked, holding the paper cup in the air.

I hesitated. For a moment I couldn't remember if my name was spelled with one *n* or two. Not that it mattered much, since by tomorrow I'd have to pick a new one.

"Joanna with two *n*'s," I replied.

He nodded, scribbled something on the cup, and passed it down the line to a girl who began preparing the order.

My drink wasn't anything out of the ordinary. A tall vanilla bean frappé with two pumps of cinnamon syrup, hold the whipped cream. Nothing too easy or too complicated. Something quickly forgotten.

Sort of like me.

Didn't matter if my hair was dyed blond, red, or even its current shade of brown, I always played the part of some random homeschooled girl from nowhere in particular who usually kept to herself. I was a mix of people you might know, but could never really remember.

That had been the story for when I was called Ana, Beatriz,

Carla, Diana, Emma, Faith, Gina, Holly, and Ivette. Joanna was no different. And tomorrow it would continue, except this time with a name that began with the letter *K*.

Over the past few years it had all become a game for me. Picking a name while going through the alphabet gave me a sense of order and predictability in my highly unpredictable life. Dad had come up with the idea back when he was still the one choosing my names, but I'd decided to continue the pattern. The question was which *K* name to choose. It could last me either a couple of weeks, like Joanna, or almost a year, like when I was Carla.

I never knew.

It all depended on when my parents said it was time to move on and start over.

"Ready?" Mom asked me, glancing around the half-empty coffee shop. She'd been standing by the door looking out toward our van while I placed my order. Her hands were stuffed inside the pockets of her quilted jacket and she looked like a ball of stress. Her appearance was the direct opposite of the two women wearing yoga pants and chit-chatting behind me as they waited to order their drinks.

"Almost," I said, stepping away from the line and moving over to the pickup area. "You sure you don't want anything?"

She shook her head and got closer to me. "No, I'm fine. Just make sure you go to the bathroom. We've got about five more hours to go."

"Seriously, Mom? I'm almost thirteen. I'm pretty sure I can figure out when I need to go. Ya no soy una niñita."

Mom tilted her head, crossed her arms, and raised a single eyebrow.

"What?" I feigned ignorance, but she was onto me. My using Spanish to soften her up or prove a point was not as effective as it used to be.

"Quizás, but you aren't grown up either." She gave me her classic "I'm not playing" stare-down. "No se te olvide."

I raised my hands in surrender. "Yes, I know. And don't worry, I already went to the bathroom. Figured that the next time might involve some sort of hole in the ground."

Mom's shoulders relaxed and her face softened. "There will be a bathroom on board, and your father has already read up on how to dump the waste. Think of it as a fun adventure."

"Yeah," I muttered. "Real fun. Can't wait to live out of an RV."

"Well, it'll be practical. We can take it with us when we want to move. Park it in another town. Have a little more continuity." Her tone was overly positive and meant to make us both feel better.

It wasn't working.

We both knew that, eventually, when we were forced to move again, we would have to leave everything behind. If it didn't fit in a suitcase, it couldn't come with us. That was another one of the rules.

Or at least it used to be. I wasn't so sure about our rules anymore, because small-town living in an RV seemed to go against all our prior moves to big cities where we could easily disappear by blending in, hiding in plain sight, and never standing out.

But an RV park in the middle of Georgia . . . that was something else completely. It felt like people there might take notice of us.

"Small-town people are friendly," Mom continued. "I still remember how it was when I was young and living in Cuba. You'll be surprised at how quickly you might be able to make a friend or two."

"Yeah, right," I muttered. Friendships took time. The only real friend I'd had was when we'd lived in Houston almost two years ago. Not too many kids like to hang out with the new kid who doesn't go to school.

"Joanna!" The girl called out my name and slid the drink forward on the counter.

Mom stuffed a handful of brown napkins into her purse and headed to the door. "All right, let's go."

I grabbed the cup and smiled as I read the name on it.

Jo Ann Nah.

So much for being accurate with my name.

"Mom. Check this out." I held up the cup as we crossed the strip mall's parking lot. "Maybe we should use this as our new last name instead of the one they assigned. I think the Nah family has a better ring to it than the Davis family."

"Hmm. The Nahs." Mom tapped the side of her chin as if seriously considering the idea before she opened the van door. Then she looked at me, the corners of her mouth crinkled into a smile, and she shook her head. "*Nah* . . . I don't think so."

"Ugh! That was painfully bad." I crawled over a couple of small suitcases, moved my sketchbook out of the way, and stretched across the third row, leaving the pile of duffel bags to occupy the two bucket seats in front of me.

"What was?" Dad turned to face me.

"Mom tried to make a joke," I said. "And it was almost as bad as one of yours." I showed him the cup with my name. "Seems like they thought I was part of the Nah family and Mom said 'nah.'"

"Ha! Amateur." His eyes twinkled under his dark-rimmed glasses. I approved of this new look. Shaved head and all. It was better than the blond toupee and blue contacts he used to wear. "I do have a new joke for you. When is it the best time to—"

"B, I think we should get going." Mom unfolded the map and fidgeted in her seat.

"Just a sec," he continued. "When is it the best time to go to the dentist?"

"Dad . . ." I cringed. It boggled my mind to think that my dorky dad could have ever been involved with bringing down one of the most notorious drug cartels in North America, but here we were.

"Come on," Dad insisted.

I relented, knowing he wouldn't stop until I played along. "No idea. Tell me. What time?"

"At tooth-hurty!" Dad laughed and slapped the side of his leg. "Get it? Tooth-hurty. Two thirty."

"Whoa . . . just when I thought they couldn't get worse . . . they do." I took a sip of my frappé and put it in the cup holder. "That one's like a little kid joke, too. Are you recycling them from when I was six?" I teased. "I probably didn't laugh back then either."

Dad shrugged and turned around. "Maybe," he muttered.

I'd hit a nerve, but really hadn't meant to. It wasn't my fault that I didn't remember anything from before I was ten. The accident wiped away almost all my memories and my parents refused to talk about our lives before the accident. It was as if my lack of memories was their most vivid reminder of the danger we were in and also an assurance that I wouldn't accidentally reveal who we really were. I could only cling to the few flashes of my childhood that seemed to live somewhere in my brain. Mom giving me a toy bunny. Dad telling me stories at night. Doctor visits. Lots of doctor visits.

And yet my parents still didn't fill in the gaps.

They liked having a clean slate to start over, but I didn't.

I hated not remembering who I used to be. It was as if none of us had existed before the accident, but I knew that we had. There was a normal life in our past—I only wished my parents would tell me about it or at least tell me our real names. I had never slipped up, not even once. Now I was old enough to be trusted. But they didn't see it that way. Which meant I had to eavesdrop and sneak together little pieces of information to learn more about who we were.

"B . . ." The concern in Mom's voice pulled me out of my thoughts. "Over there." Mom pointed to a car with dark-tinted windows parked on the corner. "It's got Virginia plates and the driver left the engine running. He's now standing by the Starbucks door, wearing sunglasses. He got out of the car and spoke to the women that were with us inside, but he hasn't gone in to get a drink. He's just looking around."

The ability to quickly notice even the smallest details was a trait that made Mom an excellent lookout. It also made her a little paranoid.

I slunk down in my seat. This wasn't the first time I'd been in this type of situation.

"It's probably nothing," Dad said, but his demeanor had changed and I could hear a bit of an edge in his voice. "X suggested the move this time only as a precaution. How could they find us here in the middle of nowhere?"

Agent X. That was the name of our contact in the Witness Protection Program. The person in charge of keeping us safe. All I knew about him was that Mom and Dad trusted him above everyone else because Dad had known him in the Before Time.

"I just don't like it," Mom insisted. "Let's get out of here."

Dad pulled out of the parking lot and headed to the main road. The van, like every car we'd ever had, was old, but it was in good enough shape to get us where we needed to go.

"All right. Which way, L?"

B and L. That's how my parents referred to each other. It was a way to simplify things and avoid messing up each other's names. It also made sense since Dad always used different names that either started with *B* like Bradley or Bernard, or a name like William or Robert whose nickname could be Bill or Bob. Mom did the same thing, except hers were usually Spanish-sounding names like Lucia or Leticia.

"Make a left on the main road." Mom studied the map in her hands. "The highway should be up ahead."

I turned around and popped my head over the top of the seat just in time to see the man jump into his car.

Mom had also been watching him through the side-view mirror. "We need to go faster. *Now.*"

"I got it." Dad's fingers were clenched tight around the steering wheel, but he remained with the flow of traffic as our van crossed the intersection and approached the on-ramp for the highway. "I'm trying to blend in."

"Dad." My voice cracked a little. I knew the story about the car accident that had almost killed my mother and me. It's what had started everything. A car had run Mom off the road in order to send a message about what happens to people who testify against the cartel. Mom hadn't been seriously hurt, but I'd barely survived. "The guy . . . he's still back there, and I think he's going to get on the highway, too."

This time Dad floored the gas pedal and we lurched forward, passing several cars. The van seemed to shake with excitement at being pushed to its limit.

I glanced ahead at the empty highway and then back at the car that was growing ever closer to us. "He's gaining on us—go faster!"

Suddenly, Dad slammed on the brakes and I went tumbling forward, slamming my head against the back of the bucket seat.

The mysterious car quickly switched lanes and zoomed by, not even giving us a second look.

"You okay back there?" Dad called out.

"I'm okay," I said, rubbing my forehead. "Should've had my seat belt on."

"You always need to have it on." His eyes met mine for an instant through the rearview mirror. "But if you got scraped up or anything, the medicine bag is in between the seats. The blue liquid for cuts and scrapes is in there."

"I'm okay," I repeated, buckling myself up. "I don't need it."

Mom chuckled nervously as we resumed a normal speed. "Guess that was a little bit of an overreaction on my part."

Dad let out a deep breath. "Ya think?" Then he cracked a smile. "But it's good practice." He reached over and patted her hand. "You never know."

I slumped back into my seat. My heart was still racing but everything was back to normal . . . or at least our version of normal.

This was the only life I knew.

A life on the run.

Never revealing who we were. Never dropping our guard. Never forgetting that there were people who wanted us dead.

Always wondering if this would be the day they'd find us.

CHAPTER 2

MEET K

THE SOUND OF PEOPLE talking right outside the van stirred me from my sleep. I lifted my head and saw my dad in the glow of the headlights, speaking to a bearded, hipster-looking guy in a flannel shirt. Off to their right was an RV parked among several tall trees, and farther down the small paved road were the twinkling lights of other trailers.

By the look of things, we had arrived at our new home.

All of a sudden, the van door slid open.

"Yes, this is our daughter," Mom said, motioning for me to get out. "And we have no pets . . . never will. Allergies, you know."

An older woman, with short blond hair and wearing reading glasses that hung at the edge of her nose, glanced around the van.

"Like I said before, not many kids around these parts, but they are allowed. Just sign the bottom where it says you're aware of the park's rules and regulations," she said to Mom as I crawled out. "Initial on the left where it says no money is due since the year was already paid for." She pointed to the clipboard Mom was holding.

I stretched my arms and cracked my back before taking a few steps away from the van.

"I think your family will really like living here," hipster guy said. "The RV might not drive very well, but it worked well enough for my uncle." Hipster guy handed my dad an envelope. "Title is in there with the keys, and I think your wife just signed everything Mrs. Huntley needed, so I guess that's it."

I took a few steps over to our new home.

It looked like an old bus with fewer windows. There was a part of it that popped out on the side, and the front windshield had a long crack running down the middle. The word *Sightseer* was scribbled along the side, but from the looks of it, I doubted the RV had seen any sights other than this trailer park. This was not a glamorous rock star bus.

I had gone up the two small steps to the front door when I heard Mrs. Huntley call out. "Mrs. Davis, Mrs. Davis! You left this line blank on the form. What's your daughter's name and age?"

Mom and I quickly locked eyes. I had fallen asleep before choosing a name for myself.

"Oh . . . um, well, that's K," Mom said. "And she's twelve."

"K-A-Y?" Mrs. Huntley asked.

Mom had just bought me about three seconds to come up

with a name. Now I had to say what my full name was or get stuck with the name Kay.

"No. It's short for Katrina," I explained. "My mom sometimes calls me K."

"Sure, whatever." Mrs. Huntley wrote my name down on her form. "If you need anything, which I expect you won't, I'm in the management office from nine to two and I live in the last trailer by the creek if there's some sort of emergency."

"I'm sure we'll be fine," Dad called out, taking one of our suitcases from the van as hipster guy waved goodbye.

"All right. Well, good night, then." Mrs. Huntley turned around and walked down the paved road, using her phone's flashlight to light the way.

"Katrina, huh?" Mom whispered as she got closer to me. "I like it."

I didn't respond since I'd learned not to get attached to any name. Instead, I pulled open the RV door and was overwhelmed by the smell of lemon-scented disinfectant. A momentary flash of being in a hospital room with doctors in surgical masks flooded my brain, but then just as quickly it disappeared. Now I could smell the mustiness that the lemon deodorizer had been trying to cover up.

Mom reached over and flipped on a light switch.

I stepped inside and analyzed what would be my home for the foreseeable future. The door had opened into what would be considered our living room, with a swivel chair to my right and a skinny, flowered sofa jutting out from the trailer wall in front of me. The front windshield had curtains drawn against it, but the driver and passenger seats still faced forward as if there was an expectation that the RV would be going somewhere.

Immediately to my left was the tiniest kitchen I had ever seen. A table with booth seating was squeezed next to the sofa. Farther down I could see the bedroom and the back of the trailer.

The "tour" of my new house didn't even take five seconds.

"Let's air this place out a bit," Mom said, opening one of the screened windows.

I glanced around the place once more. "There's no bathroom?" I asked with dread.

"Of course there is," Dad answered, stepping inside. He opened up a small door across from the refrigerator to reveal a toilet, shower, and sink. "There's even a closet in here for storage."

"And I'm guessing this skinny thing is my bed." I patted the floral couch under the window.

"It's not just a sofa—watch what it does." Dad walked over with a bounce in his step as if he was a little kid showing off his newest toy. He pushed and pulled the top of it. "Wait, I know there's a trick." He adjusted the bottom and then the seats slid forward, with the back falling flat to create a bed. "Voilà!"

"Very nice, B," Mom said very matter-of-factly. "It will

suit our needs just fine." She gave Dad a peck on the cheek. "This will work."

"I think so," he said, adjusting his glasses and smiling at her. "This Winnebago may have seen some better years, but it'll do . . . at least for a while."

Mom opened up the suitcase with some of our clothes and began putting them in the drawers. "So here we are, the brand-new Davis family. Bingham, Laura, and Katrina. Just a typical family wanting to live off the grid for a while . . . everyone got that?"

"Got it," Dad replied with a smile.

I stayed silent. They knew I didn't like this plan.

"M'ija?" Mom asked, putting a hand on my shoulder.

"Yeah, I know the drill." I shrugged her off and headed to the door. "I'm going to get my things. Maybe I can make friends with the squirrels or whatever else lives out here."

"Sweetie." Dad took a step toward me. "You know we—"

"B." Mom blocked him. "Give her some space."

I was almost at the van when I heard a rustling in the bushes nearby. My ears perked up and my body became very still.

We were in the middle of nowhere and who knew what animals called this place home.

I waited, but there wasn't another sound except for the loud droning noise of crickets or cicadas or whatever nasty insects were out in the woods.

"Just get your stuff and go," I said to myself, inching

toward the van with its open door. The overhead light was on and I could see my large duffel bag wedged between the middle seats. I pulled on the straps, but it was stuck.

There was no sound or movement, but something made the tiny hairs on the back of my neck rise up. I was keenly aware of my surroundings and something felt off. I crawled back out of the van and looked around. I got the sensation that someone or something was watching me.

It was fight or flight. I could run back inside the RV or face my fears and get my bag.

It didn't take me more than a second to decide.

Even though all my family did was run away, that's not who I was going to be. I'd be a fight-not-flight kind of girl.

I crawled back into the van and found the strap that'd been caught under one of the seats. Moving it aside, I dragged the bag out with me until a hand grabbed my shoulder.

Instinctively, I screamed at the top of my lungs, dropped the bag, and swung my fist.

"Whoa! Hey! It's just me," Dad said as the porch light from the closest trailer flickered on.

My heart was beating so hard that it felt like it would pop through my sweatshirt. "Oh," I said, trying to catch my breath. "Right."

So much for my warrior attitude. I had reacted like a scared little girl with my punch flailing through the air.

"Guess our neighbors now know we've arrived." Dad chuckled as he handed me the bag.

"Yeah, I didn't mean to mess up our low profile."

Dad cupped my face in his hands. He kissed my forehead like when I was little. "It's not even nine o'clock. It's fine to let them know that the Davis family is here. Hopefully we'll be here for a long while."

I glanced over at the neighbor's RV, where I could now see that whoever lived there had set up some plastic flamingos and a collection of garden gnomes along the front. The one saving grace was the fact that there was a skateboard shoved under one of the Adirondack chairs.

I sighed.

Maybe there was a chance that this place wouldn't be completely awful.

CHAPTER 3

THE PARKER INITIATIVE

THE NEXT DAY MY parents woke up with a plan to make the RV feel more like home. After a morning spent putting away all our belongings, Mom made a list of things we needed, including new curtains, outdoor chairs, and groceries. Dad, meanwhile, inspected every nook and cranny like he always did when we moved someplace new. Soon I was given a choice. Either go to Walmart with Mom or stay and help Dad. The decision was easy.

I'd stay with Dad.

"So, you want me to teach you how to empty the tanks?" Dad asked as soon as Mom left in the van.

I was sitting outside on the RV's lowest step with my sketchbook on my lap. "Do I really have to learn how to do that?" I asked, fearing what his answer might be.

I'd chosen to stay behind because I wanted to finish the drawing of our former neighborhood before the details began to fade. My sketchbook was the only recording of where we'd been and the people we'd met. It was my alternative to photographs since those were strictly forbidden. As was all internet or cell phones, for fear that they could somehow be traced.

Dad gave me a wink. "Just kidding, pumpkin. But let me know if you find anything broken or loose. I'm playing the role of Mr. Fix-It today."

"And tomorrow?" I opened the book to a page with several apartment buildings and a lone tree on the corner. "What role will you be playing then?"

Dad raised his hand in a mock salute. "World's Best Short-Order Cook is here and ready to find a job!"

"Again?" I shook my head. "I thought you were going to pick something else this time."

"Meh." He shrugged. "I put myself through grad school doing that and no one seems to ask too many questions. It's not a bad gig."

I gave my dad a long look. A while back Mom had let it slip that she and Dad used to be research scientists. Dad was always in a lab and she would hide away in libraries, but destiny brought the two of them together. They ended up working on projects together and fell in love. Then, because Dad made one mistake and got involved with the wrong people, this was his life.

This was *our* life.

"Hey, don't be staring at me like that," he said. "This isn't going to be forever. One day it'll all be over and things will go back to normal, okay?"

I nodded, not really believing him. "Okay," I said, looking down at my sketchbook.

"It will get better," Dad muttered as he opened the kitchen door. "It has to."

I didn't argue with him. I also didn't want to think too much about the future. Eventually, I would be too old to be on the run and living with my parents . . . then what? Would I have to choose between them and having a normal life?

I focused on my drawing instead of thinking about those things.

I thought about the people I'd met back in Oakland. The guy who ran the bodega and the little girl who lived across the hall from us. I wasn't that good at sketching faces, but I was getting better. I hadn't lived there long enough to miss anyone, but it was still important for me to have a record of them.

Minutes became hours. One drawing became two, which then became four. Mom came back and was giving the RV a thorough cleaning, but I barely moved. I was completely focused, taking only a short break for lunch and to switch over to one of the lounge chairs Mom had bought and placed in front of our trailer.

"Parker! Parker!" a raspy voice yelled as the sun began to set.

I glanced up to see our new neighbor, a heavyset woman wearing several blue rollers in her gray hair, yelling toward the woods. She had a large red purse under one arm and was trying to straighten one of the plastic flamingos that wanted to remain tilted at a forty-five-degree angle.

"Hey, neighbor!" the woman called out to me. "Been watchin' you over there all day. Busy doing some homework, huh?"

I gave her a small wave and stayed quiet. The art of keeping secrets began with not answering questions.

"You seen a boy about your age around here?" she asked. "He's not answering me."

I shook my head.

"Figures. Wouldn't be the first time he wandered off. Got no initiative for schooling or otherwise. If he pops up, you tell him I went to Suzanne's and he's on his own for dinner."

"Um, maybe it'll be easier if you send him a text," I suggested, not wanting to be a messenger.

"If I could do that, why would I be asking you to tell him?" she scoffed as she walked to her green pickup. "Kids always think they know so much."

The moment the truck disappeared down the street, a boy about my age with black curly hair popped out of the woods. Our eyes locked and he grinned. A lopsided, mischievous one that made me crack a smile.

That seemed to be the only invitation he needed to come over.

"Thought she'd never leave," he said, plopping down on the lounge chair next to me. "So, I guess you're the newbies."

I looked around to see where Mom and Dad were, but

they were busy inside the trailer. Not that I should worry about them seeing me talk to someone. We were loners, but we weren't completely rude either.

"FYI . . . there isn't much to do around here. Not sure where you're all from, but this place is beyond boring." He stuck his hand out. "I'm Parker, by the way."

I hesitated for a moment and then shook his hand. "I figured."

Parker chuckled and leaned back in the lounge chair. "Yeah, unfortunately, you'll probably be hearing my name yelled all the time. Seems like there are always chores for me to do. That's why I disappear sometimes."

"She mentioned that," I answered.

"Oh, I'm sure she did. Probably talked about my 'lack of initiative,' too. She always likes telling people that. You'd think she gets paid to say that."

I didn't confirm or deny.

"By the way, do you have a laptop or phone I could use? I haven't been on the internet in forever."

I shook my head. "Sorry. My parents like being off the grid. They're weird like that."

"No worries. Mrs. Anderson only lets me use her old flip phone when I go out so I'm basically cut off, too."

I wasn't sure who Mrs. Anderson was, but I figured that it was likely the old woman. Before I could ask, Dad poked his head out the door.

"Hi there." He gave Parker a slight wave. "Are you one of our new neighbors?"

Parker jumped up. "Uh, yes, sir. I live right over there." He pointed to the trailer next door. "The gnome home."

Dad tried not to smile, but the corners of his mouth lifted ever so slightly. "Gnome home . . . funny," he muttered, before becoming serious again.

I rolled my eyes. He *would* like something corny like that.

Dad stepped out of our RV and walked toward Parker with his hand extended. "I'm Mr. Davis."

"Parker," he said, shaking hands with Dad. "Parker Jimenez."

"Nice to meet you." Dad gave Parker the once-over. "And how old are you, Parker?"

"Thirteen."

"Mm-hmm." Dad evaluated his height and build. "Pretty tall for your age, huh?"

Parker shrugged. "I guess."

To me he seemed like a regular, skinny kid. I couldn't understand why Dad was acting so strange.

"Do you go to school around here?" Dad asked him.

"No." Parker looked down at the ground and shifted his weight from one foot to the other.

"No?" Dad waited for an explanation.

"Um, no, sir. I moved here a few months ago, at the end of January. I did online schooling, but I'm sure the local school is good. Mrs. Anderson knows a bunch of people and—"

"Oh, I'm homeschooled, so you don't need to explain that part," I said, interrupting him.

Dad got closer to us. "And who is Mrs. Anderson? Is that your—"

"Da-a-a-d." This was starting to feel like an interrogation.

"What? Just getting to know our new neighbor. You don't mind, do you, Parker?" Dad smiled to soften all the questioning.

Parker's eyes locked in on my dad's. "She's my foster parent," he said without blinking or smiling. "My mom died a while back."

"Oh, I see." Now Dad was the uncomfortable one. "I'm sorry about that."

Parker glanced over at his trailer. He was probably thinking that being with Mrs. Anderson was better than getting the third degree from some stranger's father.

I had to stop this. "Hey, Parker. Mrs. Anderson wanted me to tell you that she went to Susan's or Suzanne's for dinner."

Parker nodded and took a step back. "Oh yeah. Thanks. Better go make myself something."

"Nonsense," Mom said through the open RV window. She had obviously been listening to the entire conversation. "I insist that you join us. I'm making burgers. It's nice for Katrina to have made a friend on her first day here. Especially a nice boy."

I could feel my cheeks getting hot and turning red.

"B, why don't you come in here and help me for a minute?" Mom added, her voice a little stern.

Dad gave Parker a last once-over before he headed inside.

I glanced over at Parker. "Please ignore my parents," I whispered. "I already told you they're weird. You don't have to stay."

Parker seemed to relax a little. "They're not so bad. And I guess you're Katrina?"

"One and only." I smiled. "And you really don't have to eat with us."

"Hmm." He held out his hands as if weighing his options. "Cereal or homemade burgers? Tough choice, but I think burgers sound pretty good."

"Not when they come with a heaping side order of my parents."

Parker laughed and it sounded a little goofy, which made me like him even more. "I'll take my chances," he said with a wink. "I like to live dangerously."

I kept my mouth shut.

He had no idea what a dangerous life really was.

CHAPTER 4

PHOTOGRAPHIC EVIDENCE

WE'D ONLY BEEN LIVING in the trailer for a couple of days, but I had to hand it to Mom—it was already beginning to feel like home. It was a bit cramped, but we were all getting into a routine. It was nice to wake up to the smell of coffee brewing a few feet away from me and, while I got dressed in the small bathroom, Dad would turn my bed back into a sofa and Mom would set up breakfast for the three of us.

"Any plans for today?" Mom asked as I slid into the booth to have my bowl of cereal.

I stayed quiet, assuming that she was talking to Dad.

"Katrina?" Mom stared at me over the rim of her coffee mug.

"What? Me?" I glanced over at Dad, who was buttering his toast, and he gave me a slight shrug.

"Well, yes. Your father's going to keep looking for some work and I thought you and Parker might have talked about doing something today."

I rolled my eyes at her. "Mom, I just met him. We're not, like, best friends or anything."

"Parker . . . humph," Dad grunted while stuffing a piece of toast into his mouth. "Have you seen how much trouble he gives Mrs. Anderson? All I hear is her yelling his name, day and night."

Mom shook her head. "I think he's a nice kid in a tough situation. Mrs. Anderson doesn't seem to be very . . . um . . . nurturing."

"I guess," Dad replied as he took a sip of coffee. "But let's talk about something else. How about I get us a movie while I'm in town? I'm thinking a comedy."

"I'll take anything that's new," I replied. "Like within the last few months. Doesn't matter what it is."

"The older ones are usually cheaper, though," Mom countered. "And your dad doesn't have a job yet."

The rest of the breakfast conversation was centered around the pros and cons of getting several old movies or just a recent one. As we put away the dishes, Mom suggested that I take the morning off from schoolwork and go to the stream by Mrs. Huntley's trailer to draw some nature scenes.

"By herself?" Dad questioned the idea, the van keys already in his hand. "We don't really know the area or the people around here. I'd feel better if you went with her."

"It'll be fine," she said. "I checked it out yesterday and it's very picturesque and safe. I'll go by after I'm done with the laundry."

I wasn't going to argue against anything that got me out of having to do schoolwork.

"Sounds great!" I grabbed my art notebook and a pencil, gave Mom a quick peck on the cheek, and dashed out the door before anything else could be said.

The morning sun was rising over the trees that lined the path to the stream, casting golden beams of light through the branches. I loved the way it all looked. The green of the leaves, the gray cracked asphalt, and the blue cloudless sky above. It all called out for me to re-create it in my notebook . . . but I'd need my colored pencils, which I'd left in the RV.

As I rounded back, I saw that our van was still parked in front. I threw back my head and sighed. I couldn't risk going inside and having Dad tell me to stay. I'd have to make do with a regular pencil.

I was about to walk back to the stream when I heard Dad's voice filter through an open window. I was still too far away to hear what he was saying, but I could tell he wasn't happy.

I crouched down and tiptoed closer. I'd discovered long ago that, in a family full of secrets, you had to take every chance to eavesdrop, because that was the best way to get information.

"I don't like it," I heard Dad say sternly as I got closer to the RV. "Not one bit. It's a bad idea. There aren't any real guarantees."

"But think about it—there has to be a way to go back to what we were doing. We can't continue like this. You are too brilliant a scientist to spend your days frying eggs. Maybe the government would allow us to go back to our old lives. X can plead our case because the impact your research would have is—"

"Is not worth it," Dad interrupted. "L, I know you're frustrated, but we're lucky to not be in jail right now. We can't take the risk."

"But the contributions you can make are bigger than just the three of us. You know that," Mom countered. "Think about it. Talk to X. He has contacts everywhere. You could resume your life's work."

I held my breath. Were Mom and Dad considering going back to being scientists? Would that mean no more life on the run?

"No. *She* is now my life's work and I won't do anything if it puts her at risk."

"Risk?" Mom sounded frustrated. "We're already at risk. Just look around!"

"I know, L. I know." I could hear the anguish in Dad's voice. "But we agreed to this life because we wanted to protect her. We're adults, we can handle the consequences . . . she's only a child."

"I'm only suggesting that we consider trying something different. We wouldn't even have to tell her what's really going on. Just that it's a new identity."

My eyes narrowed and I could feel the anger in my chest rising. More secrets? *That* was Mom's solution?

"Maybe we should tell her why we're here," Dad replied.

"Tell her what exactly?"

I held my breath, not wanting to miss a word that was about to be spoken.

"Everything," Dad replied. "We should probably tell her everything."

"Are you out of your mind?" I could imagine Mom shaking her head in disbelief. "She'd never see you in the same way if she knew the truth about what you did. Everything would change. And she's not ready to cope with all of it . . . not yet, at least."

My stomach felt queasy. What had Dad done that was so bad? Did I really want to know?

Dad didn't say anything for several seconds.

"B, she's not going to discover anything by accident. We'll tell her when the time is right, but for now we can't say anything." Mom's voice had changed and had a more soothing tone to it. "You agreed to move to a small town so that she could have some friends in a more controlled environment and become more independent. Let this play out a little. Then we can discuss things again."

I could hear Dad pacing around in the RV. "You're right, of course. I just wish things were different. That we could give her a more normal life."

"Well, part of being normal is having friends, and Parker seems like a good one."

"Humph. He seems like trouble."

Mom chuckled. "I think any boy would look like trouble to you."

Dad's voice softened. "Maybe."

"Listen, whether it's him or someone else, we can afford to give her some more freedom here. Better to start now than when she hits the teen years and really wants to rebel against us. This will keep her happy for a while."

Buying me off with a little bit of freedom. That's what Mom was trying to do, but it wasn't going to work. Not anymore. I now knew that Dad wanted to tell me things and I'd just have to wait for the right moment to get some answers from him.

Spying most definitely had its benefits.

"A teenager." Dad sighed. "I don't know. I like the little girl we've raised."

"Well, we're all going to have to make adjustments. Best to start wrapping our heads around it. Changes are coming whether we like it or not."

⸻

Seven days.

One measly week.

That's all it took for me to completely change my mind

about moving to a small town. Sure, there were a lot fewer people than what I was used to, but I kind of liked that. I especially liked that Parker and I had become friends. That might not have happened in a big city, where he could have hung out with tons of other people. Here, I was his only choice.

"Hey, Katrina!" Parker called. "Check this out!" He zoomed by, popped up his skateboard, flipped it in the air, and then stuck the landing before spinning to a stop. "Sweet, huh? Want to try?"

"Can't. Have to finish my work." I lifted up my notebook as proof.

"Take a break. Come on. It's a perfect day. Sun is out, it's pretty warm, and Mrs. Anderson is still out bowling. The math or English you're doing can wait." He held out the skateboard. "Come on, I'll show you how to do it."

"I know how to ride a skateboard," I said, tossing the notebook on the lounge chair and walking over to him. "And today it's Russian, but I get your point."

"Russian? Isn't that kind of a weird thing to be studying?"

"Have you met my parents?" I tossed my hands in the air in mock exasperation. "They are the definition of weird. My mom figured that if she learned it when she was in school in Cuba, then I should, too."

"Cuba? So, you're Latina!" He gave me a half smirk. "No wonder we get along so well." He studied me for a moment and nodded. "Guess I can see it. You look like you could be anything, though. A big mix of stuff. Sorta like me. My mom was from Virginia, but my dad is from Santo Domingo."

I nodded, unsure what else to do or say. I wanted to pull back everything I had just said.

How could I have been so careless in sharing a real fact about my family? I shouldn't have mentioned being part Cuban. The backs of my ears were getting hot and I could feel myself starting to sweat. *Are my parents right that I can't be trusted with too much information?*

"Hey, so do you know Spanish?" Parker continued. "'Cause mine sucks and I can barely talk to my dad's family back in the DR. Maybe you could help me out when I call them."

"Sure," I said, taking the skateboard and placing it on the ground. "If you want me to."

"That'd be awesome. I'm trying to work some stuff out to maybe go live there, but they still think it's better for me here. I need to convince them otherwise."

"I'll do what I can," I said, and pushed off on the skateboard, trying my best to stay balanced and get some distance between us.

"Cool. Hey, so what about your dad?" Parker called out as I rolled down the street. "Where is he from?"

"American," I answered vaguely, making a wide turn on the skateboard and heading back. "And you said your dad is from the DR, right? Is he over there now?" I asked, wanting the focus to go back on Parker and not me.

"Who knows." He shrugged. "He bailed on me when I was

a baby, but I have my grandpa over there . . . but he's pretty old and not really with it anymore."

I rolled to a stop in front of Parker as he let out a long sigh. "I've talked to a couple of my dad's stepbrothers . . . guess they're like my stepuncles. Never met any of them, though. Those are the ones you can help me with."

"Uh-huh." There was too much talk about families. I needed to change the subject. "So, those quick turns on the board . . . can you teach me how to do them?"

"Yeah, sure. They're easy. Here, I'll show you." Parker stepped on the skateboard. "It's called a kick turn and, when you're riding, you put your back foot on the tail and let the front lift up." He did it as he explained. "Then swivel in the direction you want to go. Now you try it . . . but slow."

"I got this," I said, not wanting to stick around too much longer in case he wanted to talk some more. I pushed off, gained some speed, and that's when I saw it. A red car with a white racing stripe down the middle. It was barreling down the road straight toward me. I tried to do the quick turn, but instead I slammed the back of the board into the asphalt, launching me headfirst into the middle of the street.

"WATCH OUT!" Parker yelled.

I froze, bracing for impact. The driver blared the horn, slammed on the brakes, and swerved, barely missing me.

Seconds later I was shrouded in a haze of dust and smoke, but alive.

"DUDE!" Parker ran toward me.

The driver, a young guy wearing a baseball cap, jumped out of the car. "Are you stupid?" He hovered over me. "You have some sorta death wish?"

Parker shoved him out of the way. "You're an idiot, Jimmy! She's the one hurt and you're yelling at her?"

Jimmy glared at Parker, his fists balling up. Both boys were about the same size and it was obvious that there was bad blood between them. This could all get ugly real fast.

I stood up and smiled, trying to defuse the situation. "I'm fine, Parker. See? Just a little accident. No big deal." I pulled Parker away.

"Aw, isn't this cute. My little cuz has a girlfriend. You think you're some sort of ladies' man now, like your pa?"

Parker glared at the boy. "She's not my girlfriend and you know we're not really family, so lay off the cuz talk."

"Sure we are," Jimmy insisted, glancing over at me. "Don't the two of us look alike?"

The two boys could not have been more different. Jimmy had pale, freckled skin with straight brown hair that clung to the sides of his neck and stuck out from the front of his cap. His eyes betrayed a shallowness and meanness that was the complete opposite of what I saw in Parker.

"Katrina!" Dad yelled, running out from the RV. "Katrina . . . are you okay?"

I turned around and waved that I was fine.

"Oh, wow. Katrina, you're bleeding," Parker pointed to my elbow, where my long-sleeved T-shirt had been torn and a deep, three-inch gash had blood oozing out.

"Nasty," Jimmy muttered, taking out his phone.

"No." I pushed his hand away just as he snapped a picture of the cut. "Delete that!" I demanded in a hushed whisper before Dad got to us. "Right now."

Jimmy shrugged. "Too late," he said, stuffing his phone back into his pocket. "Just shared it with my fans."

"You did what?" I knew all about social media and how dangerous it could be for us.

"Don't worry," Parker reassured me. "No one pays attention to his boring stories. It'll disappear with barely any views."

"Katrina," Dad interrupted us. He was a little out of breath, but his focus was on me. "What were you doing?" He turned my arm over and saw the large cut. "Look at this!"

I couldn't say anything. Thoughts were flying through my head. Not about the cut, but about the picture. Dad might not have noticed the photo being taken, but I knew the rules. No pictures. Ever.

"It's my fault, Mr. Davis," Parker said. "I was trying to teach her how to ride my skateboard and—"

Dad didn't want to hear it. He turned his back on Parker, pulling me along with him. "Let's get you cleaned up before your mother gets home."

I didn't care about my cut or the throbbing in my arm.

The only thing I could think about was Jimmy taking the photo and whether I should tell Dad. He always said that technology could be used to find us. Facial recognition software and GPS tracking were our enemies.

But my face wasn't in the picture, just my elbow. And if I told Dad about it, he would probably insist that we move again. I'd lose my one friend and the little bits of freedom I was slowly gaining. Why should this be my last day as Katrina because of some stupid picture of my bloody elbow on social media?

I glanced back at Parker and made my decision.

Silence was the only option.

CHAPTER 5

BLUE

"KEEP YOUR ARM STILL," Dad instructed as I rested my elbow on the small table. "This may sting." He dipped the eyedropper into the bottle of blue liquid and squeezed several drops onto the gash in my forearm. The liquid foamed upon contact, but didn't hurt. It was one of the few things still left over from our old life. A treatment for cuts that Dad had been working on in the lab before everything went horribly wrong.

"You doing okay?" he asked, his voice having lost the edge it had while scolding me a few minutes earlier.

I nodded, not having said much since coming inside. I knew that Dad's anger never lasted very long, especially if you let him get it out of his system.

"You know that I get worked up because . . . because I worry about what could have happened." He placed a large bandage over my cut. "That car could have really hurt you."

"But it didn't. I'm fine." I grabbed a plaid flannel shirt that I'd left in the corner and slipped it over my torn T-shirt. "Are you going to tell Mom? I mean, it'll just worry her for nothing."

"I guess we *could* forget to mention it," he said with a wink. "Just make sure you keep that cut covered so that it doesn't scar and heals quick."

"No worry there," I answered. "Your cure makes sure of that. Magic mermaid potion, remember?" I gave him a half smile, hoping that all his anger had finally subsided.

Dad laughed. "Wow. You haven't called it that in a long time. I think you used to get scratched up just to have me put some on."

"You know . . . one day when this is all over, you can sell that stuff and make millions of dollars. Revolutionize the world."

"Yeah, well, we'll see about that." He tapped my hand and I could see the shadow of sadness cross his face. "For now, it'll stay our secret."

Another secret.

We were all about secrets, but maybe this was the moment I'd been waiting for. A chance for Dad to tell me the truth.

I covered his hand with mine and held it. "Dad, was this what you were working on before the accident? The blue potion." My voice pled for a morsel of information. "I know you were a brilliant scientist and nothing heals skin like that stuff." I thought about the words Mom had used when trying to convince him about looking into another path for us. "Was it your life's work? Please talk to me."

Dad stared down at our intertwined hands. "My life's work," he muttered, and then lifted his head, but now his eyes had a faraway look, as if he had been transported back in time. "My priorities were so different then."

I leaned forward and instinctively lowered my voice. "Tell me about it." I wanted him to see that I was older now and that secrets didn't need to be kept from me. "I want to know. What was our life like . . . *before*?"

"Before . . ." A wave of sadness seemed to creep over his expression. He reached over and stroked my cheek. "You were the one who taught me what was really important. Being your dad is the best thing I've done."

"But what did you used to do? How did we get here, Dad?"

Dad pulled his hand away and straightened his back. The walls that usually kept out the past rose up again.

"I've already told you," he said in an almost monotone voice. "I lost my way in life and fell into a bad crowd for a while. There was only one way to get out, so I did what I had to do. I betrayed them. It was the right thing to do, even if this is the price we have to pay. Now let's talk about something else."

"NO!" I stood up from the table. "You don't get to push me aside again with a vague story." I stared at him. "I want to know *why* we live like this. Why the cartel is still after us." I paused to gather my courage. "I want to know exactly what you did. I deserve the truth."

I held my breath. I'd never spoken to Dad like this. Mom and I were the ones who usually argued, and even those were never really big fights.

"You don't . . ." he mumbled, and gazed out the window.

"I don't what? Don't understand? That doesn't work anymore, Dad."

He shook his head. "You're still too young."

"I'm almost thirteen . . . you owe me the truth!" I could feel my heart pounding at my temples. I had never been this angry with him. "Tell me!" I demanded.

"Owe you?" Dad looked me in the eyes. "I *don't* owe you anything." He got up and turned his back on me. "This conversation is over."

His words sliced through me. It was a wound deeper than anything that the magic mermaid potion could ever heal.

I took a step back, and with tears threatening to explode from my eyes, I ran to the door, flinging it open. I glanced at him still turned away from me. "Then you can stay living with your lies and I'll find my own truth. I wouldn't trust what you said anyway."

I stormed outside and froze, my anger momentarily paralyzing me. I wasn't a little kid anymore who he could simply push aside. I took a deep breath and looked around. I wanted answers, but how do you search for answers when you can't risk anyone else finding what you uncover?

My heart beat a little faster.

This was now my mission. The truth couldn't be concealed forever. There had to be a trace of it somewhere, but where? The only thing I knew was that a drug cartel was after us, so maybe I could start with that. Look into drug cartels that had made the news around the time of my accident. It wasn't much, but it was something.

But I'd need help. Help from someone who didn't keep secrets from me.

I glanced over at the gnomes and flamingos in front of Parker's double-wide trailer.

Parker. He was my best shot at getting some answers.

I marched over to the trailer and before I had gone up the steps, the front door flung open. "He hates me, doesn't he?" Parker blurted out, shaking his head. "I don't think he liked me much before, but now . . ."

"Who? My dad? He's fine. Don't worry about him." I paused for a moment to calm myself down. I had to be sure about what I was going to do.

"Yeah, but I should have thought—"

"Listen," I interrupted him. "You mentioned that you do online schooling. That means you're good with computers, right?"

"Well, yeah. Who doesn't know how to use a computer?" Parker scrunched his eyebrows. "What's going on?"

"We live off the grid, remember? So, I need some help doing some research. Can you help me look things up?"

"On the computer? Sure, if I still had it." Parker glanced back inside. "Hold on a minute." He took a couple of steps, and I could see Mrs. Anderson was sitting in a big chair facing a large TV. "Um . . . Mrs. Anderson, I'm going to see if the laundry's ready."

"Yeah, yeah, all right." She waved him off, noticeably bothered.

Parker walked out and closed the door behind him. "She hates to be interrupted during her soap operas. She probably wouldn't have even noticed that I'm gone." He gave me a mischievous smile. "Now, about that computer research."

"Right," I said as we walked toward the park's laundry building. "I need to look some stuff up for a project I'm doing."

"Cool. I can totally help you. All you need to do is have your parents talk to Mrs. Anderson and ask her to give me back my laptop. She gave it to Jimmy about a month ago."

"Jimmy the cousin-who-almost-ran-me-over?"

"Yeah, and he's definitely *not* my cousin. At least not by blood." Parker kicked a rock off the dirt path as we walked toward the main office and laundry shelter. "My mom's cousin is his stepmom. She took me in for a while, but that didn't work out, mainly because of Jimmy, so I got sent to Mrs. Anderson. That's all Jimmy and I have in common."

"But why did Mrs. Anderson give him your laptop?" I asked.

"She's his grandmother on his dad's side. I was only allowed to use my computer while supervised and she thought it'd be easier to just get rid of any temptation. I didn't think finishing my classes early meant losing my laptop."

"Why can't you use it unsupervised?" I asked, realizing how everyone seemed to have their own share of secrets. "Unless you don't want to talk about it."

"No, I don't mind telling you." Parker watched me out of the corner of his eye. "I have a thing with computers. I mean, not a thing, it's just I'm really good with them. Like crazy good." He paused to see if I said anything before continuing. "Anyway, one day I realized that I didn't have to get bad grades in school anymore. I could get all As if I hacked into my school's server. Ended up changing some grades for me and a few other people. Made a little money on the side."

"Oh." I didn't know how to react. It wasn't good, but it also didn't seem to be too bad. Not when you compared it to whatever my family had gotten involved with.

"Yeah, it was ridiculously easy and so I kept trying bigger challenges. Then my mom got sick and I changed some bills. After she died, I got put into foster care and I used my skills to do some other stuff to sort of get by. I even changed some computer records to get moved to a couple of different homes." He paused. "Long story short, I finally got caught when I tried to hack into the Pentagon."

"Whoa." My mouth was slightly open. This was some serious stuff. Maybe Parker wasn't the right person to approach or maybe this made him the perfect person. I wasn't sure anymore.

Parker stared at me for a moment, then doubled over laughing. "The look on your face . . ."

"Wait." I gave him a big shove, almost pushing him to the ground. "You're lying. You didn't do any of that stuff. You didn't hack into the Pentagon."

He spun around, gave me a shrug, and raced down the path. "Maybe I did and maybe I didn't. Get me a computer and find out!"

I caught up with him at the storm shelter where all the coin-operated washing machines and dryers were housed. "Tell me the truth," I said as I followed Parker over to a small bench in front of a dryer that was still shaking with its full load.

"I'm really good, but the cops caught me when I was careless with a bank. So maybe not quite Pentagon-busting good, but close." He slid a dingy white plastic basket with a broken handle in front of the dryer. "So, what do you think? Want to get the laptop for me? I mean for your project. I'm sure your parents can convince Mrs. Anderson."

"That's the thing . . ." I bit my bottom lip before going on. "My parents don't want me using any technology. I'm sort of doing this without their approval."

"Ooh." Parker smiled. "That's even better. I knew you'd add a little excitement to this place."

I sighed. "But that means we can't get the laptop."

"Not necessarily." Parker had what I could only describe as a sly twinkle in his eye. "There is a way, but it'll mean bending some rules and telling a couple of lies. You okay with that?"

I nodded. "Oh yeah. Lying is not a problem."

CHAPTER 6

BOWLING FOR ANSWERS

WHILE THE TOWELS DRIED, Parker and I hatched our plan. Parker explained that he had once tried paying Jimmy five dollars an hour in order to "rent" the laptop from him, but that Jimmy had backed out of the deal because he was afraid of what his grandmother might do if she found out. But if I was the one doing the "renting," then Jimmy might do it and we could use the Wi-Fi at the diner where Jimmy worked.

The only problem was that this meant I'd have to get permission from my parents to go to town with Parker . . . unsupervised. Not so easy.

That night, while Mom was serving dinner, I began laying my trap.

"The pasta looks good, Mom," I said, trying to butter her up. "¡Y tengo un hambre!" I rubbed my belly while looking at my plate. "I could eat a horse."

"Oh, good. I made plenty. Wasn't sure if Parker would be joining us tonight."

"Nope, Mrs. Anderson is cooking," I explained. Then, trying to keep things as casual as possible, I initiated phase one of my plan. "In fact, speaking of Parker, he asked if I wanted to go into town one of these days."

"Oh, that's nice," Mom said as she passed Dad a plate with a little bit of the alfredo sauce dripping off the side. "With Mrs. Anderson?"

I knew that if I was going to have any chance of success, then I had to stay cool, calm, and collected. I also had to blend the truth with the lies.

"Um . . . no," I said, taking a bite of pasta. "We'd just walk there by ourselves. Parker's gone before to run some errands. No big deal."

"No way," Dad said. "You don't even know the area."

"But Parker does," I answered a little more sharply than I had wanted to.

"Parker and his great ideas," Dad muttered.

"Sweetie, that's a pretty long walk." Mom tapped my hand and gave me a smile. "At least a few miles. Maybe I can take the two of you. The three of us can wander around a bit. Get some lunch. It'll be fun."

"But that defeats the purpose," I blurted out.

"And what purpose would that be?" Dad had a suspicious tone in his voice. "You know, I bet that boy can find trouble under a rock, and that's something none of us need."

"B!" Mom scolded him. "What's gotten into you?"

"That's not true and you're being completely unfair!" I lost all pretense of being relaxed and glared at Dad. He was still holding Parker responsible for my little accident with the skateboard. "You just don't like him."

"It's not just me." Dad had a callous look on his face. "I've spoken to Mrs. Anderson and she told me that he's been sent to six foster homes. Bet neither of you knew that."

"Did you know some of those people beat him?" I spat back. "What do you expect him to do? Take it?"

I had no idea if anyone had ever beat up Parker, but lying came naturally, so I went with it.

"Poor Parker," Mom mumbled, shaking her head.

Neither Dad nor I said anything else.

Mom watched our stare-down. "Did something happen between the two of you today?" she asked suspiciously.

"No." Dad and I replied at the same time.

"Uh-huh." Mom served herself a plate of food and sat down at the table.

We all ate in silence for several minutes until Dad broke the ice.

"L, I've been thinking . . ."

"Uh-oh." Mom chuckled, trying to lighten the mood. "That can't be good."

I didn't react. I still wasn't ready to be on good terms with Dad, but I couldn't keep fighting with him if I wanted to get permission to go to the diner with Parker.

Dad glanced at me. "It's time to start thinking of making some real changes."

"Changes?" Mom questioned. "Like what?"

I wasn't sure if I liked where Dad was headed with all this.

"What you said this morning. About getting back to our old jobs and lives. It's got me thinking . . ."

Mom widened her eyes. "Why don't we talk about this later, B."

"B." Dad shook his head. "I can't believe that we've gotten used to not even saying our real names." He sighed. "And with Katrina making it abundantly clear to me that she's not a little girl anymore, it's all just confirmed my thinking . . . we can't keep going like this. We shouldn't have to."

Mom was rubbing her hands like she did whenever she got nervous. "Okay, but why don't we go for a walk to talk things through?" She stood up.

"Or to get away from where I might hear things," I added, crossing my arms in disgust. I was being left out of the big decisions once again.

Dad looked at me from the corner of his eye. "We can talk now, and in more detail later. But I've been thinking about this all afternoon. We should work out a plan to implement a real exit strategy. One that allows us to fully disappear."

An exit strategy? What was he talking about?

"That's . . . um . . . cryptic." Mom picked up her plate and took it to the sink. "But I'm sure you can bring up your idea with X next time we have contact."

Dad shook his head. "No, I don't want to use X for this."

"I thought you trusted him?" I asked, not expecting to receive an answer. "Not that I know much about him."

"I do trust him." Dad looked at me strangely. As if he were suddenly realizing how old I was. That I wasn't a little kid anymore. "He's always been a good friend to me and, if things go poorly, I don't want this to blow back on him. He's already risked a lot."

"But isn't that his job?" I asked. "To protect people like us."

"It's complicated," Dad said.

"B, we need to talk about things later." Mom glanced over her shoulder to look at us. "Not now."

"Fine. But I've already decided. I want to leave tomorrow so I can be back by Saturday . . . Sunday at the latest."

"What?" Mom spun around, soap bubbles covering her hands. "Are you crazy? What in the world for?"

"Relax. Just trust me. I have contacts. People who can get us foreign passports and . . ."

"So, you think you can run around and act like a secret agent. Hate to break it to you . . . you're not X. You're only a . . ." She caught herself before saying anything else.

"I know exactly who I am." Dad's voice had a sharp edge. "And we both know why we're here."

I didn't dare move. Obviously, I'd gotten to Dad, but maybe not in the way I'd wanted.

"We can talk later, but you know it's time," Dad replied while he dabbed the side of his mouth with a paper napkin. He stole a quick glance at me before looking back at Mom.

"Accidents can happen, will eventually happen, and we need to be able to leave the country . . . if necessary."

"Leave the country?" I shrieked.

Mom took a deep breath and slowly let it out. She took a couple of steps and leaned on the table in front of Dad. "B, just because you two had a fight . . . about who knows what because neither of you wants to talk . . . that's no reason to make drastic, radical moves."

"That's not why I'm doing this. It's a precaution. You were thinking of alternatives, too." Dad looked out the window. "I've made up my mind and I'll explain later. I'll only be gone for a day or two. Now is the safest time period because we just got here and it'll be a while before we can get tracked."

"But . . ."

"No buts. The two of you can drive me to a bus station and—"

"A bus station?" Mom threw her hands in the air as if she couldn't believe what he was saying. "Where you can be spotted? You're not even thinking logically."

I watched the back-and-forth like a tennis match.

Mom narrowed her eyes and focused on me. "You want to tell me what led to all this? I know something must have happened today."

I shrugged and tried to look as innocent as possible.

"No clue, huh?" She let out a huge sigh and resumed talking to Dad. "Fine. We'll talk about your backup plan later, but for heaven's sake, if you go anywhere . . . take the van."

"You might need it," Dad countered.

"If there's an emergency I'll drive this thing out of here and meet you in Atlanta."

The safe house in Atlanta. It was a place we all knew about. An address to be memorized, but never discussed.

Dad reached out and touched Mom's hand. "Trust me."

She sighed again. "I always do."

The rumble of thunder, a howling wind, and the hammering sound of rain woke me from a deep sleep the next morning. I sat up and peered through the mini-blinds at the dark skies and raindrops sliding down the window. My shoulders drooped. Mother Nature was putting a kink in my plan B . . . to simply sneak off with Parker without permission. I wondered if it had delayed Dad's plans, too. He and Mom had gone for a walk after dinner, and when they returned, Mom announced that we'd be on our own for a couple of days. No matter how much I'd asked for some more details, the decision had been made to once again shut me out.

"Good morning, sunshine," Mom said, poking her head up from a book titled *The Hieroglyphics of Horapollo Nilous.* "Looks like a good day to stay inside and read, huh? Want me to make you some eggs?"

I glanced around.

"He left a couple of hours ago," she said, knowing what I was thinking. "Gave you a kiss before going."

My heart twinged with guilt for not squaring things up with him last night, but I wasn't going to get sidetracked. My parents were still choosing to keep me in the dark about what was going on. And just because Dad was on some sort of quest of his own in order to have us disappear to another country didn't mean I was going to stop looking for answers. In fact, it meant the opposite. I needed to hurry up and get going.

"I'll just have cereal," I said, stuffing my sheets and pillow into the drawer before turning the bed back into a sofa.

"Still don't want to talk about it?" she asked.

"Nothing to say."

"You and he are so much alike sometimes," Mom muttered, shaking her head. "Stubborn as anything."

I stayed quiet and served myself breakfast.

The storm continued to rage for hours. Mom had our small radio tuned into the local station that liked to play classic songs from the '80s, and the DJ had announced that we'd be having storms like this for the rest of the day. By nighttime, Mom and I had already decided that if the tornado sirens went off in the park, we'd run over to the laundry shelter. Even though that building didn't seem very strong, it was better than staying in the RV.

The next morning the battering rain had turned into more of an annoying drizzle, but it was still keeping me inside.

Mom seemed content to read and study her notes on ancient languages, but I was anxious. All I wanted was to get to a computer and research who I used to be.

A knock on the door changed everything.

"Hi, Parker," Mom greeted him, and motioned for him to come in from the rain. "Great weather, huh?"

"Yes, ma'am." He took a step inside. "I mean ... no, the weather is pretty bad." He glanced over at me. "Um, Mrs. Anderson is going into town for her Saturday bowling league and said Katrina and I could go with her." He paused. "Maybe even go visit my cousin Jimmy at the diner for lunch ... if that's okay?"

I could feel the excitement in my stomach as if someone were tickling me from the inside. Parker had found a way to get us into town to do the research.

"Oh, well ... that's nice, but, um ..." Mom turned to face me.

I could see she was unsure, but she had been the one who had wanted to give me more freedom, so I thought she could be convinced. "Mom, please," I whispered. "I don't ask for much." I didn't want to beg in front of Parker, but I'd do whatever it took. "Mrs. Anderson is going with us."

"You've never even bowled," Mom whispered back.

"So? Isn't it about time I learned?"

"Why don't I go with you?" Mom replied to Parker, trying to sound perky and upbeat. "I haven't bowled in years."

"Oh, that'd be great, Mrs. Davis, but our truck doesn't have a back seat. It only fits three." Parker took a step toward the door. "But we can all go next time when you have your van." He put his hand on the doorknob. "See you later, Katrina."

"No, wait." I clasped my hands together and stared at my mother. "Please. Por favor."

"I don't like this," she muttered, but I could see her resolve starting to crack. "But you are growing up."

I held my breath.

"Okay." She smiled. "But take an umbrella. And let me give you some money."

"Great, I'll go tell her that you're coming. She's waiting in the truck," Parker said, running back outside.

"Thank you, thank you, thank you!" I exclaimed, and threw my arms around Mom's neck.

As Mom went to get her wallet, I grabbed my backpack, which was bulkier than usual. "What's in here?" I asked, opening up the large middle pocket.

"Oh, I forgot. I threw some things in there last night in case a tornado alarm sounded and we had to make a mad dash to the shelter. It's just a couple of T-shirts, some snacks, the medicine bag. Just take it all out and—"

From outside I heard a long beep.

"Forget it. They're waiting." I checked that my wallet was still in the bag's front pocket. "I have to go."

"Okay, but here. Take this." Mom handed me a ten-dollar bill. "Is that enough?"

"Yeah. Sure." I didn't mention that I already had all my money, all fifty-four dollars, in my wallet.

"Here, take ten more. Just in case you want to eat something."

I smiled, took the money, and gave her a kiss goodbye. Now I had seventy-four dollars to bribe Jimmy.

I was ready for some answers . . . no matter the price.

CHAPTER 7

EMERGENCY CALL

IN THE TRUCK, NONE of us spoke. Mrs. Anderson had a country station on full blast and was humming along to every song on the radio. She looked happy, and neither of us wanted to do or say anything that might change her mood.

As we approached the bowling alley, Mrs. Anderson finally spoke up. "Well, that's not good." She pointed to the empty parking lot and the darkened building. "Stay here while I go find out what's happening."

She parked the truck right by the glass door and went over to peer inside.

"Looks like the place is closed," I said.

"The electricity is out," Parker replied matter-of-factly. "Storm damage."

"How do you know?"

Parker gave me a wink. "One of her bowling league ladies may have called while she was in the shower. I also called Jimmy and he said he'd rent you the laptop for ten bucks an hour . . . but I'm kinda hoping we can convince him to do a different deal. How much money did you bring?"

"Seventy-four dollars. Why? What's your idea?"

"Well, I heard that Jimmy's car is messed up and he needs money to fix it. Figured he might be desperate enough to sell us the laptop outright since it's just a paperweight for him because I never gave him the password." He tapped his black backpack. "That's why I brought this along. So we can hide it in here."

"Whoa. You think he'd do that? Sell it to you?" This plan was getting better by the minute. "I mean, sell it to me?"

"Maybe. I have a hundred and sixty-eight, so between us we can probably get him to do it."

"But how are we going to get over to the diner if—?"

Mrs. Anderson opened the truck door. "Sign says they're closed till tomorrow. Seems like they had some damage from the storm." She shook her head. "You'd think one of the ladies would've called me or something."

"That's too bad," Parker said. "But maybe you can drop us off in town and we can run some errands for you. That way it's not a wasted trip."

Mrs. Anderson gave him a side-eyed glance. "Whatcha up to, Parker? You're not usually so . . . *helpful*."

"Nothing. Just being nice, that's all. I was even thinking about stopping by the diner and asking Mo if she needed help. Maybe make some extra money."

Mrs. Anderson leaned over the wheel and chuckled. "Uh-huh. New Jersey got you worried, huh?" She then stared at me sitting quietly by the passenger door. "Or maybe having a girl around is doing you some good. Best behavior and all."

I could feel my cheeks turning red, but I said nothing.

"Well, all right. No matter the reason, I guess." She thrust the truck's gear into reverse. "I guess I could use a couple of things from the grocery store."

"If you give me your flip phone, we can call you when we're done." Parker smiled, his knee pressing against mine for a moment as we drove down the street. "That way you don't miss any of your shows."

"Well, I'm not your personal driver, so I'll call *you* from the house phone when I'm good and ready to pick you up."

As we pulled into a large strip mall and stopped in front of the Winn-Dixie, Mrs. Anderson rattled off her grocery list. "Now remember, I want a box of Bisquick, some decaf . . . the one with the green label . . . and the paper towels that are on sale." She handed Parker a twenty-dollar bill and the flip phone. "And if you buy anything else, it better be with your own money, 'cause I expect my receipt and change. You got that?"

"Yes, ma'am," we both said in unison.

"Don't go getting into any trouble, you hear?" she said as I jumped out of the truck with Parker right behind me.

"Never," Parker said with a smile.

"Humph!" she scoffed just as Parker slammed the truck door shut.

"That was brilliant," I whispered as we walked into the grocery store.

"Yeah." He shrugged, blowing off the compliment. "It was even easier than I thought . . . but Jimmy might be a different story."

Five minutes later we were headed out with everything Mrs. Anderson wanted in the big brown paper bag that Parker was carrying. We had walked a few blocks when Parker motioned with his chin that we'd have to cross the four-lane highway. "The diner is over there," he said. "I told Jimmy to have the laptop ready and fully charged."

"But will he be there now?" I asked while we waited for an eighteen-wheeler to pass by.

"He should be." Parker looked both ways to make sure the road was clear, before crossing. "Mo has him working there every Saturday." He shifted the bag to carry it in one arm and with his free hand pointed to the truck stop down the road. "The diner's been getting a bunch of business lately 'cause the food got better ever since Mo took over for her dad. He was the original Mo."

We walked in between several long trucks lined up next to one another at the far end of the lot. They seemed to form a protective wall in front of the gas station and the small brick building with the Mo's Diner sign on top.

"So, what should I tell Jimmy?" I asked as I peered through the diner's front window and saw Jimmy wiping down a table. There were a few men sitting at the counter, but the place didn't seem very busy.

"Just follow my lead and let me do the talking." Parker pushed open the glass door and a small bell tinkled overhead.

"Be right with—" a woman called out from behind the cash register, but stopped when she made eye contact with us. "Oh, hey, Parker. What are you doing here?"

"Hi, Mo." Parker gave her a friendly wave. "Just here to—"

"He's here to see me, Aunt Maureen," Jimmy interrupted, slapping the dirty rag over his shoulder. "I'm gonna take a five-minute break, okay?"

His aunt shrugged. "Sure. Better now than when the lunch crowd gets here." She waddled a little as she walked toward the kitchen, and that's when I noticed that she was very pregnant. I made a mental note to tell Dad when he got back because she might need a short-order cook to help out. "Anyone interested in some leftover crumb cake?" Maureen asked.

"No. They won't be staying that long," Jimmy answered for us as Maureen shrugged and went into the kitchen. "You got my money?"

"Yeah, about that." Parker put down the bag of groceries on an empty table and reached around into his backpack. "Heard you needed some extra cash. I was thinking Katrina here could have a long-term lease. Say for a hundred bucks." He pulled out some cash and held it in front of Jimmy.

Jimmy tipped his head to the side, considering the

offer. "I'm actually surprised you showed up at all considering what's going on with your girlfriend," he replied matter-of-factly. "You must really want that laptop. I've got it there behind the counter. But it'll cost you more."

"She's not my girlfriend," Parker hissed. "I've already told you that. And why wouldn't we show up?"

"Wait a minute." Jimmy took a step back. "You don't know?" He glanced at me and smirked, seeming to enjoy whatever bit of information he held. "Oh boy." He shook his head. "Seriously? Neither of you know? Well, no, she has to know . . . it's her dad, after all."

"What about my dad?" A bit of panic filtered into my veins.

"Ten bucks." Jimmy held out his hand. "No, twenty. 'Cause it's big."

Parker leaned in until he was almost nose to nose with Jimmy. "Just tell us what you know."

Jimmy sucked on his teeth and stayed quiet.

I had already reached into my own backpack and taken out some money. "Tell me." I shoved the cash toward him.

Jimmy took the twenty-dollar bill and stuffed it into his back pocket. "Two feds came by here a little while ago. They were looking for your dad. Say he's wanted for something."

"You're insane." Parker rolled his eyes. "That's the stupidest—"

My heart dropped. "Feds? Are you sure?"

Jimmy shrugged. "They showed me their badges. Looked legit."

Parker shook his head. "Katrina, this guy is a huge liar. Don't believe a word he says. It's probably part of some scam. Think about it . . . why would feds ask this jerk about your dad?"

"Because, Mr. Know-It-All"—Jimmy sneered at Parker—"they saw the picture I posted of her elbow and he was in the background."

"Yeah, right. You've got an answer for everything," Parker replied. "But I know a liar when I see one."

I doubted that those were real agents. It was probably someone from the cartel. I tried to remain calm, but it felt like I was frozen in place and the world was spinning out of control around me. That stupid photo had put us all in danger. "What . . . what did you tell them?" My voice cracked as I asked.

Jimmy's face twitched. "Listen, I'm no snitch. I told them where I took the picture, but that was before they said they were looking for your dad."

"I have to get to my mom," I muttered. "Warn her."

Jimmy got closer. "So, what did your dad do? Gotta be pretty bad to have the feds here."

I didn't know what to do. It felt like my legs were crumbling under the weight of the news. I had to tell Mom. We had to get out of town and meet up with Dad, immediately. But how was I supposed to do that? We didn't even have a phone at home.

"Back off, Jimmy." Parker gave him a shove, but before Jimmy could react, Maureen called him over.

Jimmy hesitated and looked at Maureen standing by the kitchen door. He sighed and whipped the towel off his shoulder. "You're lucky I'm at work," he growled under his breath before heading toward the kitchen.

"Anytime, Jimmy!" Parker puffed out his chest and shouted at him as he disappeared. "Anytime!"

I grabbed Parker's arm. "Listen," I whispered. "You've got to help me warn my mom before those guys show up at the RV park."

"Seriously?" Parker studied my face. "You really think Jimmy's telling the truth?"

I bit my lip and slowly nodded.

"Oh." The seriousness of the situation seemed to dawn on Parker. "Ohh!"

All of this was my fault. If I hadn't been so selfish. If only I had told my dad about Jimmy's picture, then they wouldn't have tracked us down. Now our only chance was to get away quick, but I'd need help.

"Let's get out of here," I said, making a beeline for the door.

"Just a second." Parker dashed behind the counter and peered over the kitchen pass-through. I heard him say "Later, Mo!" as I walked outside.

I ducked behind a dumpster on the side of the diner, and kept running through different scenarios as I waited for Parker. I didn't have very many options.

"Dude, I thought you took off on me!" Parker exclaimed,

hurrying over. "And you don't have to freak out . . . I figured out what's going on."

"You did?" I scrunched my eyebrows in disbelief.

"Yeah. Agents show up looking for your parents and you act all weird after telling me your mom was from Cuba . . . you're running from la migra, right? Immigration?"

My mouth dropped a little. He was completely wrong, but his story actually made sense. I could work with that lie, avoid revealing the truth. "Um, yeah."

Parker gave me a knowing nod. "It's okay. That happened to my dad, too. He got picked up in a sting when I was three . . . part of the reason I think he took off on us. But maybe if you get a good immigration lawyer . . ." He let the sentence trail off.

"Uh-huh. Maybe," I responded. "But right now, I just need to get ahold of my mom."

"Here." Parker held out Mrs. Anderson's flip phone.

I shook my head. "We don't have a phone, remember? We live off the grid."

"You don't even have one for emergencies?"

"No, but maybe you can call Mrs. Anderson and have her get my mom on the phone?" I suggested. "Tell her it's an emergency."

Parker scoffed. "Um, have you not met her? She's not really into doing favors for people . . . especially when they interrupt her shows."

"You have to try. Please."

Parker opened up the phone and dialed. After a few seconds he shook his head. "She's not answering," he said.

"Try again. We have to get ahold of my mom."

He dialed again. "What do I say if she asks what's the emergency or . . ." His face changed and he held up a finger as I heard an irate voice on the other end of the phone.

"No, I'm not in any trouble. I just need you to go over to the Davises' place and . . ." He paused as I heard Mrs. Anderson's muffled voice complaining about something.

I waited. A bead of cold sweat trickled down the side of my body.

"What do you mean she got arrested?" Parker's eyes widened.

I twisted his hand and leaned in so I could hear her, too.

". . . and I saw her sitting in the back of their car. Figures that you'd get involved with people like that, 'cause you always seem to find trouble one way or another. But I told them to send you my way as soon as they picked up the girl 'cause New Jersey is your next stop."

I felt like I couldn't breathe. Couldn't move. My mom had already been taken and who knew if they had my dad. I was alone and could be next.

"Wait . . . you told them where we were?" His voice was rising. "Why would you do that?"

"Don't take that tone with me and . . . well, what was I supposed to do? They said they were looking to place her with some family . . . not that it's any of my concern. I told them that I'd dropped the two of you off at the grocery store and that—"

"How long?" Parker interrupted. "How long ago did they leave?"

"I don't know. Few minutes ago. I was about to call and tell you to behave yourself around those agents. You don't need that kind of trouble with your record."

"I gotta go."

"Parker, don't go getting any foolish ideas. You mind your own business and—"

He hung up the phone and grimaced. "I'm so sorry, Katrina. But if you were born in the US—"

"I have to get out of here," I mumbled, not sure where I should go, but knowing that I couldn't stay there.

"Okay. Do you have any friends or family nearby?"

"No," I muttered. This was another casualty of being in the program. No real friends or family to reach out to. At least none that I remembered.

"Well, if you don't have anywhere to go . . ."

But I did have somewhere to go. The safe house. It had been created for moments like this. A place of last resort. I could go there and get help.

Parker was still talking. ". . . we could try to do it together. I think it'd be better than—"

"I need to get to Atlanta." I adjusted my backpack along with my attitude. "How do I do that?"

"Um, I'm not sure," Parker said. "What's in Atlanta?"

My mind was going into overdrive. Every minute I wasted here was another minute when my parents and I were in danger. "You think you can find someone to take me? Like right now?"

Parker shook his head. "Not really. That's like two hours away, but there might be a bus or something."

"No." I glanced over my shoulder as the voices of a couple of truckers carried through the alley. "They might be looking for me at the local bus station. In fact, this whole area is probably going to be watched."

"Immigration isn't going to come after you. I'm surprised they've gone through this much trouble just for your parents. Worst case . . ."

Parker didn't understand. This was about life or death.

Mainly death.

I needed help in getting to the Atlanta safe house, but I also needed Parker to understand the stakes in all this. I took a deep breath, knowing that I was about to break the most important rule of the Witness Protection Program. I was going to trust someone with the truth.

"Are you listening to me?" Parker asked, and I realized I hadn't been.

"No, but that's because I have something to tell you." I paused, reconsidering for a moment what I was about to do. "I'm going to tell you something, but you have to swear not to tell anyone. Even if you choose to not help me, you can't tell anyone. Not Mrs. Anderson, not the police, not anyone."

"What are you talking about?" Parker asked.

"Do you promise?" I insisted on an answer. "I'm trusting you with . . . well, with everything."

"Um, okay," he said hesitantly. "Sure."

"Those men that took my mom . . . they aren't with Immigration. My parents aren't being deported." I paused for a second, knowing that I was going against everything I'd been taught. "We're in the Witness Protection Program and those supposed agents are probably showing fake badges and really work for the drug cartel. They want us dead."

For a moment Parker's face showed no reaction; then he slowly took a step back and let out a nervous laugh. "You're kidding, right?"

I shook my head. "Wish I was."

Parker slow-blinked. "So, those men . . . you've been running from them . . ."

"For years," I said, feeling a sense of relief at being able to finally talk about things with someone. "And now they have my mom."

"What about your dad?"

"I don't know. He left yesterday and I don't have any way to get ahold of him. That's why I need to get to Atlanta. There's a safe house there where I can get help. Maybe he'll be able to meet me there."

"Wow." His shoulders slumped a little. "This is all . . ."

"I know, I know. It's not what you expected, and I wouldn't

have gotten you involved at all if I didn't need your help in getting there."

"Uh-huh." Parker paced alongside the dumpster. "Okay, give me a second to think." He stopped and shook away an idea. "Jimmy can't be trusted."

"But I need a way to get out of here and over to Atlanta."

Parker snapped his fingers. "Cows."

"Huh?"

He peered around the corner of the building. "All right, I have an idea. There's an empty livestock trailer out there. You can get in the back and no one will know you're there."

"But how does that get me to Atlanta?" I asked.

"It doesn't. I mean, it might, but it'll at least get you out of town. The Atlanta part can be figured out later. The trailer had something on the side about being Georgia's best dairy, so it's not like it's going to Florida or something. What do you think?"

This didn't seem like a good idea, but time was running out and I couldn't come up with anything better.

"I'll be the lookout. Trust me?" he asked, glancing toward the line of trucks and trailers.

I took a deep breath and nodded. "Let's go."

CHAPTER 8

SMELLS LIKE COW

PARKER SIGNALED ME THAT I was clear to cross the parking lot toward the livestock trailer that was sandwiched between two semis.

As I sprinted over, I noticed the aluminum trailer had POWELL'S DAIRY—GEORGIA'S PREMIER ORGANIC DAIRY FARM emblazoned on the side in bright blue letters and there were metal slats stretching across the open-air top. It would be too high and too tight of a squeeze for me to slip through, and I spotted a padlock hanging on the back door. We'd have to come up with another plan.

Panic was starting to build up inside me. The cartel's guys could be here any minute. "Maybe there's another truck I can sneak into," I said, crouching down next to Parker.

"Why?" Parker stood up and lifted the latch on the gate-like door. The padlock wasn't closed. "Your ride is ready," he said, opening the door. "Get in and I'll close it behind us."

"Us?" I said as I jumped into the trailer and crouched down on the dirty metal floor to stay out of view.

"Um, yeah. I'm not letting you go by yourself." Parker

closed the door, stretched his arm through the opening to close the door latch, and hung the open lock back on.

"Parker, these aren't people that you play around with."

Parker shrugged. "I don't have too much to lose. Plus, what kind of friend would I be if I let you go by yourself . . . in a cow trailer."

I sniffed the air. "It does smell like cow."

"More like cow poop," he said.

I chuckled, but looked around to make sure there wasn't actual cow poop in the trailer. Thankfully, there wasn't.

"Did you see the truck door?" I said, looking out at the highway in case a suspicious car pulled into the truck stop. "It says the dairy is in Grayson, Georgia. Do you know if that's near Atlanta?"

"No, but at least it's not anywhere near here, and that's what matters, right?"

"Definitely. I just—"

"Get down!" Parker said in a loud whisper. "I think our driver is walking over." He peered through the metal slats that ran along the top half of the trailer.

I hunched down and carefully peeked over the metal siding, and saw a man wearing a plaid shirt, jeans, and a cowboy hat. He was texting on his phone and not even looking up as he walked over.

Parker and I crouched down next to each other in the corner by the door and waited.

As soon as I heard the truck's engine start and the trailer begin to roll forward, my shoulders relaxed. I was going to disappear from this place without a trace. The cartel would have no idea where I'd gone.

The trailer gently shook as it rambled along the highway. Oddly enough, it had a soothing effect on me. My thoughts felt more focused as all the other noises were muffled by the whistling wind flowing through the open-air top.

My parents never liked buses or trains, but if where we ended up was too far from Atlanta, that might be my only choice. I'd just have to blend in with all the other passengers. Or I might even need to get a taxi if the dairy was really remote.

I reached into my backpack and felt for my wallet. Fifty-four dollars wasn't much, but maybe I could ask Parker to loan me the rest if I needed it. I sighed and leaned my head back.

I could do this. I *would* do this.

I stared up at the blue sky above and waited. For the next couple of hours, there was nothing to do except sit and worry about my parents.

***

"I think we're almost at the dairy," Parker said as the truck and trailer turned onto a bumpy dirt road.

I jumped up and held on to a metal slat for balance. In the distance I saw a barn next to a silo. There were cows eating grass in the pasture next to the road.

Parker pointed to something on the other side of the road as the pickup slowed down. "Check it out."

It was a huge sign in the shape of a cow next to a brick building. POWELL'S ORGANIC DAIRY FARM—VISITORS WELCOME was written on the side of the cow sign.

We both shrank down next to the trailer door as the truck came to a full stop. We'd have to wait for the driver to leave before sneaking out, otherwise we risked getting caught.

"No issue with the transfer, Keith?" a woman's voice called out as I heard the pickup's door slam shut.

"Not a one. The heifer didn't even seem bothered by any of it."

"Good. Well, I got some lunch inside . . ." The voices drifted away.

"You think they're gone?" Parker whispered.

"Think so," I said, inching up and trying to keep as low a profile as possible. "Now's our chance."

Parker stood up, reached out through the door opening, and quietly lifted the latch. The door creaked a little as I slowly pushed it open, but it wasn't enough to attract any attention . . . not even from a nearby cow.

"All right," Parker said, jumping out of the trailer and closing the door. "What now?"

He thought I had some sort of plan. "Um . . ." I glanced

around, hoping to see a bike or something. "Depends where we are. Maybe there's a bus or train station nearby that'll get me to Atlanta. If we're close enough, I could just get a taxi."

"So . . . we need info." Parker tapped his backpack and gave me a sly smile. "And I'm the master of information. Whatever we need is here."

"Huh?" I watched as he unzipped his bag and pulled out a laptop. "Is that . . . ? Did you steal it from Jimmy?"

"Can't steal what's already yours." He crouched down and opened the computer. He typed something in, then grimaced. "No Wi-Fi but at least it's got a full battery."

I peered around the corner of the trailer to scan the area. There wasn't anyone outside. "What if we go over there?" I pointed to a row of tall bushes that lined the side of a brick building. "Looks like it's an office or something. They might have a signal."

Parker stuck his head out next to mine. "Yeah, it's worth a shot." He closed the laptop. "Let's make a run for it."

The two of us darted out and ran toward the building. We hid between the bushes and the wall, a few feet away from a closed window.

Parker flipped open his laptop again and gave me a thumbs-up. "This is easier than I thought. It's unsecured."

"What do you mean?" I whispered.

"No password. Not that a password would have slowed me down much." His fingers were flying across the keyboard as location maps popped up on the screen. "Looks like the nearest town is a few miles away and Atlanta is about forty-five miles from here."

"Can I take a taxi there?" I asked.

"To Atlanta?" Parker kept typing. "That's going to cost about a hundred bucks."

"I need to get there as fast as possible, Parker." I looked at him. "I've got fifty-four dollars left and I'll make sure you get reimbursed if you loan me the rest."

"I don't mind loaning you the money." He paused. "I'm worried about you. Why don't we just ask the police to help?"

"We can't. They have no record of my being in the Witness Protection Program and by the time the right people get notified, the cartel might find me."

Parker shook his head. "But that doesn't make any sense to me. How can the drug dealers be monitoring everything? I mean, sure, they might have some people on the inside, but it's not like they're everywhere."

"It's the way things are," I snapped.

"But think about it—"

"Look, these rules have kept us safe for years and I'm going to follow them." I bit my lip and took a deep breath. "I appreciate your help, but like I said . . . it's the way things are. I'm in this situation because I messed up and broke one of the rules. I'm not breaking another."

"Okay, I get it." Parker pulled out his flip phone and

handed it to me. "Here. Call the taxi. I'll give you all the money I've got."

The call was easier than expected. The taxi company said they'd send someone in about twenty minutes after I told them that they'd be picking up my "niece" to take her to Atlanta and that she'd be waiting for them by the main road at the entrance to the dairy.

"Niece?" Parker asked as I gave him back the phone.

"Don't want anyone questioning why I'm traveling alone." I stood up. "Cover stories are kinda my thing. Now let's get out of here before someone sees us."

As Parker and I walked toward the main road, neither of us said much. I pretended to be somewhat interested in the cows roaming the pasture and, in the distance, I could see a tractor kicking up dust in a field. We were definitely in the middle of nowhere.

We took refuge from the sun by sitting under a large tree next to the quiet country road. The tranquil setting with birds chirping and a soft breeze blowing was completely opposite from how I was feeling. Inside I was a flurry of activity, with thoughts racing through my head and every instinct on high alert. A more appropriate setting would have been New York City in the middle of rush hour.

Parker suddenly broke the quiet. "So, you said you're really good at cover stories . . . I'm guessing Katrina isn't your real name, huh?"

"Just the most recent," I said, unsure if this was the conversation I wanted to have.

Parker plucked a blade of grass and crinkled it in his hands. "How many names have you had?"

"Eleven." I watched him out of the corner of my eye, but he stayed focused on the grass. "Letters *A* through *K*. I was already working on *L* names, just in case."

Parker's eyebrows crinkled as he looked over at me. "Just in case?"

"In case our ID change came up sooner than expected."

"Oh." Parker nodded and yanked up another blade. "What would your new name be?"

"If I told you, then I wouldn't be able to use it when I get to Atlanta."

"Oh. Right." He flicked away the little green ball in his hand. More silence.

"I'm thinking Lily or Layla," I said, realizing that at this point there was no harm in telling Parker as much as he wanted to know. "Because names have to match the person."

Parker stared at me for a second. "You look more like a Layla than a Lily, I think." He smiled and straightened up. "What about me? What name suits me?"

I gazed at him from head to toe. "Can't see you as anything other than Parker."

"I was thinking Peter," he answered. "Then I could say I was Peter Parker . . . like Spider-Man."

"Nope." I shook my head. "You'd just be Peter because

once you have a new name, you can't really use your old one again . . . even if you wanted to."

"That makes sense." Parker leaned closer to me. "Do you ever want to go back to your real name?"

I shrugged. "I don't even know what it is."

"Really?"

"That's what I wanted to research on the computer. I don't know anything about my old life. At least prior to being in the program."

"And how long has that been?"

"About three years. I was almost ten when my mom and I were in an accident caused by the cartel. They ran us off the road and I ended up with amnesia. It's what made my parents realize that we wouldn't be safe unless we went into the program." I sighed, but it felt good to talk about it all with someone.

"Wow."

"Yeah. Since I don't remember much from my old life, it feels like it never existed. Although I do have some flashbacks about living somewhere near a desert when I was little, but it's like remembering old photographs. I just wanted to learn more about who I am and what my dad did to get the cartel so angry that they'd want to hunt us down."

"Well, you have to be sure you want to know stuff like that," Parker said. "Not knowing might be better."

"It's not," I answered. "Trust me. Not knowing the truth is the worst."

"I don't know," Parker mused. "I sometimes wish I didn't know some stuff about my past."

"Like what?" I said, realizing that I wasn't the only one who had secrets.

Parker stared at the ground. "You know how I mentioned that when my mom got sick, I changed some bills."

"Yeah."

"Well, she wasn't actually sick," he said. "I found out that she had a drug problem." He sighed. "I couldn't do much except change some bills. She eventually overdosed and died."

I put my hand on his knee. "I'm sorry."

"Yeah." He shrugged. "It's fine. Kinda been on my own ever since, you know?" He looked up at me. "Just make sure you want to know your parents' secret."

I nodded, leaning against the tree.

We both grew quiet, lost in our own thoughts.

A few minutes later a car could be seen coming down the road. "That's probably the taxi," Parker said, standing up and taking a couple of steps toward the road.

"Um, yeah. About the money . . ." I lingered for a few seconds under the shade.

Parker turned to face me. "I was thinking about that. I think it makes more sense for me to go with you instead of getting stuck here in the middle of nowhere." He held his hand above his eyes to reduce the glare bouncing off the black asphalt. "If that's okay with you, I mean."

"Sure," I said. "I can drop you off wherever you want."

"I've come this far, might as well make sure you get to the safe house." Parker gave me a lopsided grin as a blue car with the word TAXI in checkered letters pulled over along the opposite side of the road. "Plus, I'm guessing the agents can make sure I don't get into too much trouble with Mrs. Anderson."

The taxi driver, an old man with a big gray mustache, stuck his head out the car window. "You asked for a cab?" he called out.

"Our aunt did!" Parker shouted.

I smiled. Having a friend who knew my secrets was something I'd never really experienced. It filled a void that I didn't even know I had. I liked it more than I'd thought possible. It was like having a partner. "Okay, we stick together until the safe house and then the agents can help get you home," I whispered as we walked over to the taxi.

"Cool." Parker let out a short laugh. "Look at me. Never thought I'd be headed toward federal agents . . . always thought I'd be running away from them."

I gave him a little shove. "You also never thought you'd meet a girl with eleven names."

"Wrong." He gave me a wink as we crossed the road. "A girl with twelve names . . . right, *Layla*?"

I felt my body stiffen. I already disliked that name. "I'm still Katrina," I replied dryly. "Don't want to change just yet."

"Right. I didn't mean . . . I just, uh, never mind." He gave me a weak smile. "Katrina. Understood," he said as he opened the back door of the taxi and got inside.

But Parker didn't understand. Katrina was the only version of me he would ever know. The moment I changed my name and became someone else, our friendship, like everything else in my life, would have to disappear. I wanted . . . no, I needed, Katrina to exist for as long as possible.

CHAPTER 9

CALL ME X

"HERE WE ARE . . . 804 Magnolia," the taxi driver said as we pulled in front of a brick house with a huge yard that had two cars parked in the driveway. "That'll be one hundred twelve dollars."

The driver had confirmed that we had the cash before starting the drive, and we'd been watching the meter, so I had $120 in my hand ready to give to him.

"Thank you." I handed him the bills and opened the car door. "You can keep the change."

"Uh, sure." The taxi driver counted out the money. "You two want me to wait and make sure you get in okay?"

"Nah, we got it." Parker closed the door and waved him off. "Thanks, though."

We waited for a moment as he pulled out of the driveway.

"All right, let's go." Parker took a few steps toward the house. "Doesn't look like much of a safe—"

I raised my hand, which had the desired effect of silencing him and making him stop.

"What is it?" he whispered, his eyes darting around.

"Hold on." I watched to make sure the taxi turned at the corner, before moving. "Okay, now we can go."

I turned and walked down the street.

"Hey, wait a minute!" Parker called out, hurrying to catch up to me. "I thought the point was to get help from the feds once we got here."

"Exactly." I couldn't hold back a grin. "You don't think I was going to give the driver the exact address of where we needed to go, did you? We're going down there . . . to 824 Magnolia."

Parker nodded in approval. "Well done. I didn't even think of that."

We headed toward a house that was shrouded by trees and had a large wrought-iron fence surrounding the property. "Yeah, well . . . I've been on the run for a little bit longer."

I approached a brick pillar by the property's front gate that had a small keypad and a camera with the numbers 824 above it. This place looked like what I imagined a safe house to be. A secure, protected location.

Parker pushed the intercom button and waited.

Nothing.

"Buzz them again," I suggested.

He pushed the button and tapped the camera's plastic cover.

"Can I help you?" a gruff voice asked through the speaker.

I pushed Parker aside. "Um . . . yes, I was told to come

here by my father . . . I'm part of the . . . um . . ." I paused. I had to be careful with what I said.

The response was short and stern over the intercom. "I'm not interested in donating. Thank you."

"Don't you have a password or something?" Parker whispered in my ear.

I shook my head. Dad had never mentioned anything except the address. I buzzed the owner again. "Um . . . sir, you might know my father as B? He said I should come here if there were any problems. If there was an emergency. We need help to—"

"Wait . . . you're B's and L's daughter?" the man asked. "Where are they?"

"Yes," I answered as a huge sense of relief filled my chest. I'd made it to the safe house. Now they'd be able to get my parents back. "They took my mom, and my dad left town and I can't reach him and—"

"And who is that with you?"

Parker leaned in front of the camera lens. "Parker Jimenez, sir."

"He's a friend who helped get me here," I explained. "I told him what's going on. We need—"

"Don't say anything else," the voice ordered as the large iron gates parted, with each half sliding across the redbrick pillars. "Both of you need to get inside the house and stay out of sight until I get there. I just opened the front door remotely."

"Let's go." Parker headed down the driveway, but I stayed back.

"So, no one's here?" I asked, peering into the camera. "I thought there'd be people to help us."

"I'm helping you right now. Get inside," he ordered. "I'll be there as soon as I can."

"But who are *you*?" I asked.

"Just call me X."

I took a deep breath, letting the huge wave of relief wash over me. I'd found the safe house and I'd found X.

"Katrina! Hurry up!" Parker shouted as the gates started to close again.

I squeezed through just before they slid together with a large clanking sound.

From where I stood, I could only see a dark gray roof hidden among a scattering of trees.

"So, this is the safe house, right?" Parker asked, glancing around. "I mean, that guy is on his way here to protect you and stuff. We can trust him, right?"

"Yeah," I said as we walked up the driveway and a small squirrel darted in front of us before running up one of the nearby trees. "He's the one who's always helped us. Agent X."

"X, huh? Seems very . . . um . . . comic bookish."

I shrugged. "It's the way things work in the program. I mean, keeping everyone's identity a secret is how they keep people alive."

"Guess so," he said. "But didn't you want some answers? Maybe we can find them inside." He pointed to the small, one-story wooden house that had come into full view. It looked nothing like the new, larger homes in the neighborhood, and I figured it was probably a throwback to what the area looked like fifty years ago.

"Answers?" I shook my head. "I think this place will only make me have more questions."

"I don't know." Parker opened the front door. "An empty safe house might still have some clues."

I stepped inside and took in the surroundings. The place had a lived-in look. There was a worn leather couch in front of the biggest TV I'd ever seen and a stack of newspapers next to the fireplace. I began searching for clues, hoping that I'd find files with information, but there was nothing. In fact, while wandering around the house, I noticed that there were no photographs anywhere. None in the master bedroom with the neatly made bed and none in the other bedroom that had been converted into a workout room with a treadmill, weights, and a stationary bike.

I came back to the family room, where Parker was sitting on the couch with his laptop open and plugged into the wall socket nearby.

"Find anything?" he called out as I opened some of the cupboards in the kitchen.

"The guy likes cereal," I said, glancing at over a dozen

boxes. I looked at the few dishes in the sink. "And I'm pretty sure this isn't a typical safe house. I think this is his regular house."

"Well, his internet security is no match for me even if he is a secret agent. The programs I designed already bypassed his firewalls and I made sure he doesn't have any interior surveillance, so we're good."

"Hold on, you designed your own computer programs?" I asked, turning around from the cupboard where all the dishes were stacked.

"Told you I was good with computers. Jimmy had no idea how valuable this laptop actually is." Parker remained focused on the screen. "I've got all sorts of software on here that no one knows about." He paused and glanced at me. "Well, almost no one. You know now."

I smiled. Secrets were better when you could share them with someone.

I went back to searching the drawers. I'd found the silverware drawer and where he kept his pans, but nothing of importance.

"Hmm. That's interesting," Parker muttered.

"What?" I asked, opening and closing a drawer full of pot holders.

"I'm on the county records website and it lists this house as being owned by Eduardo Krajewski," Parker replied. "Ever hear of that name?"

"Nope." I opened the last of the drawers and discovered

the messy junk drawer. It had three different spools of ribbon, an assortment of pens, a paper-clipped stack of receipts, and scissors in all different sizes.

"Krajewski could be X's real name," Parker mused as he kept typing. "But I'm not getting any real information on that name."

I was rifling through the receipts when a folded green sheet in the back caught my eye. It looked like it was about to slide into the abyss behind the drawers, so I carefully pulled the drawer all the way forward and grabbed the paper. It was a receipt for Baaqir Yusuf for a hotel stay in Morocco four months ago.

"Try looking up Baaqir Yusuf," I suggested. "There's a receipt with that name in the drawer." I pulled the drawer out completely to see if anything else had fallen behind it, but there was nothing except little balls of dust.

Parker set his laptop on the coffee table in front of the couch. "What we need to find is this guy's computer so I can hack into his personal stuff. Have you seen one anywhere?"

"No." I tried fitting the drawer back onto its track, but it wouldn't slide shut. "And wouldn't he have it with him?"

"Not necessarily." Parker was now on the hunt, searching all around the house.

I kept trying to get the drawer to fit on the tracks, but wasn't having much luck.

"Problem?" Parker smirked as he came back into the kitchen and saw me battling the drawer.

I pulled it out one more time and set it on the floor. "Stupid drawer," I muttered, giving it a little kick with my foot. "Did you find a computer?"

"No." Parker opened the refrigerator. "Hey, aren't you starving? Let's see what this guy has to eat."

As if on cue, my stomach rumbled.

I glanced at Parker standing with the refrigerator door wide open and saw a whole lot of nothing on the shelves.

"He's got beer, some expired salad dressings, and a half gallon of milk." Parker pulled out the carton of milk. "Guess we're having cereal."

"There's Cocoa Krispies, cornflakes, and Raisin Bran up there." I pointed to the cupboard above the microwave. "I'll take the Cocoa Krispies."

"Um, yeah." Parker took out a couple of bowls while I got the spoons. "We both will."

After a couple of bowls of cereal, Parker and I started our search of the house again . . . this time for any type of clue about who lived here. After about thirty minutes of scouring the place and looking under beds and through books on the shelves, it had become obvious that Agent X didn't leave any personal information out in the open for someone to find. But there had to be something more than the receipts I'd found in the drawer.

"Parker? Parker!" I called out as I walked back to the living room. "Where are you?"

"Over here," he said.

He was sitting on the floor of the kitchen with all the receipts and papers from the drawer spread out around him.

"What are you doing?"

"Trying to see if there is a pattern or something with all these receipts. They don't have a name on them, but they're mostly from airport restaurants. Weird, right?" Parker looked up at me. "Why would he keep them?"

I shrugged. "Maybe he just empties his pocket and throws stuff there instead of the garbage?"

The sound of a car pulling up in front of the house made us both freeze.

"He's here," I said. "Put everything back and help me get this drawer into place."

Parker tossed everything into the drawer and lifted it over his head while I tried to guide the side wheels onto the tracks.

"Hey, there's something under here." Parker let go of one side just as I got it to slide smoothly in.

He pulled out a black flash drive that had been taped to the underside of the drawer.

The door alarm chimed as it opened. Parker quickly shoved the flash drive into his pocket and I closed the drawer as quietly as possible.

"Hide. Just in case," I whispered as I snuck behind the kitchen counter and Parker rushed to crouch behind the sofa.

I held my breath as the footsteps grew louder and closer.

"Hello? B's daughter, where are you?" a voice called out. "It's safe to come out."

I poked my head over the counter. A man wearing a light blue business shirt and dark pants stood at the entrance to the kitchen. He had dark hair that was turning gray along the sides and lightly tanned skin. "There you are," he said, a polite but somewhat insincere smile sliding across his face. "It's nice to see you again. You're going by Katrina this time . . . correct?"

"See me . . . *again*?" I responded, rising to stand as tall as I could, hoping that this would create the illusion that I was strong and brave. I'd heard of Agent X from my parents, but was pretty certain that I'd never met him in person. Yet there was something vaguely familiar about him. A distant memory of some sort. "I don't recall . . ."

He looked around. "You were much younger back then." He tossed his keys from one hand to another. "But that's not surprising. You might say I'm in the business of not having people remember me."

X took a few steps toward me and I instinctively retreated until my back hit the refrigerator.

"Where's your friend?" he asked, glancing around the kitchen.

Parker stood up from behind the couch, looking a little nervous. "Here. I . . . um . . . I'm Parker . . . Katrina's friend," he said.

"Yes. Parker Jimenez." X spoke very matter-of-factly.

"Originally from Chicago. Entered the foster care system about four years ago. Been in eight homes."

My eyes widened at the mention of eight homes. I thought it had been six, and that was already way too many.

"Recently got sent to Georgia to live with a distant relative after getting into some trouble for hacking a few government sites." X grimaced. "I now know *all* about you."

Parker's jaw clenched, but he didn't say another word.

"Parker helped get me here," I said, trying to defuse the tension. "If it weren't for him, the cartel might have taken me along with my mom."

"The cartel?" X glanced from me to Parker and back to me again.

"It's all right," I explained. "I told Parker, but he won't tell anyone. He understands the rules of the Program."

"The Program," X repeated. "You told him about the Program."

"Yeah." Parker nodded. "But don't worry, I get all the secrecy with being in the Witness Protection Program. I won't say a word about any of it."

"Hmm." X didn't seem convinced, but he wasn't going to press the issue. He turned to me. "Now tell me exactly what happened to your parents. Start with your dad."

"Well, um . . . he left yesterday . . . I don't know where exactly. He's supposed to come back tomorrow."

"Why?" X pulled out a pack of gum from his pocket and slowly unfolded the silver wrapper. "Why did he leave?"

"Um . . ." It felt strange to tell X when Dad had specifically wanted to exclude him, but it didn't seem like there were any other options. "He mentioned wanting to get some passports in case we needed to leave the country, but . . . he . . . um . . . he didn't want you to know. I think he wanted to protect you in case something went wrong."

X's jaw tightened and he shook his head. "That idiot," he muttered, popping the stick of gum in his mouth. "Thinking he can do what I do." X paced around the room. "What about your mother?"

"Parker and I were in town when Mrs. Anderson told us that my mom had been taken by some men pretending to be cops."

"Feds," Parker corrected me. "They were pretending to be feds and they were looking for Katrina, too."

"That's not good," X mumbled.

"Yeah." I sighed. "I know."

"But you can fix it, right?" Parker prompted. "Get other agents to go look for her. Warn her dad and stuff."

"I've already made some calls." X walked over to a closet and pulled out a duffel bag. "But we need to get out of here."

"Well, Parker just needs a ride back to his house. He—"

"He's not going back." X pulled a seascape painting off the wall to reveal a safe. "I've had to make some other plans for Parker."

"Excuse me?" Parker had a confused look on his face.

"What?" I stared at Parker, horrified at the mess I'd made

of his life. "No. This is all my fault. He shouldn't get in trouble because of helping me."

"This isn't about getting in trouble. It's about keeping you safe." X put his finger on a scanner and typed in a code. "It'll appear that your friend here has run away once again. Later we'll let Mrs. Anderson know that he was found and sent to another home." X glanced at Parker while holding the safe's handle. "Seems there were already some plans to send you to a relative in New Jersey next week, right?"

Parker met X's strong gaze with one of his own, but didn't respond.

"Wait." I looked at Parker for an explanation. "Is that true? You were leaving and didn't tell me?"

"I was going to, but . . ." He paused. "And let's not point fingers about keeping secrets."

He had a point, but his secret wasn't necessary. Mine was.

"But why do we have to leave this place?" I said as X took out several bundles of cash and placed them in the duffel. "I thought this was where we were supposed to go. That this was a safe house."

"Sure, but I'm guessing that the two of you probably left a trail, and that complicates matters." He took out what looked like a large stack of passports and threw them in the bag. "That's why we have to leave before anyone confirms that you were here."

"No one knows we're here," Parker replied.

"Right." Agent X closed the safe and hung the picture back

on the wall. "Then how did two kids manage to get here? I doubt you drove over."

"We stowed away in a cow trailer to some random dairy farm and then we took a taxi that dropped us off down the street. Not even in front of this house," I said, confident that we had covered our tracks perfectly.

"A taxi. Great." X shook his head in disgust. "And I'm sure the taxi driver didn't . . ." He paused. "Wait a minute." He took a deep breath. "Please don't tell me that you have a cell phone and that you've been using it."

"Um . . . yeah." Parker glanced at his backpack by the sofa.

"Ugh, and it keeps getting worse," X muttered. "Give it to me."

Parker hesitated.

"Never mind." X walked over and picked up the backpack. He searched inside and pulled out the phone, dropping the bag back on the floor. "At least it's an old flip phone. Much more difficult to track." X took out the battery and dropped both the battery and the phone into a nearby trash can.

"Hey, that's mine," Parker complained.

"Not anymore." X picked up the duffel bag and walked toward the bedroom. "Stay here," he ordered. "I'll be right back. Need to get a few more things before we go."

I didn't say anything, but I didn't like how X was treating us. I had come here for help and it didn't seem like I was any safer or closer to rescuing my parents. Maybe this had been a mistake.

Maybe there was a reason why Dad didn't want to get X's help anymore.

The moment we heard X close the bedroom door, Parker rushed over to his backpack. "Cover me," he whispered, sitting on the floor out of view from the hallway. "Make sure he doesn't come back yet."

"What? Why?" I asked as he took out his laptop from under the sofa. "What are you doing?"

"I've been downloading whatever was on that flash drive. Good thing I didn't have it in the bag when he searched it."

I glanced over at the hallway that led to the bedrooms. "You think there's something on there about me?"

"Maybe. We'll have to check it out later." Parker yanked the stick out from the side of his computer and gave it to me. "Here. Put it back before he goes looking for it."

I grabbed the flash drive and ran to the kitchen, opening the drawer and pulling back the duct tape. Just as I re-attached the flash drive and closed the drawer, X walked in.

"I got you two some baseball caps and . . ." He stopped mid-sentence.

I smiled innocently from behind the counter. He had changed into a pair of khakis and a long-sleeved button-down. He had a couple of caps and sweatshirts in his hands.

"What are you doing over there?" he asked.

"Just looking for something to eat before we go."

X glanced at the empty bowls of cereal in the sink.

"Some people like to eat more than just cereal," Parker added.

"Uh-huh." X flung an olive-green baseball cap at Parker and slid a white one toward me. "Put these on. We can get some food on the way." Next, he placed the sweatshirts on the kitchen counter. "You can each use one of these for now and I'll try to get you different clothes later on."

I held my breath as X walked over to the drawer and slid his fingers underneath it. Would he notice that the flash drive had been moved? I needed to keep him distracted. "I have a change of clothes in my backpack that I can wear . . . if you want to take a look." I pointed to the bag in the corner.

X glanced over to where I was pointing. "What else do you have in that bag besides clothes?" I went to grab it but still saw him pull out the flash drive and slip it into his pocket.

I brought over the bag, happy for the distraction. "It's just stuff my mom threw in there in case of an emergency because we were under a tornado warning last night. I didn't really look through it."

"I see." X unzipped all the pockets and pulled out one of my flannel shirts, a pair of leggings, our first-aid kit, a small towel, duct tape, and my wallet. "Looks like L packed you some granola bars and a bottle of water, too," he remarked, stuffing everything back inside. "You two can have those when we get to the car. Now let's get going."

"Um, where am I going exactly?" Parker asked, his

backpack slung over his shoulder. "Because I'd rather stay with Ka—"

"We'll discuss that later." X slipped on a pair of dark sunglasses, picked up the duffel bag with the money, and walked to the front door. "We can't waste any more time here. I'm not sure who might show up . . . or when."

"But couldn't it be my dad who'll show up here? If we leave, how will he know where to find us?" I asked. X didn't pause, smoothly punching in a code on the house alarm.

"Don't worry. He'll find us or I'll find him," X said as he opened the front door. "But we need to go . . . now. This location is compromised."

Parker and I exchanged a quick glance before following X to the car.

Leaving the safe house without information on my parents seemed like a bad idea, but what other options did I have? My fingers lingered over the door handle.

"I don't like this guy," Parker whispered. "Something is off. Don't you think?"

My gut had been telling me the same thing, but my parents knew X and trusted him. I shrugged. "Maybe he—"

"Get in!" X ordered, already starting the car. "Now!"

"If you want, I'll stick with you until they find your dad," Parker said as I opened the car door. "I don't care what this guy says."

I nodded and slid across the seat as Parker followed me in. "I'm really sorry for getting you involved in all this." I leaned close to Parker. "I thought you'd be on your way home by now."

"It's all good." Parker looked out the window. "Like he said, things weren't that great anyway. It's not like anyone's going to be writing me a note saying they miss me." He put his head back as the driveway gates opened.

"Wait!" I shouted, suddenly coming up with an idea as the car started rolling. "Can we at least leave a note or something . . . in case my dad does show up? Something that only he'll understand. So he knows I'm okay. Or maybe we can come back tomorrow and see if he came by."

X shook his head. "It doesn't work that way." He paused to look back at the house. "Chances are, none of us will be coming back here. It was a nice place while it lasted."

Parker sat up again. "So, you're just going to leave all your stuff?"

"Casualty of the job," X replied. "In this business you can't have attachments."

"What exactly *is* your job?" Parker stared at X's reflection in the rearview mirror.

Agent X said nothing, acting as if he hadn't heard the question.

An uneasy silence followed.

Parker glanced at me before continuing. "Well, can you at least tell us where we're going?"

"Somewhere safe," he said.

"But where is that?" Parker persisted. "Or do you not know?"

I widened my eyes at Parker. There was no reason to antagonize X. He was our only chance at reaching my dad and helping my mom. We needed him on our side.

"I suggest you not ask so many questions, Mr. Jimenez, and simply remain quiet," X advised. "Otherwise, I may have to silence you myself."

CHAPTER 10

RULES FOR LYING

THINGS WEREN'T ADDING UP.

Parker's suspicions were starting to grow in my head, too.

We'd been driving south on the highway for almost an hour, but X still hadn't told us anything about where we were actually going. Why had we left Atlanta? Wouldn't there be government offices or other safe houses in such a big city?

I leaned forward, sticking my head between the front seats. "Listen, X . . ." I said in a low voice, "I know we live in a world of secrets, but we've been driving for a while and I think I should know what's going to happen next. This involves me directly."

X didn't respond. He didn't even look at me.

"What about my dad? You still haven't explained how he's supposed to find us."

Silence.

"Come on, dude!" Parker was exasperated. "What's the point of not telling us where we're headed when we can see where you're driving. It's not like we're blind."

X slowed down the car and pulled onto the highway's shoulder.

I glared at Parker. He might have just given X an unwanted idea and taken us from a bad to worse situation.

X reached over and opened the glove compartment, taking out a screwdriver.

We were in the middle of nowhere, with the sun starting to set, and no backup plan. I thought about darting out of the car, but where would I go? Maybe Parker and I could overpower him together. But then what?

X turned around, whipped off his sunglasses, and studied the two of us for a couple of seconds. "All right. Since it seems like the three of us might be stuck with one another for a bit . . . I'll let you in on a few things."

I pushed the small of my back against the seat to brace myself for whatever was coming next.

"One." He held up a finger. "Where are we going? Miami." He lifted a second finger. "Two. How will your father find us? I've left him a message through a back channel that we use, and no, I'm not telling you what that is." A third finger came up. "Three, and this is the last one. What happens next? That's not up to me. I react to the situation as it presents itself, always keeping my cover, and I suggest that you do the same. Do that and hopefully we all come out of this unscathed. Understood?"

"But what about my mom? Do you know where they took

her?" I asked. "Are people working on getting her back? How will we know if they do?"

"I'm working on that, too." He sighed, and his face seemed to soften a little. "L is a smart woman. She should be fine for now."

"But how can you be sure?"

X's eyes darted over to Parker, who was listening intently to everything being said. "I know these people. They won't harm her. She's not the one they want."

"She's a bargaining chip," Parker added. "They'll trade her for Katrina's dad. Right?"

X nodded. "Something like that." He lifted up the screw-driver. "Now, I'm going to switch the car's license plate to give us a little more anonymity while we're driving." He opened the car door. "And I usually don't work with kids, so I'd appreciate it if you two stayed quiet so I can think of how we're going to get out of this mess."

Parker and I glanced at each other, but did as we were told.

Neither of us said another word for hours.

I stared at the passing scenery. It was mainly trees with the occasional town until we crossed the Georgia-Florida border. It was then that X slowed down and pulled off the highway. I knew that Miami was all the way at the bottom of the state, so there had to be another reason why we were stopping.

"What's going on?" Parker asked.

"Getting us some gas and food. We still have a long ride."

X pulled into a gas station where we were the only car. "You can eat anything, right? No allergies?"

We both nodded.

"All right. Stay in the car," X ordered as he got out.

We watched as X walked around the gas pump and into the convenience store.

The moment the door closed behind him, Parker started talking. "None of this feels right." He pulled out his laptop. "How can we be sure he's who he says he is?"

"Who else would he be?" I fidgeted in my seat but kept my eyes fixed on the convenience store windows where I could see X walking around. "I know that it's weird that we didn't go to some government office, but he's always been the one to help my parents. Even if you don't like him, we've got to trust that this is just the way things are done."

"But how do you know *he* was the one helping them." Parker kept typing on the computer. "What if he isn't even Agent X? Maybe he's pretending to be him and it's just a clever way to kidnap us. Do you know what Agent X looks like?"

"No." I bit my fingernail. "But something does feel familiar about him. I can't explain it. Like I have some old memory of him. My gut says it's him."

Parker kept typing, then hit the side of his laptop in frustration. "Ugh . . . Wi-Fi isn't strong enough here! I can't do research on this car's plates or anything!"

"But what about the stuff you got from X's flash drive? Maybe there's something there."

"I tried." Parker sighed. "They're encrypted, so it'll take some time." He turned to look at me. "Maybe we can make a deal with the cops. Tell them what we know and have them help us."

"Cops? Are you serious? We're with the feds already . . . why would we go to them when we don't know anything?" I shook my head. "No way. X is the only link to my parents. I'm not going to lose that."

"Okay, but then what do we do? Go along without asking questions?"

"He's coming!" I slapped Parker's laptop closed as X approached the car holding a bag. "Act normal."

Parker slipped the laptop back into his bag and pushed it under the seat. "Keep him busy," he said. "I have an idea."

Before I could ask him anything else, X opened my door.

"Here," he said, thrusting the bag toward me. "There weren't any healthy options."

I peered inside and saw chips, beef jerky, candy bars, and a couple of bottles of water.

Parker opened his door and stepped out.

"Hey, what do you think you're doing?" X walked quickly around the car. "Get back inside."

"I need to go to the bathroom," Parker stated, looking directly at X. "It's an emergency."

"Now? You can't wait?" X asked in a hushed voice.

"Nope." Parker shifted from one foot to another. "Gotta

go . . . right now." He pointed to the empty station. "And no one's here. Don't you have to pump the gas anyway?"

X sighed. "Fine. Just hurry up." He looked over at me. "Can you wait or do you suddenly have to go, too?"

I wasn't sure what Parker was up to, but he probably needed me to stay and distract X. "I'm fine," I said as casually as possible. "I'm just going to stretch my legs."

I strolled around the car, but X kept his focus on Parker. Both of us could see him talking to the clerk behind the counter, who promptly gave him a key and pointed to the back of the store. Parker quickly glanced outside before disappearing behind some cases of bottled water.

I needed to give Parker time. Plus, this might be my chance to get some answers. Maybe X would speak more freely without Parker around.

I walked around to where X was pumping the gas.

"Can we talk a little bit about what's really going on now that Parker isn't here?" I said, mustering up as much confidence as I could. "About what you're planning to do."

"Nope." X remained laser focused on the convenience store.

Seconds passed, then a minute.

X hung the gas nozzle back on the pump and checked his watch. Parker was taking longer than expected.

I had to come up with something

"I know what this is all about," I said.

X turned to face me. "You do?" He analyzed me, my reactions. "You got your memory back? After all these years?"

I didn't bat an eye. A good lie always includes the truth. Something you know to be true and then you allow the deception to spread from there. It was how we had survived for the past few years. Those were our rules for lying.

"Some of my memory," I said. "But Dad filled in the gaps."

"He did, huh?" X raised an eyebrow, not believing me. "That's surprising. Doesn't sound like your dad."

I shrugged. "He thought I'd eventually learn the truth and that it was better if I heard it from him. Mom wasn't too happy about it, though."

"I imagine she wasn't."

"Plus, I was having more flashbacks."

"Flashbacks?" X closed the lid on the car's gas tank. "Like what?"

"Like from when he was a scientist. I mean, he's still a scientist. Mom even mentioned having him go back to . . ." I deliberately paused. This was about all I knew, but X didn't need to know that. "Wait, how do I know that *you* know everything? My parents told me not to discuss this with anyone. They didn't carve out an exception for you." I paused. "For all I know you aren't even the real X."

"Then who would I be?" he asked, leaning against the car. "You came to me, remember?"

I crossed my arms and waited. "Trust, but verify."

"I remember your mother once saying something very

similar to me. Guess the apple doesn't fall far from the tree."

"Part of our core values."

X laughed. "Now *that* sounds like your dad."

"Huh?" I didn't get what was so funny.

"Apple from the tree . . . *core* values," X explained. "It sounds like one of your dad's puns."

"Oh yeah, guess it does." I tried relaxing my shoulders to make it seem like I was dropping my guard . . . even if I wasn't. Although him knowing my dad's love of bad jokes seemed like confirmation that he actually knew my parents and wasn't some imposter.

I stayed quiet, waiting for him to say something else.

Another rule of lying was to get the other person talking. Mom would tell me that it helped establish a connection. Something to use in order to build a relationship. Even if it was a fake one.

"So how long have you known my dad?" I asked as casually as possible.

X scanned the area to make sure no one was approaching while we waited for Parker. "Since we were kids. He loved bad jokes back then, too. He was the brain and I was the muscle." X took a long, hard look at my face. "He's always been the smartest guy I know."

"Dad doesn't talk much about when he was kid. Where did you two grow up?" I asked, hoping it might be the same place I remembered in the desert southwest.

"Nowhere special." He cocked his head to the side and

smiled. "But let's go back to you. Tell me what your dad told you."

It was my turn to answer some questions, but I couldn't.

I didn't know anything, but this was where my years of training had to come into play.

I saw Parker come out of the store. "I can't. Not now." I pointed to Parker. "He's coming back and he thinks that I don't know anything about what my dad did . . . only that people are after us. I didn't want to give him the details."

"Smart move," X muttered to me before turning to face Parker. "You took long enough," X complained as Parker got closer.

"Well, I had to do my business." Parker fanned his nose. "And you do NOT want to go in there."

"Ugh!" I recoiled at Parker's comment.

Parker grinned. "Just be glad I went when I did. It would have been worse if I'd stayed in the car."

X walked around the car and opened his door. "Let's just go."

As Parker and I got in the back, he discreetly gave me a thumbs-up.

I scrunched my eyebrows because I had no idea what he'd just done. All I could hope for was that, whatever it was, it wouldn't come back to haunt us.

CHAPTER 11

A FACE WITH NO PAST

FOR HOURS THERE WAS nothing to do in the car except stare out the window. I saw the sun set and cast the sky in pink and purple hues as we stopped for a brief bathroom break at a rest stop, then nightfall crept in and enveloped the car. I couldn't believe that it had only been that morning when my biggest concern was sneaking into town with Parker to get his laptop. It all seemed so silly. So trivial compared to our current situation.

Most kids my age had spent nights away from their parents—at a sleepover with friends, or even at camp. But I'd never spent the night away from my parents before. They were all I'd ever had.

I stared at the darkness outside the window. At first all I could see was the silhouette of trees against the star-filled night, but then my eyes refocused and I saw my reflection. A face with no past.

I kept trying to sort out everything I knew about my

parents and my past while my eyelids got heavier and heavier. Without even realizing it, I drifted off to sleep.

And it wasn't a light nap.

No, this was a deep sleep. The kind where your mind shuts off and there are no dreams, no awareness of what's happening around you.

I felt someone tug on my arm, but I wasn't able to react.

A fleeting image filled my brain. Something I hadn't seen before.

No, it was a memory. I had seen it. I had lived it. I just couldn't remember it before that very moment.

Mom was pulling my arm as I tried to slip out of her grip and run toward a mountain range that loomed in the distance. There was a playground nearby, but I didn't want to go on the slide or on the swings.

I tugged at her arm, trying to get away.

There was a sense of fear growing inside me. A sense of desperation.

On a far bench I saw Dad wearing his lab coat and speaking to someone who had their back to me.

I twisted my arm and squirmed my way out of Mom's grasp.

I felt free and happy. I sensed the sand and gravel crackling under my shoes as I raced toward the mountains.

"Eva, stop!" Mom shouted. "STOP!"

The way she yelled at me made me pause and turn around.

There was the playground, a large three-story building

behind it, my father with the man on the bench, and Mom.

She was still holding my hand.

I was confused. Had I never broken free of her grip?

My hand got pulled again, this time with more force.

"Katrina," someone whispered, fingers around my wrist. "Wake up."

I opened my eyes, disoriented. It was pitch black outside and I could feel a breeze coming in from the slightly open windows.

"We stopped." Parker pulled out his laptop. "X went inside and said for us to wait here while he got some supplies."

I sat up and looked around. We were parked in front of a twenty-four-hour Walmart, but my thoughts were still in the past. I had lived that moment, I was sure, even though it seemed like an impossible dream.

"Everything okay?" Parker asked without really looking at me.

"Um, yeah." I rubbed my eyes, forcing myself to pay attention to the present. "Are we in Miami?" I asked, unsure how long I'd been sleeping.

"Nah, we passed a sign about thirty minutes ago that said it was two hundred miles away." Parker typed something in his laptop.

Even though I was more alert, I tried to keep my connection to that far-off world I'd just seen . . . to the most important word.

Eva.

The name reverberated in my head, silencing everything else around me.

I had finally discovered who I used to be. At least a small piece of the puzzle had been filled in.

Names were something we tossed away with each new move, but a name was significant.

A name has importance.

A name has meaning.

And I now knew my own.

"The Wi-Fi here is super weak," Parker complained, staring at his laptop. "I'd have to get closer to the store, but X might catch me. I don't think we can risk it."

I didn't say anything, still thinking about my discovery. Did I feel like an Eva?

"Hello . . . are you listening?" Parker asked.

"No, sorry," I muttered, collecting my thoughts as best I could. "It's just that something happened when I fell asleep. I remembered a piece of my past from when I was little. I was at a playground and my dad was talking to some man—"

Parker looked intently at me. "Was it X?"

"No, it was someone else, but I heard my mom call out my name. I think I know my real name." I braced myself, as if saying it out loud would trigger a tsunami of emotions that I wasn't prepared to handle.

I took a deep breath. "It's Eva."

"Whoa. That's huge." Parker's fingers hovered over the

keyboard, itching for a little more information. "What else do you remember? Maybe a last name that we can look up?"

"No. It was like a quick snapshot. My mom yelled it out when I ran away from her. We were in a desert with some mountains in the distance."

"Hmm." Parker mulled over everything I was saying. "That doesn't give us much, but it's a start." He bit his lip. "Do you still want me to call you Katrina?"

Katrina versus Eva. It was more than just a name, but I wasn't sure who I wanted to be.

I didn't remember being Eva.

And at least I had chosen the name Katrina, and it was while being Katrina that I had met Parker.

"I like Katrina." I gazed at Parker's open computer. "But we should try to find out more about what you downloaded . . . while we have the chance."

Parker nodded. "And I have a program that will help break any encryption, but first, check this out." Parker shifted in his seat and pulled out a small plastic pineapple from his pocket. "I got us our backup plan."

"A toy pineapple?" I was completely confused.

He grinned and pulled the top off. "It's a flash drive. We can make our own backup of the stuff we got from X's drive. Pretty good, huh? I bought it while you guys thought I was pooping my brains out."

"Yeah, about that." I sat up a little more. "You can't take off and do stuff without telling me. We're in this together, okay?"

Parker rolled his eyes. "It wasn't a big deal. I wasn't going to do anything drastic."

"But how would I know that? We've been friends for, what . . . a week and a half?"

"Feels longer, but you're right." I saw Parker's jaw tighten. "I guess we don't really know each other that well."

Now I felt bad. "That's not what I meant." I sighed, realizing that Parker was my only friend and I was already messing things up. "Listen, I trust you, but I need to know what's going on. I've never had a friend who knows my secrets. Who knows my name."

Parker's face softened. "Yeah, I've been on my own for a long time, too. Not really used to checking with anyone before I do something." He gave me his goofy, lopsided grin. "Guess I need to remember that we're partners in this."

"Partners and friends." I pointed to the flash drive. "Now tell me about that pineapple thing. How does that help us when we already have a copy on your computer?"

Parker plugged it into the side of his laptop and resumed typing. "It's insurance . . . like in the movies. Where if something happens to us, it gets sent to the cops." He wiggled his eyebrows. "I'm a genius, right?"

"Um, sure," I said, not wanting to offend him, but still not understanding how it would help. "I just don't get who'd send it to the cops? And how would this person even know that something happened to us?"

Parker's shoulders drooped a little. "Um, I haven't worked out all the details." He shrugged off the doubts. "But I will. In the meantime, let me see if I can break any of these encryptions." He typed quickly, his eyes focused on some elaborate coding on the screen.

I once again tried reviewing that little scrap of memory that had poked through the fogginess of my past. Pushing myself to expand on it. Trying to remember something from before or after that moment.

But there was nothing.

No, that wasn't true. I could feel something there.

An entire lifetime hidden in my brain, waiting to remind me of my life before the accident.

"I got something!" Parker pointed to the screen. "It's a log of online access for some place called Sterling BioGenysis." Parker faced me. "Does that name sound familiar?"

I shook my head.

"Okay, since there's no Wi-Fi, we'll have to look it up later." He studied the information on the screen. "Looks like most of the entries are by Bennet Fisher and a couple by Geoffrey Sterling."

"Bennet Fisher could be my dad," I mused. "He always picks names that start with B, but that's just a guess. Can you see what Bennet Fisher was doing?"

"Not yet, but there was something that I might be able to access. Hold on." Parker continued pulling up different screens and typing different codes on the laptop. "There was something in one of the subfiles that just might . . ."

"What?" I asked, staring at what seemed to be a list of jumbled letters and numbers.

"Here." He pointed to a photograph that appeared on the screen. "This JPEG file wasn't like the others and just required a similar log—"

I couldn't hear what he was rambling on about. All I could do was stare at the picture that had appeared on the computer.

It was a screenshot of me lying in a hospital bed, connected to a bunch of wires with electrodes on either side of my forehead. It looked like a still from a security camera.

"Whoa . . . that's you, right?" Parker asked in a hushed voice.

I felt a huge knot in my throat as I stared at myself. "It must be from when I had my accident."

"The bottom says it's from about three years ago."

"Yeah, that's when I lost my memory." I turned the laptop to get a better look. *EIIIA exp.* was written before the date. "What do you think that means?" I asked, pointing to the words. "Some sort of code?"

"Could be the name of the machine recording the image," Parker suggested. "Might not mean anything."

"But why would this picture be saved?" I scanned the black-and-white image for other clues. "It must mean something."

The lights in the car turned on and the doors unlocked remotely.

X was coming back with a shopping cart full of things.

"We'll have to look for more clues later," I said as Parker slipped the laptop back in his bag and hid it under the seat. "For now, we need to go along with whatever X is planning. Until we can get ahold of my dad."

Parker nodded as X put the bags in the trunk.

"You took a while," I said as X opened the door to get behind the wheel.

"Had to get several things," he said curtly, turning on the car. "Don't usually need to plan on bringing along two kids when starting phase two of an operation." He shifted the car into reverse and pulled out of the parking space.

"Phase two?" Parker questioned. "What was phase one?"

"Phase one is escaping," X explained, driving out of the parking lot. "Phase two is disappearing. That's why I bought everything we'll need to establish our new identities."

"Is there a phase three?" I asked as we merged onto the nearby highway.

X glanced at me through the rearview mirror and nodded. "That's when we implement the mission." He hit the accelerator as we raced into the darkness. "The rescue mission."

CHAPTER 12

CLARK KENT

I LOOKED AT MYSELF in the bathroom mirror of the dingy motel where we had spent the night. It was another day and another look for me.

And I actually didn't look too bad. It had taken a while to bleach my brown hair to blond, but the new color reminded me of the days when I went by the name of Carla and we lived in Memphis.

I grabbed a pair of brown-framed nonprescription glasses from the shopping bag and put them on to complete the transformation.

I no longer looked like Katrina.

Once again, I was a different girl.

And yet it didn't faze me. After changing appearances so many times, I still knew who I was inside, regardless of my name or hair color.

But apparently Parker didn't feel the same way, because when I opened the bathroom door, he and X were still going back and forth about shaving Parker's dark, curly hair.

"You have limited options." X turned to look at the new

me. "See . . . *she* doesn't have a problem with changing her look."

X had already transformed himself into someone else. He was wearing a silver wig that looked like it was his real hair and a fake mustache. It was obvious that he had done this all before and was a master of disguises.

"I don't care," Parker insisted. "I'm not shaving my head." He pulled down the baseball cap he was wearing. "This covers my hair and . . ." He walked over to where I was standing and took the glasses off my face. "If I put these on . . ." He slipped them over his ears and smiled. "Ta-da. It's like I'm Clark Kent. No one can recognize me."

I bit my lip.

We were in a dangerous situation with a man we didn't fully trust and yet, somehow, Parker seemed to lighten the tension in the room.

At least for me.

X was not amused. But he also didn't want to argue the point any further. "Fine, whatever. But the cap and glasses stay on at all times when we go out." He picked up the pillow and blanket off the floor where he'd slept and tossed it all on one of the beds. "This is why I hate working with kids," he muttered, grabbing his duffel bag and setting it all on the small table by the window.

"Are we going to try to meet up with my dad today?" I asked.

"Maybe." X turned around with the small camera in his

hand that he had pulled out of his duffel bag. "I sent him a message so he'd know not to go home and where to rendezvous with us. I'll see how he responds." He pointed to the bare wall next to the far bed. "Stand over there. I need to take a headshot of each of you. And don't smile in the picture."

"Why do you need photos of us?" Parker asked as we both did as we were told and stood side by side against the wall.

"IDs," X replied, snapping a picture of each of us.

I took a doughnut from a box on the nightstand and sat next to Parker on the bed. We silently watched as X pulled out a tiny printer, a tackle box, and several passports from the duffel bag.

Parker and I glanced at each other as X hunched over the passports with a pair of tiny scissors.

Leaving the country had not been part of the plan. X's actions were becoming more and more suspicious. None of this was adding up. The government wouldn't give us fake passports . . . they'd be able to give us real ones. "Um, why do we need fake passports?" I asked. "I thought we were going to Miami to meet Dad there."

"I'm traveling with two kids," he said, not bothering to look our way. "Need something to show we're a family. Plus, what other type of ID would kids have?" He shook his head as if he couldn't believe he needed to explain things. "And I need to keep our options open."

"But won't people be able to tell those are fake?" Parker asked as X turned on a tablet that he'd had in his duffel bag.

X ignored him. "Tell me what you want as a first name," he said while connecting the tablet to the printer. "We'll all be part of the Garcia family. I already have a passport with that name and this disguise. You two can be my kids . . . from different mothers."

I looked at Parker sitting next to me on the bed. He didn't need to be here. "Parker, this really is more than what you bargained for. If you want to go—"

"It's too late for him to back out at this point." X typed something into the tablet. "It was actually too late the moment he took off in that horse trailer with you."

"Cow," Parker corrected him.

"Huh?" X scrunched his eyebrows and glanced over at us.

"It was a cow trailer," Parker said, his arms crossed and his face clearly showing his annoyance. "And not that I'm backing out, but why is it too late? Maybe Katrina and I are better off on our own."

"On your own?" X scoffed, as if the idea was ridiculous.

"Yeah." Parker stood up and got closer to me. "I've got my own resources. I know people."

X's expression seemed to change. It was as if he was seeing us for the first time. Me, a girl completely willing to change everything about herself, who had lost the only two people who really knew her, and Parker, a boy who had bounced around from place to place and always tried to be self-reliant, but was clearly in over his head.

"Listen." X sighed and his shoulders relaxed a bit. "I know this is all a bit intense. But the people we're dealing with . . . they don't mess around. I'm sure they've figured out that you were helping her, and they can't take any chances on what you may or may not know."

"But he doesn't know anything," I said.

"I get that." X nodded. "I do. But they won't care. Parker isn't safe anymore. He's in as much danger as you . . . probably more."

"More danger?" Parker repeated, a little incredulous. "Than Katrina?"

X shrugged. "You're dispensable. She's not."

"Oh," Parker and I said in unison, realizing what he meant.

"So, at this point, I'm going to try to protect the two of you." He leaned back in his chair. "Listen, your father trusted me with his secrets. He trusted me with you. I hope you do the same."

My father and his secrets.

It always came back to this.

"Protect us from who exactly?" I asked. "We should at least know who's after us."

X's eyes narrowed and he cocked his head to one side. "I thought your father had told you everything."

Ugh! I had messed up my lie from the night before. "Well, he told me most of—"

"Stop." X raised his hand, holding back a smirk. "Don't bother lying. You might be good, but I'm much better and you didn't fool me with your little ploy at the gas station." He paused. "Nice try, though. Now let me get back to—"

"No!" Parker jumped up from the bed. "Nothing is going to happen until we get answers. Real ones, because I don't think you're really with the government."

X remained quiet.

"Are you?" Parker persisted. "Are you a government agent?"

"I am," X said. "But not like you think. You'll never find my name on any government payroll. My role is . . . more nuanced."

"Are we really in the Witness Protection Program?" I asked as plainly as possible.

Inside, I was trembling, but I tried to keep my emotions in check. I couldn't let the creeping fear of finding out the truth stop me.

"No," X answered. "But your parents thought it best to have you believe that. I've been using my resources to create their own type of protection program."

My heart sank inside my chest. Not because I didn't expect the answer, but because I did. It had been something that I'd never wanted to face. There'd been clues for so long, but I'd put on blinders in order to keep the lie going.

Parker glanced over at me, then back at X. "But then who exactly are we running from? It's not a drug cartel, is it? Because if it were, we'd be with some real feds by now."

"Smart kid." X took a deep breath and slowly let it out. "Neither one of you is going to let this go, are you?"

We shook our heads.

X's eyes narrowed as he decided what to say next. "It's a powerful conglomerate with an even more powerful man in charge. You've probably never heard of them, but they have their hands in a lot of things that the public never finds out about. They control a lot of things."

"Sterling BioGenysis," I said, gauging X's reaction.

"That's one of their companies, and your dad is someone they want . . . at any cost." X turned around to face the desk.

"But why do they want to kill him? Kill us?"

X shook his head. "Your father can answer those questions. Right now, I need to finish these passports." The conversation was apparently over . . . for now. "Give me the names you want to use. Just the first name."

"Um . . . how about Carlos?" Parker suggested. "That's my dad's name."

X shrugged. "Sure."

"Make my name . . ." I paused, then plowed ahead with my idea. "Eva."

I could see X's body tense up for a second. "No. Pick something else," he replied in a very businesslike tone.

His response seemed to confirm that the flash of memory I'd had was real. My name had been Eva.

"How about Layla?" Parker suggested, using the name I'd mentioned to him. "You were thinking of that name anyway."

"I guess." It was strange. For the first time, I didn't want to change my name. I still wanted to be Katrina.

"All right." X continued working at the desk. "Those are your new names. I'm using Henry Garcia. We'll go over a backstory later, but for now I'm just a somewhat absentee dad who hasn't been in your lives too much . . . except for this trip that we're taking to Miami." He paused for a moment. "Not that anyone should be asking."

"What about—"

X raised a hand, cutting off Parker's question as he focused on the passports. "I need to concentrate, so no more talking."

"Well, in that case, I'm going to take a shower." Parker stood up and grabbed some of the new clothes along with his backpack.

"Mm-hmm." X didn't turn around.

Parker stopped at the door of the bathroom and pointed to his backpack. He gave me the thumbs-up before shutting the door.

He was going to do some more research. We now knew about Sterling BioGenysis, my name being Eva, and that X wasn't with the Witness Protection Program.

I trusted that Parker would be able to find something more.

The minutes passed and X stepped outside to make a call on a satellite phone that he claimed was untraceable.

Through the motel window I could see him pacing around our car, which was parked outside the room. I couldn't hear anything he was saying, but he didn't seem very happy.

I glanced at the closed bathroom door. The shower was still running, but Parker had been inside for too long. X would notice it and become suspicious as soon as he came back inside.

"Parker, hurry up," I whispered, knocking on the door. "X will be back soon."

The door opened.

"Back?" Parker asked, peering into the room. He was already dressed in his new clothes and was wearing his fake glasses. "Where did he go?"

I pointed outside. "He's making a call. Did you find out anything?"

"On a cell phone?" Parker shook his head. "Didn't he get angry at me for using mine?"

"It's a satellite phone. He said it was secure." I shrugged. "I don't know. Who cares?"

Parker mulled it over. "Hmm, probably some type of encryption software like what I have on my laptop. I used it when I got on the motel's Wi-Fi. It masks the IP address and reroutes—"

"I have no idea what you're talking about." I pulled back the curtain a bit and saw X leaning against the car. "Just tell me what you found out before he comes back."

"Oh, right. Well, there's not much about X. The car's original license plate was listed under the same name as the house . . . Eduardo Krajewski. The new plate belongs to the name he's using now . . . Henry Garcia."

"And we know those names are fake." My finger tapped the side of my leg. We were running out of time. "What else?"

"Yeah, but the names we saw on the access log were real. Geoffrey Sterling . . . he's the CEO of Sterling BioGenysis and he's, like, a gazillionaire. No one even knows exactly how much money he has." Parker paused. "And um, Bennet Fisher . . ."

I twisted the side of my pants, not wanting to get my hopes up too much. "Yeah?"

"It's definitely your dad," Parker said.

Bennet Fisher.

My dad's name.

Which made me Eva Fisher.

"I found a picture from a charity event from about twenty years ago . . . but it's him," Parker continued. "He worked as a scientist for BioGenysis and they have their main lab outside of Ashe, New Mexico. So, I figured that might be the place you were describing and started looking for birth certificates in New Mexico."

I couldn't say anything. I was trying to absorb all the information about myself and my family.

Parker glanced out the window. "I couldn't find a birth certificate, but I did find a marriage certificate. Bennet Fisher married Lydia Nikitin about fourteen years ago. I think that might be your mom."

Bennet and Lydia.

B and L.

It all made sense.

I now knew our family names. Questions were being answered. We weren't the mystery we once were.

Unfortunately, the price to be paid for having this information was the possibility that I'd never see my parents again.

"Change of plans," X announced, thrusting the door open and catching both Parker and me by surprise. "Hope neither one of you gets seasick."

CHAPTER 13

LESSONS IN GEOGRAPHY

A BOAT.

Our mission to rescue my parents now involved being out on the water until we contacted Dad. X explained that a boat gave us more mobility while being less visible, so we'd wait for Dad to communicate with us on the high seas. And Dad was the key to rescuing Mom.

It took us about two hours to drive to the marina in Miami. During that time, X quizzed us on our backstory. For the time being, we each had to play our part in a somewhat dysfunctional family. In addition to memorizing our made-up birthdays, we had to be able to give a short explanation of who we were and why we were traveling together.

Parker's story was that he lived in Chicago with his mother. Her name was Susan Conrad and she worked at a bank. My mother was Doris Hernandez and she was a teacher in Oakland. Both mothers had agreed to let us come with our father, who we hadn't seen in years, to visit our sick grandmother in the Bahamas for a week.

Parker stuck his head between the two front seats and gazed out the window at the boatyard up ahead. "You don't think it all sounds a little simple?" he asked.

I turned to look at Parker from the front passenger seat. X had said it looked suspicious to not have one of us call shotgun, and so he chose me to sit up front with him.

"Simple is best," I answered as we entered the Grove City Marina. "You start with a bit of truth and keep the lie as clean as possible. Nothing too crazy."

"Listen to your friend there," X replied, pulling into a parking space next to some large boats. "She's been doing this for a while."

"Yeah, sure." Parker gazed out the window. "I thought the ocean would look different. Kind of looks like Lake Michigan."

"That's because that's not the ocean." X turned off the car. "It's Biscayne Bay."

"It leads to the ocean, though," I said. "I remember how the bay in Oakland went out to the Pacific."

"You two continue the geography lesson while I see someone about the boat." He opened the door and gave us both a smile as fake as our names. "I'll leave the car running with the AC. All right, Carlos and Layla?"

"Sure . . . *Dad*," I responded with my own phony grin.

Parker gave him a thumbs-up. "You got it, *Father*."

X sighed and closed the door behind him.

We watched him go into the small marina office next to the open-air restaurant near the docks. It was close to noon and there were several people sitting at the tables right by the water.

"Think it's time for a little more research, don't you?" Parker smirked as he unzipped his backpack. "You know what to do."

"I'm on the lookout," I said, keeping my eyes on the office door. "Anything you can find out about my dad or BioGenysis might help us figure out where my dad went, 'cause X might be good at disappearing, but I'm an expert on my dad."

"Got it," Parker said, opening his laptop. "Aw, crap. I don't have a strong enough signal here from the restaurant's Wi-Fi." He pointed to the people having lunch. "We need to go there."

I shook my head. Parker wasn't thinking things through. "We can't. X will see that we left."

Parker grabbed a napkin from the floor and handed it to me. "Leave him a note."

"And say what?"

Parker shrugged. "I don't know. You're the lie expert, remember? And it's not like he's our real dad and can tell us what to do anyway. Just keep it simple."

I rolled my eyes, but he was right. X trusted that we weren't going to run away and we trusted that he wasn't going to leave us behind. There was no reason why we couldn't go to the restaurant, especially if we were in disguise and being careful. Plus, information was critical at this point if I was going to help find my dad and rescue my mom.

"Fine." I took a pen from the door's side pocket and wrote a quick note on the napkin. "I'll say that we went to get a drink and stretch our legs."

"Perfect." Parker turned off the car, slipped the key into his pocket, and slung his backpack over his shoulder. "Let's go before he comes back."

We raced over to the restaurant, where the hostess escorted us toward a table near the water's edge where we could catch a breeze on what was a hot, cloudy day. There were people at the tables next to us and I could hear pieces of their conversations as we passed by.

Not the most discreet of locations.

"Could we sit over there?" I pointed to a table all the way in the back of the restaurant, away from the dock and close to the bathroom and back door. There was no one sitting in that area.

"Um, sure." She gave a small shrug and walked us there. She plopped two menus on the table as I took a seat facing the boats and the parking lot.

"Oh, and I'm just ordering a Coke," I said, thinking about the little cash I had left in my bag.

She sighed and picked up the menus. "I'll tell your waitress."

Parker sat down and waited for her to leave.

"Okay." He unzipped his bag. "I can—"

"Don't do it here," I cautioned. "Someone might mention to X that we have a computer." I pointed to the bathroom. "Go do it there."

"The bathroom? Again?" Parker pursed his lips. "The toilet is not the best place to do research. Plus, won't X get suspicious if he finds out that I'm in the bathroom . . . *again*?"

"Nope." I shook my head and tried to hold back a grin. "You've got IBS. Irritable bowel syndrome. And when you're stressed, you go to the bathroom a lot."

"Really?" Parker did not look pleased with my idea. "I poop a lot?"

"You said it yourself. X isn't your dad. He doesn't know anything about you that's not in a file somewhere. It's totally plausible."

"Fine. Just give me a heads-up when you see him leave the office." Parker stood up. "And order me a water. Extra ice."

The minutes ticked by as I sipped on my Coke. X was taking a lot longer than expected, which was a good thing. I had already paid for the soda and thought about checking in on Parker to find out what he'd discovered so far, but I knew it was more important to give him the extra time to do research. Plus, I wasn't too eager to hang out in the smelly men's bathroom.

As I stared out toward the dock, I noticed X pacing. He was speaking on the phone again and stopped next to one of the restaurant's wooden columns, in an area that was closed off from the public.

This was my chance. I'd gained lots of information over the years from eavesdropping on my parents . . . this would be no different.

My heart pounded as I hurried around the bar stools that blocked that portion of the restaurant and snuck behind the other side of the column.

I could feel my ears twitch as I concentrated on listening to whatever X was saying.

"I understand, but I have a plan. My sources tell me that the Russians and Chinese are aware of the entire project at this point. I've gone dark with the agency, but we have to assume they know as well." X paused, then added, "We don't have much time . . . you'll have to trust me."

A wave of relief washed over me. He had to be talking to Dad. We were now one step closer to rescuing Mom. But why were they talking about the Russians? And Chinese?

I took a step forward, wanting to talk to Dad myself and get answers directly from him.

"Of course, Fisher is the key," X said. "But I need another day or two to get him . . . force his hand."

I spun back behind the column, holding my breath. X was talking to someone else . . . about Dad.

"You need him because at this point, everyone knows about the experiment even if no one admits its existence. They'll want Fisher to explain how he did it or they'll simply try to reverse engineer it if they can get ahold of it."

It was one of my father's experiments that had gotten us

into this mess. Something so valuable that people would kill for it.

My eyes flicked over to where my backpack sat resting on the table next to my Coke and Parker's ice water.

Inside was Mom's little emergency medical kit.

I touched my elbow where I had fallen the other day. It had already perfectly healed. Dad's miraculous cure-all, the thing I used to call the magic mermaid potion, could be what got us into this mess. I had told Dad it was revolutionary. Maybe it really was.

I started to feel sick to my stomach.

My thoughts kept racing as X kept talking.

"Listen, I'll try to convince him to go back, but you have to keep the wife safe. I'm sure I can get him to hand over the experiment in exchange for certain assurances. I can be very convincing."

The blue liquid, I thought. *He doesn't know I have it! I could give it to X right now, bypass Dad, and trade it for Mom's safety. It was selfish of Dad to risk our lives for some stupid experiment.*

Before I could think it through, X said something that changed everything.

"As long as I get paid, I don't care what happens to them . . . and I always tie up loose ends."

A shiver ran down my spine. The one who was supposed to protect us was actually the one betraying us.

I felt overwhelmed and alone. X was my dad's friend

and had helped us for so long; why was he doing this now? What had changed?

None of it made sense.

But one thing was certain . . . I had to get away.

I inched away from the column just as X began to walk toward the parking lot.

My heart beat so hard that I could hear it in my head.

There were only seconds to spare before X would realize that Parker and I had left the car.

Parker.

I had to warn him.

I ran to the table, grabbed my backpack, and headed to the men's room. "PARKER!" I shouted while pushing open the door. "WE HAVE TO GO!"

"Hey!" Parker opened up the stall where he had been sitting on the toilet seat. "What are you doing? This is the men's room. Someone else could've—"

I grabbed him by the arm and pulled him toward the exit as he clutched the laptop in his other hand. "It's X. You were right to not trust him." I was speaking as fast as I could. "He's working with BioGenysis. He's not trying to help us, he's just using us to get to my dad. He sold us out."

"What?" Parker stuffed the computer in his bag while following me out the restaurant's back exit. "How do you know?"

We were in an open area that led to a park. I didn't know where to go, but I knew we didn't have much time. "I heard him on the phone." I started running toward the main street, where an orange-and-green trolley-like bus had stopped at the corner. "We have to get on that thing."

Parker and I ran faster, hopping on just as it was about to pull away.

"How . . . how . . . how much is it?" Parker asked the driver as he tried to catch his breath.

The driver, a large woman wearing sunglasses, smiled and motioned for us to take a seat on one of the wooden benches behind her. "Trolley is free," she said as the doors behind us folded close. "Which stop do you want?" She pointed to the map plastered along the edge of the ceiling next to an ad for teeth cleaning.

I looked out the back window and could see X in the marina parking lot looking around for us. We'd hopped on just in time.

The sign above us had several stops, but there was one that would help us get farther away from X.

"The Metrorail station," I said.

"Then you're on the right trolley," the driver answered. "Just take a seat and I'll get you there."

Parker and I sat down on one of the long wooden benches that lined either side of the trolley. There were a few other people on board, but no one seemed to pay much attention to us.

"I don't think he saw us get on, so we should be okay," I whispered, still a little out of breath from running.

"Even if he did . . ." Parker pulled out the car key. "He's not going anywhere without this."

I could feel my body relax a little. I had forgotten that we had it with us when we went to the restaurant.

"So . . . what did you hear, exactly?" he asked in a low voice as my heart rate settled down.

"You were right to be suspicious of him. I think he's working with the people who kidnapped my mom." I took a deep breath before continuing on. "I heard him say how they should keep my mom safe until my dad made contact. That he'd be able to convince my dad to turn over his experiment . . . probably because he'd tell him they had us and my mom."

"Experiment?" Parker asked.

"Yeah." I opened my backpack and, without taking it out, I unzipped the red first-aid kit. "I think it's this." I pointed to the bottle with blue liquid. "My dad came up with this drug that basically makes your skin heal really fast."

"Uh-huh." Parker didn't look convinced.

I rolled up my shirtsleeve. "Remember the gash I got from skateboarding? Look at it now." I showed him my elbow.

"There isn't even a scab or a scar." Parker lifted my arm up for closer inspection. "But that's amazing."

"I know." A strange sense of pride welled up inside me. "And it healed after just a few hours."

"And you think your dad came up with this?"

"I know he did."

Parker widened his eyes and stared at the little blue bottle. "I mean, selling that could make anyone billions of dollars."

"I know. But for some reason my dad didn't want that to happen." I shook my head at the realization of what both my parents had done . . . not just my dad. "It seems like my parents were willing to go on the run for this stuff. Risk our lives. I just don't know why."

Parker pursed his lips. "Maybe there were weird side effects. That happens in the movies. It turns people into zombies or something."

"That can't be it. My dad wouldn't use it on me if that were true, and I've been using it for as long as I can remember with no side effects."

"That you know of." Parker cracked a smile.

"Very funny," I said, rolling my eyes at him. "But whatever my dad invented, X thinks that the Russians and Chinese are after it, too. I heard him say so on the phone."

"Man." Parker leaned against the wooden seat back. "This is getting more and more complicated. Especially with what I discovered."

"What were you able to find out?" My voice was a bit shaky from the excitement.

"I'll show you." Parker opened his laptop and showed me a spreadsheet full of dates and numbers. "These are bank transactions going back several years. I paired up the sequencing and they are all overseas accounts. Someone is getting a lot of secret money."

"Well, it wasn't my family. We just get a little money from . . ." My voice trailed off.

"From X, right?"

I nodded.

All the money for our moves had always come from him. I'd been told that it was from the Witness Protection Program, but now I knew better. Had he been funneling us money from Sterling BioGenysis? The same people I thought we were running from? That wouldn't make sense. Why not turn us over to them? If he was going to betray us, why wait until now?

Parker let out a breath that sounded like a balloon losing air.

We were both deflated.

Nothing made sense.

The only thing we knew was that we were all in danger.

Parker glanced at me. "I can't believe I'm going to say this, but I think we only have one choice left."

"What?" I wondered, not coming up with any options of my own.

"We have to go to the feds," Parker said. "The real ones."

CHAPTER 14
GOVERNMENT CENTER

THE METRORAIL STATION WAS relatively empty. It didn't seem like it was used by very many people. We bought our tickets from the automatic kiosk and took the stairs up to the platform. From that vantage point, I could see the tops of palm trees and the highway down below. The train itself ran above the city, bypassing all the traffic.

Parker and I had found the station map, which pointed us to where we wanted to go . . . Government Center. It would be there that we'd ask for help and turn over the files we'd copied from X.

It was the opposite of everything I'd been told to do, but apparently everything I'd been told was a lie. Now it was up to me to make my own set of rules and figure out the best way to save my parents.

"Train is coming." Parker pointed down the tracks.

I didn't look up. Both of us had been keeping our heads down as much as possible, knowing that there were cameras everywhere—on the trolley, at the kiosk, on the platform, and in the train. Although it seemed that Parker forgot more often than I did.

"According to the signs"—Parker motioned over to the billboard next to the stairs—"once we board, we'll have access to Wi-Fi. We can figure out where we need to go. Make sure we get this information to the right people."

"I'm not even sure who the right people are anymore," I muttered.

The train squealed as it stopped in front of us and the doors slid open. No one got out, and there was only one other person getting on in a different car. Inside, there was a guy with dreadlocks sitting in the far corner listening to music on his headphones and an older woman holding a large bag in her lap right by the door. Parker and I avoided eye contact with both of them, choosing seats as far away from them as we could.

"We should ask for an agent who works these types of cases," Parker suggested as he looked up the FBI's Miami office on his laptop. "A specialist, don't you think?"

"A specialist in what?" I scoffed. "In parents who lie, who choose some experiment over their own daughter? What kind of agent specializes in that?"

"Hey, don't take it out on me." Parker kept typing. "I'm just saying that it'll be better if we go in there with a name of who to ask for."

A second later, Parker slapped the side of the computer. "Of course, this would be our luck!"

"What?" I looked at everything written beneath the website, titled Miami FBI Office.

Nothing stood out.

There were articles about someone being captured, a list of the most wanted fugitives, a community service project, and instructions on how to report suspicious activity.

"It's in Miramar," Parker said, pointing to a small map at the bottom of the screen.

"Huh?" Not sure what he was talking about.

"The Miami office isn't even in Miami . . . it's in some city called Miramar." He hit a few more keystrokes and the entire screen turned into a map. "And that's like twenty miles away."

"Well, we'll just have to go there." Having the FBI help us was our last resort and I wasn't going to let something like this stop us. "We'll take a taxi or something."

"We're basically broke," Parker pointed out. "This just gets worse and worse."

"Seriously? Given the circumstances, I don't think ditching a cabbie is a big deal . . . especially for someone like you." I pointed to the name of the special agent in charge. "Now look this guy up."

Parker stopped typing and looked me squarely in the eyes. His jaw stiffened. "And what's that supposed to mean exactly?"

"Huh?"

"That comment about someone like me." He crossed his arms. "What did you mean by that?"

"Nothing." I shrugged, not sure why he was getting so upset. "Just that for someone who's lived in, what . . . eight homes and been in trouble with the police . . ."

"So? Just because people have ditched me doesn't mean I'd be fine doing the same." Parker's eyes flashed with anger. "I didn't skip out on you, did I? Then again, look where it got me." He waved his arms around. "Running for my life for reasons neither of us understand."

"Hey . . . I never asked you to get in that cow trailer," I argued, refusing to be made to feel guilty. "Or go with me to Atlanta. I tried to stop you."

"Stop me? You asked me to help you get away when we were at the diner," he pointed out. "Or did you conveniently forget that part?"

I stayed quiet.

He was right. There was nothing I could say that would change that. It was my fault he was here. We hadn't even been friends for very long and he had risked everything to help me. Even if neither of us had realized what he was risking at the time.

Tears started to burn my eyes. "I'm sorry. I did do that."

"Ugh, don't cry." He gave me a slight nudge. "Forget I said anything. I shouldn't blame you. You tried to warn me."

"But I should've done it on my own. None of this was your

problem." I wiped my eyes, refusing to let the tears fall. "I really wish you weren't caught up in all this. That you could just bail out and go home. But I don't think I could've gotten this far without you." I bit my bottom lip for a moment. "I know that I couldn't have."

Parker looked out the window as the train came to its first stop. "Yeah, yeah. I'm amazing."

"You really are," I said, knowing that I couldn't afford to lose my only friend. Parker was the only person I trusted. Maybe even more than my own parents.

"Vizcaya Station," a voice announced as the doors opened.

The old woman got off the train and a teenage boy jumped on.

Parked turned to me with a lopsided grin on his face. "But I guess I am kind of awesome, aren't I? Getting all the information and breaking the encryptions."

I gave him a slight shove. "Don't let it go to your head too much."

"Ah, but you agreed with the fact that I'm amazing." He wagged his finger at me and then refocused on the laptop. "Won't let you forget that. But for now, let's see what else we can find out about BioGenysis before we lose the Wi-Fi."

Parker began doing his thing with the computer. Typing away and pulling up all sorts of documents. The company apparently did lots of different kinds of research, from cancer cures to bacteria research that would help with waste management. But there was one picture that made a shiver run up my spine.

"Stop. Go back to that article," I said, drawing closer to the computer screen.

I recognized the man I'd seen arguing with Dad in that flashback I had. Reading the caption, I saw it was Geoffrey Sterling—the CEO of Sterling. In the photo, he was standing next to a woman wearing a lab coat. She was the one who I instinctively feared. The article praised the company's scientific discovery of a new drug to treat migraines after a series of clinical tests by Dr. Olga Porchencko.

"Dr. Porchencko . . . I've seen that doctor before," I said, my voice barely above a whisper.

"After your accident?" Parker asked. "Or before?"

"I . . . I don't know. Before, I think. It just feels like there's something about her that my brain doesn't want me to remember. Something important. Something bad . . . almost evil."

"Evil? As in bad-guy evil?"

I tried to force myself to come up with when and where I'd seen her. All I had was this overwhelming sensation that told me that she had done something bad. That I had seen her do something.

"It sounds strange, but my gut tells me this woman is dangerous."

The train came to a rumbling stop.

"Government Center." The name was announced as the doors opened up. Parker and I jumped out and headed down a set of stairs as the roar of the train leaving vibrated overhead.

We crossed the turnstile and looked out at the city. Downtown Miami lay ahead of us with all its tall office buildings. We'd soon be engulfed by people walking around and, from where we stood, I could already see a line of taxis parked down the street.

This was what I liked.

We could get lost in a crowd.

It was how my parents had trained me. Blend in and don't get noticed.

"Let's go," I said, and headed toward the yellow cabs.

A cool wind blew through my newly blond hair as dark clouds gathered in the distance. A distant rumble of thunder warned of an impending storm.

Parker was one step behind me as we wove through the large cement pillars that held the train tracks above us.

I glanced up at the menacing skies. It seemed like we only had a few minutes before we'd get drenched. We had to hurry up and get to the taxis.

Just as I was about to break into a run, a hand reached out and grabbed me by the arm, yanking me away from Parker.

All I heard was a voice whisper in my ear, "Scream and you're dead."

CHAPTER 15

NOT THE HERO

I STARED AT MY reflection in X's mirrored sunglasses. The initial shock was gone, but his threat lingered heavy in the air. He had a strong grasp around my arm and held me close against him so that there was no room to wiggle away.

"Go," I mouthed to Parker, urging him to leave me. He had the laptop; he could go to the feds and get help.

"Not a word," X sneered. "Just walk." He glanced at Parker, who hesitated as we took a couple of steps forward. "Go at your own risk," he warned him. "You won't survive the day."

X quickly led me across a large parking lot away from the taxis. I glanced at Parker, who was right next to me. He had chosen to come with us, not that X was offering him much of a choice. The way X was speaking to us, there was no doubt that he meant business. I didn't know what kind of weapon he had, but his threats felt real. Very real.

To my surprise, the car was parked nearby with the back passenger-side window broken and shards of glass scattered across the back seat. X opened the front passenger door and pushed me into the seat.

He paused to look at the two of us. "Which of you has my key?" he asked.

Neither of us said anything.

"My key," X demanded. "I'd rather not have to hot-wire my own car again."

"What are you going to do, shoot us?" Parker challenged him.

Lightning flittered across the sky.

X lifted a single eyebrow, as if he was bored with the conversation. "At this point, if I have to . . . I will."

A loud rumbling of thunder followed, as if to emphasize X's threat.

Parker stuck his hand in his pocket and pulled out the key.

X snatched it from him and muttered, "I hate kids."

"How did you find us?" I asked as he slammed the door in my face and walked around to the driver side. "There's no way you'd know that we were going downtown. We didn't even know that we were headed there."

"Deductive reasoning." The edges of X's mouth turned slightly up as he opened his door. "And you took my key."

"So?" I didn't understand the connection.

"The key. It's rigged," Parker answered while cleaning off some shards of glass from the back seat. "Should've thought of that."

I looked back at Parker. "I don't—"

"GPS," Parker explained, gingerly tossing the glass pieces to the floor. "His key chain must have a tracker on it."

"Makes losing keys less of a problem." X started the car and shifted into reverse.

"Hey!" Parker jumped in and closed the door. "I wasn't even sitting down yet."

"You are no longer my concern," X answered. "You want to stay alive, then you stick close by. You can't keep up, that's not my problem."

"Wait a minute," I protested as we turned down a busy downtown street and the windshield became splotched with large raindrops. I could see a long ramp up ahead that led to a highway that stretched over the Miami streets. We were on the move and once again I had no idea where we'd end up. "You can't just dump Parker—"

"I can and will," X retorted. "My focus is you."

"Is it because you're working with them . . . Sterling BioGenysis." I seethed as I spat out the name, wanting him to know that we knew the truth. It was time to lay our cards on the table. "You were never going to help get me to my dad. I'm just something that you can trade for his experiment."

X stayed silent as we got onto the highway leaving downtown. We passed over the tops of palm trees, and on my right I could see residential neighborhoods stretched out in little grid patterns while the city skyline remained on X's side.

The dark rain clouds above us lingered, but refused to release their load. Only the occasional raindrop seemed to land on the car.

"Not much to say, huh?" Parker said from the back seat.

More silence.

"That's because he knows he's betrayed his friend for money," I said, accusing him of what Parker and I had discovered, hoping to get a reaction out of him where he might reveal something. "How can you even live with yourself?"

"I live very well," X replied. "And the two of you really know nothing."

I glared at him. The man who had betrayed my father, had betrayed us.

"I know enough," I countered as a light sprinkle of rain began to fall and X turned on the car's wipers. I didn't have time to think through a strategy or a game plan. I was too angry and desperate for answers at this point. I blurted out everything. "Back at the restaurant. I heard you talking on the phone. You said that you just needed a couple of days to convince my dad to hand over the experiment. That they needed to keep my mom safe until then. You were talking to the people who took her!"

"Again," X replied calmly, "you know nothing."

"So, you're not even going to deny that you're working with the BioGenysis guys and not the government?" Parker shook his head incredulously. "Amazing."

"I told the two of you that I have a nuanced role with certain government agencies and that sometimes means having relationships with unsavory people." X snuck a glimpse at me from the corner of his eye. "Your father knew that, and it was his idea that I begin working with Sterling. It was part of his plan to escape from BioGenysis with ... with your family."

"My dad planned it? Right." I wasn't going to believe anything that this master liar said to us.

"Believe what you want." X got off on one of the exits. "What you heard on that phone call was me improvising and getting us a couple of extra days. BioGenysis doesn't know that you're with me and it has to stay that way."

"I guess you could've just turned us over ..." Parker mused.

"Not if he's holding out for more money," I countered, refusing to fall for whatever mind game X was playing.

"Listen," X continued. The rain was coming down so hard now that he had to raise his voice. "Listen," he said again, more loudly. "I know you're scared and worried about your parents. I'm not the enemy ... even if it may seem like it."

"Well, if you're not the enemy, then what are you?" I asked.

"That's a good question." X took a moment to think as the rain outside subsided just a little. "Been trying to answer that question most of my life. But for now, I'm your dad's friend and your best chance at getting out of this mess."

"If you really want us to trust you, then tell us more about what's really going on," I suggested, hoping for information that would help everything make more sense. "About that experiment I heard you mention."

"Can't," X said as the quick downpour eased into a heavy

drizzle and we turned onto the road that led back to the marina. "I swore to your dad that I wouldn't."

"Maybe Olga Porchencko will," I said, expecting him to ignore me.

X slammed on the brakes, causing us all to lurch forward.

"How do you know about her?" he demanded, peering straight into my eyes. "What do you remember?"

Most of my liar training went out the window. I withered under his stare. "Nothing . . . just the name. I have a bad feeling about her, but I don't know who she is."

X took a deep breath and slowly let it out, regaining his composure.

Parker poked his head around the seat back. "Who is she?"

X shook his head. "Someone dangerous. Who you'll hopefully never meet."

"Why?" I asked as X started driving again. "Is she involved in all this? You can at least tell us that."

"She works at Sterling BioGenysis," X answered, to my surprise. "She replaced your dad when he . . . um . . . when he got taken off some of his projects. She's still there, though she hasn't had much success since your father left."

"Then she has something to do with the experiment that they want back, doesn't she? The one that you said the Russians and Chinese are after." Lightning once again filled the sky as if in response to my statement.

"Seems like you heard quite a bit of my conversation," X

muttered as we pulled onto a long dirt road that bordered the marina. "I need to be a little more careful in the future."

"My dad stole it, didn't he?" I continued, realizing that for some reason X was being a little bit more cooperative with us. "The experiment that they all want."

"It's hard to steal what's already yours," he replied as the road hit a dead end.

"But *was* it his?" Parker asked as X parked next to some mangroves. "I mean, why would they come after him if he really owned it? And why wouldn't he just give it to them instead of going on the run?"

"Things are complicated. But he's definitely . . ." X's lips got tighter as he paused to choose his next words. "Let's just say no one 'owns' what your father helped create, and he's definitely the only one who knows how to replicate the process." He shook his head. "As smart as B is . . . he just didn't foresee everything Sterling had in mind. Once he realized the extent of what Sterling wanted to do . . . well, it was a little too late. That's when he reached out to me for help."

"What kind of help?" I asked.

X checked the skies, where the sun was already peeking out from between the remaining dark clouds, but he stayed quiet.

"If you want us to trust you and go with you willingly," Parker said, "you'll answer Katrina's question. What did you do?"

"Layla's," X corrected him. "Her name is Layla."

The three of us stared at one another for several seconds. It was a standoff where neither Parker nor I had much leverage, yet unexpectedly, X caved.

"Fine, I can tell you this much. B came up with a plan for me to infiltrate BioGenysis so that Sterling would eventually include me in the hunting down of your family. That way we'd always be one step ahead of them. To your dad's credit, it worked for several years." X scanned the area before turning off the car. "And that's about all I'm willing to say."

It wasn't enough.

I still didn't understand why keeping a healing drug secret would be worth putting your entire family at risk. And why would X agree to help Dad with stealing it?

"So, what if you got hold of the experiment?" Parker asked as we all got out of the car. "Would you give it back to Sterling BioGenysis? Trade it for everybody's freedom?"

I shot Parker a look. We couldn't even hint at the fact that I had some of the liquid with me. X had mentioned reverse engineering it on the phone call and I couldn't let that happen until my parents were safe. Plus, I didn't trust X . . . no matter what he said.

"Not a chance." X took the duffel bag from the trunk and headed toward a long dock that didn't seem to be part of the main marina.

"Why not?" Parker and I followed him as he walked past the dock and continued along the seawall, where a couple of small boats were tied.

"B and L would rather die than let that happen," X replied, pushing back the branches of some overgrown mangroves that were blocking the edge of the seawall.

Parker pulled me aside. "I don't want to die for some stupid experiment," he whispered. "Do you?"

I shook my head. We had to find a way out of this.

"So, what are you planning to do once we get to wherever we're going?" I asked as X continued walking toward a small inlet around the corner.

"What I've been doing all along." X paused and looked back at Parker and me. "Saving you . . . even from yourselves."

CHAPTER 16

C WORTHY

"HOLD UP." PARKER STARED at the boat. "*This* is yours?"

I couldn't believe it either. We had walked into an inlet where a small yacht was docked. It had the words *C Worthy* written in gold letters along the back.

"Don't act so surprised," X replied, taking off his shoes and tossing them onto the boat before hopping aboard. "Different identities require . . . um . . . different lifestyles." He dropped the duffel bag. "It's one of the perks of the job. *C Worthy* was something I picked up a couple of years ago. It'll keep us mobile and serve us well until I hear from B."

"Mm-hmm." I still doubted everything X said because I knew what I'd overheard on his call. It didn't matter what he tried to have us believe.

I glanced around to see if there was some way for us to escape, but the place looked deserted. Plus, where would we go?

"Listen, I already told you that Sterling believes that I'm a hired gun whose job it is to find your father. Being on the inside was the only way we could keep tabs if they were getting close to your family." X held out his hand to help me aboard. "It was part of your father's plan."

"So you say," I muttered as I purposely ignored his outstretched hand and stepped up onto the boat, only wobbling slightly. I trusted X's explanation as little as his silence and secrecy from before. I walked away, straight up the steps to the main deck, and Parker followed me without a saying a word.

"Take off your shoes!" X called out as I opened the glass door that separated the outdoor lounge area from the interior of the boat. "Both of you!"

I rolled my eyes as I kicked off my sneakers, and Parker slowly walked around, his fingers gliding over the high-gloss wood that surrounded the ship's navigation controls.

"Hoo-wee." He whistled. "This is one fancy boat." He jumped into the captain's chair and put his hands on the steering wheel. "It's like being in a fancy cockpit."

"What do you think of what X said?" I said, looking out at X, who was untying us from the dock. "About my dad's plan?"

Parker shrugged. "I don't know. I mean, if he wanted to turn us in . . . he could've done it already. I can't see how keeping us around helps him. He may be legit."

"I guess." I looked out to the open water. Pretty soon we'd be out there with nowhere to run to. No way of escaping.

"I'm going to check things out below deck," Parker said, heading down the interior stairs. "You want to come?"

"Not right now," I said. I wanted to think things through. Go over everything X had told us.

Even though I had my doubts, X seemed to have a reasonable explanation for what I'd overheard. Plus, even if I didn't fully trust him, he was the best chance we had at meeting up with my dad. Without him, I wouldn't know how to find him.

Suddenly, I felt the boat begin to drift a little. We were on our way.

"This boat might be bigger than some of the places I've lived in!" Parker yelled from below deck. "But there's three of us and only two bedrooms."

"Only?" I mocked.

"They're called cabins, and I'll sleep up here on the bridge." X had entered the bridge area and was pointing to a long leather couch. He calmly sat in the captain's chair and started the engines. "You two can decide which cabin you want."

Parker poked his head up through the opening in the floor. He couldn't hold back his grin. "Check it out, Katrina." Parker ducked back underneath. "There's a TV in, like, every room. And the refrigerator down here is fully stocked."

X shook his head. "Her name is Layla, and take off your shoes!"

"*Carlos* is new at this stuff," I said, showing off a little, and trying to excuse Parker's lapse with our new names.

"Mm-hmm." X didn't seem pleased. "Sooner we get out of here, the better."

I climbed down the metal steps to where Parker had gone

and landed in the middle of a small kitchen with marble countertops. A table with bench seating, similar to what I'd had in the RV, but a whole lot nicer, was pushed up against the wall.

Parker opened a door behind me.

"This is one of the bedrooms, and the other one is over there toward the front of the boat." He pointed past the table and a TV that hung on the wall. "Take your pick."

"I don't care." I shrugged. This wasn't some type of luxury vacation. We were on the run and dealing with my parents' lives. "Whichever one you don't want."

"Well, this one is a little bigger and—"

"Then I'll take the other one," I interrupted, wanting Parker to refocus. "You're already inside that one anyway."

"You sure? Because I don't—"

I pushed Parker farther into the room and closed the door behind me. "Listen." I lowered my voice, knowing that X was close by. "We need to get as much information from those files as we can. X mentioned that we'd be staying out at sea waiting for my dad to respond. Do you have everything you need to keep digging?"

Parker hesitated. "I've never been out to sea. I don't know if there's Wi-Fi or anything. Maybe if he has satellite service or something hooked up."

"Well, we have to try," I insisted.

The boat swayed and the engines revved up even more, causing the floor to shake a little.

My stomach churned in response.

I wasn't sure if it was the boat's movement or the idea that we'd be floating around in the middle of nowhere . . . We'd be away from anyone who might hurt us—or help us.

"Listen . . ." Parker took the laptop and power cord out of his backpack and hid it under the bed's mattress. "Tonight, when everyone goes to sleep, I'll work on trying to hack the passwords on some of the documents we have."

"Carlos!" X shouted.

I froze, thinking someone else had boarded, before realizing that X was calling Parker by his new name.

"That's you," I whispered, and pointed to Parker's shoes. "And take those off."

"Carlos," X repeated. "Come up here."

Parker kicked off his sneakers and opened the door. I followed him up to where X was sitting behind the wheel. The boat wasn't moving very fast yet, so I had a good view of the coastline. There were large mansions and condo buildings dotting the shore and barely any other boats out on the water with us.

"Yes, Dad?" Parker responded. "Need something?"

"A first mate," X replied. "Once we get far enough out, I need you to be able to take over for a bit while I dismantle some things."

"Like what?" I asked.

"Equipment that could be used to track us," X replied. "Just want to make sure we completely disappear."

"Why not do that before we left?" I asked.

"Why do you ask so many questions?" X shook his head, but relented. "Because it's better to be out of reach and then disappear than to be seen on the dock for too long. It's bad enough that your little escape attempt delayed us. The longer we're in one place, the riskier things get."

"What do I have to do?" Parker got closer, intrigued by all the controls.

"Shouldn't we both learn?" I pushed my way between the two of them. "Why does it have to be Pa—I mean Carlos, and not me?"

"Fine." X shrugged. "I don't care." He then began to go over the basics of boating.

"The main thing is keeping the wheel steady and having your eyes peeled for any other boat traffic. Where we're going there shouldn't be any, but you never know." X stepped aside and pulled me in front of the wheel. "Now let me see you navigate this boat for a bit."

I held the leather-covered wheel in my hands, sensing the power of the engines. After about a minute, X pushed the throttle that was next to me forward, increasing our speed for the next few minutes as land disappeared behind us.

"Now you." X pointed to Parker.

After a few minutes of Parker steering the boat, X shut down the engines and let us drift in the open ocean, the waves gently rocking us side to side.

"Now what?" Parker asked as X opened a drawer under the leather built-in couch.

"You two stay here and keep an eye on things." He took out a toolbox and pulled out some wire cutters and a screwdriver. "I shouldn't be long. Shout if you see anything."

X disappeared downstairs.

I couldn't see land anymore, but there were still a couple of seagulls who squawked as they flew past us, so we couldn't be too far from shore.

It worried me to be out here. Even if Parker was with me.

So much had happened in the last couple of days. Nothing and no one seemed, as Parker called it, legit. All I knew was that my dad was still out there and he had the answers we needed.

Parker sensed my dilemma.

He dashed over to the toolbox and grabbed two flat-head screwdrivers. He stuck one in the back of his pants, and gave me the other one. "Protection . . . just in case," he said. "To give us a fighting chance."

It wasn't much, but it was something. I tucked it in my pocket and let my long shirt cover it.

Right now, it was a pair of screwdrivers, Parker, and me against a huge conglomerate with infinite resources.

Yeah, this wasn't going to be a fair fight.

CHAPTER 17

FACE IN THE CLOSET

IT WAS NIGHTTIME WHEN we dropped anchor. I couldn't see anything other than the black ocean beneath us and the dark sky lit by a crescent moon that seemed to pop in and out among the clouds.

Parker and I had spent most of the day gazing out at the sea, trying to figure out where we were headed. As far as I could tell, we had made a quick pit stop at some Bahamian marina to refuel and had continued east. I assumed we were still somewhere in the Bahamas, but I wasn't sure.

The good thing about all this was that we were definitely not roughing it on board the yacht. We'd eaten a good dinner of steaks, baked beans, chips, and potato salad. The full-size refrigerator was completely stocked with all sorts of foods, and Parker had discovered that the drawers in his cabin held a complete wardrobe of X's clothing.

"I think I'm going to go to bed," I announced even though

it was only a little past ten. We had been up on the bridge for about an hour with the glass door open, breathing in the ocean air.

Parker knew what I was doing. The sooner X thought we were asleep, the sooner he could start deciphering the codes on X's files.

"Yeah." Parker raised his hands over his head in a long stretch and gave the most pitiful fake yawn I'd ever seen. "Me too. I'm beat."

X didn't seem to take notice of Parker's awful acting. "Sure, go to bed. There are a couple of DVD documentaries if you're interested in watching them and I've got some decent books in the master cabin, too."

"I think I'll just go to sleep." I stood up and headed to my room.

Downstairs, Parker gave me a thumbs-up sign before closing his cabin door.

The plan was underway.

I stepped up to the large platform bed in my cabin. I had put the screwdriver under my pillow and it made me feel better. I slowly drifted off to sleep.

"Eva! Eva!" A light, cheerful voice was calling me. It was my mother.

In the dream, I opened my eyes, but darkness obscured my surroundings.

I was hiding.

Crouched down. My back against the wall.

I felt my heart beating hard against my chest and blood rushing to my head. I closed my eyes again.

"Don't say a word," someone whispered from the shadows next to me. "She might find you."

I nodded. For some reason, I trusted this person more than my own mother.

"Eva . . . I know you're here." A light turned on outside, shining from beneath the door of the closet where I had sought refuge. "M'ija, they just want to ask you some questions. It won't be like last time . . . I promise," Mom cajoled. "I'll stay with you. Don't make this worse than it has to be."

"It's too late," the voice next to me said. "You have to go. But don't tell her I'm here, okay?" Our pinkies hooked together. "Pinkie promise?"

I nodded.

Slowly I stretched my cramped legs and stood up, parting clothes as I reached for the door.

The metal doorknob felt cold under my fingers as I turned it little by little, not making a sound. I didn't want to leave the closet.

"Go," the voice said. "It'll be okay. We'll be okay."

I glanced back as I opened the door. The light from the room was scattering the shadows and revealing the face of the person who had been telling me what to do. The person I most trusted.

It was me!

The shock jolted me awake.

My palms were sweaty and my breathing was short, panicked.

I looked around the cabin. Everything was quiet and dark.

I tried making sense of the dream. It felt real, like another memory trying to push its way to the front of my brain, but it didn't make much sense. It had to be a dream.

Maybe it was my subconscious trying to get me to trust myself over my parents. There was plenty of proof that they'd been telling me lies for years.

I got out of bed and slowly opened the door.

The boat was rocking softly, but everything else felt still.

Trying not to make noise with my bare feet, I walked into the kitchen. The digital clock on the microwave showed that it was 3:43.

I crept up the first two steps and poked my head onto the bridge. I could see X sleeping on the long couch.

Without making a sound, I inched back down and lightly turned the doorknob of Parker's cabin.

As I opened the door to the darkened cabin, I saw Parker scramble to hide the laptop.

"Shh!" I whispered. "It's me."

"Is everything okay?" His worried face was made visible by the moonlight coming in through his cabin windows. "Why are you up?"

"Just a weird dream."

Parker let out a big sigh and pulled the laptop back onto his bed.

"Have you found anything else in the files?" I asked, sitting on the bed next to him.

"These files are, like, super protected. Stuff I've never even seen before." He cocked his head to the side. "And I'm good. Like really, really good."

"Uh-huh." I wasn't sure about Parker's boasting.

"See." He pointed to the screen. "These documents aren't just file protected, they're coded within the documents themselves, with each page having a different encryption."

"Okay . . . I have no idea what that means."

"It means that even if you are able to open the nearly-impossibly-protected files, which I, by the way, have already opened . . . then you are still stuck with more protected pages." He pointed to a bunch of random letters and symbols. "There is a second level of coding that blocks you from seeing the pages."

My shoulders slumped. "So, we have nothing?"

"Well, I was able to get something by running a program that searches for repetitive permutations and . . ." He noticed the confusion on my face. "Yeah, never mind how I got it." He typed something into his computer and went to a different page. "This doc discusses chemical equations and use of something called a CRISPR. Do you know what that is?"

I looked over the page and shook my head. "It looks like they were trying to come up with a formula for something. There were a lot of experiments."

"Yeah. I know." Parker scrolled down. "There's a chart that goes on for several pages listing them. The first section starts with Alpha I Alpha and keeps going until Alpha V Omega, then the next one starts with Beta I Alpha and so on. The last one listed is Epsilon V Alpha. But I don't really understand all the scientific stuff in each section about the cells and stuff."

I reached over and pressed the down arrow on the keyboard.

"Hey!" Parker pushed my hand away. "Don't touch it. You could mess it all up."

"I just want to go to the bottom. There might be some sort of conclusion that might explain it all?"

"Yeah, but I'll do it . . . not you." Parker moved the cursor to the end of the document. "And there *is* something there." He pointed to the last lines. "Here in Recommendation. It says, *Based on the unexpected development of Experiments Epsilon III Alpha and Epsilon V Alpha, researcher insists all future projects be halted pending further evaluation for potential viability and future cross-purposing.*"

"They stopped all the experiments?" I muttered, glancing over at Parker. "Why?"

"I don't know." Parker shrugged. "I'm a hacker, not a scientist. But something must have gone really wrong with those two experiments to make them call it quits on the whole project."

"Or it's the opposite," I said. "Maybe the results of those two experiments were so good that they only wanted to just focus on them . . . because look." I touched the screen. "It's signed Dr. Bennet Fisher," I whispered. "My dad. This is probably the blue healing liquid he created."

"If that's the case, then no wonder they're angry with him." Parker leaned back on his elbows, the laptop balancing on his lap. "He had them focus on those two experiments and then stole them."

"But that's not like him. There's got to be more to it. My dad wouldn't just steal it for no reason." I took the laptop and pointed to the last two words. *Cross-purposing.* "X mentioned that Dad wasn't aware of Sterling's plans, so maybe he discovered that the cross-purposing for the blue liquid wasn't to help people, but instead it was for something bad. Something evil."

"You sound like you're describing a movie more than reality," Parker said dismissively. "In my experience, people usually steal things for one simple reason . . . money. They take off when things get tough. So maybe he might have wanted to sell it to the highest bidder or something. Set your family up to be super rich since it was his idea and take off before he got caught."

My ears got warm as my temper flared. I jumped off the bed, causing the laptop to almost tumble onto the floor. If it hadn't been for the fact that I might wake up X, I would've stormed out of the room and slammed the door behind me. Instead, I glared at Parker.

"You keep suggesting that my dad put us all at risk for money," I seethed, keeping my voice below a whisper. "He isn't like that!"

"Relax. I just mean that desperate people can do desperate things. He might have had a good reason." Parker sighed. "I've seen it happen."

His feeble attempt at compassion made me even angrier. "I don't know what things you've seen because you've never told me about them, but you can keep all your secrets . . . I don't care. Just know that this isn't one of your poor foster home situations. My dad isn't like that. You'll see when we get more answers."

I grabbed the doorknob and turned it as slowly as I could. The motion reminded me of the closet in my dream-like memory.

It reminded me of what I'd learned when I turned and saw my own face. *I* was the one giving me advice.

I had to trust myself and my instincts more than anyone else . . . including Parker.

CHAPTER 18

CONTACT

THE QUIET OF THE boat was both comforting and disturbing. It meant that we were relatively safe, but it also felt like the calm before the storm. Something was brewing and we'd soon have to face whatever was on the horizon. But for now, there was nothing to do except wait.

I woke up around mid-morning and found X already up and sitting in the captain's chair playing solitaire. He didn't seem to take much notice of me other than a garbled good morning when I came up to the main deck to eat my breakfast in the fresh ocean air.

Spoonful by spoonful, I had my Frosted Flakes while gazing at a deserted beach not too far from where we were anchored. It looked like a postcard. There wasn't a cloud in the sky, and even from a distance I could see the white sand and palm trees around the tranquil cove. There were no houses or rooftops of any kind and the island itself didn't seem bigger than a few blocks long.

The minutes passed and the sun continued rising higher in the sky.

Parker was still sleeping and, truth be told, I was glad he wasn't up.

Just the thought of him made me angry all over again. He was making assumptions about my dad without knowing all the facts.

Facts that X might have.

"How will we know if my dad makes contact when we're way out here?" I asked, breaking the silence that had existed between us for about an hour.

"I'll know," he replied, flipping another card over.

"But how?" I persisted.

He pulled out a small tablet from a side slot next to the captain's chair. "I've got ways . . . even out here." X placed the tablet on the chair and crouched under the seat, pulling out a tackle box similar to the one he'd had in the motel room. It had a combination lock that he quickly opened, and from where I stood, I could see that there was some sort of electronic equipment inside. "Let's see if there's been an update."

It was at that moment that I wished Parker were here to witness what X was doing. He'd know what equipment X was using and if he could hack into it later.

I started to inch closer to X to get a better look, but X's stare stopped me where I was. I couldn't take the risk that he'd shut everything down if I got too close.

"Hmm. He read the message that I left, but still hasn't responded," X said, pursing his lips together. "He may think

I've been compromised." X turned to me. "Tell me something only you two know."

"Are you kidding?" I scoffed. "I'm the one who everyone keeps all the secrets from. I don't have any of my own."

"There's got to be something. I already told him to meet me for the best margaritas, but he won't come if he isn't sure you're safe."

"Margaritas?" I questioned.

"He knows the best margaritas are at a place in Palm Beach," X explained. "But I need to make sure he knows you're with me and no one else figures that part out." He tapped the side of his head as if mocking me. "Now think."

I didn't know what X wanted from me. I didn't have a special nickname that Dad called me or anything . . . I barely had a name at all. "Um, I choose my names according to the alphabet, so maybe something about that?"

"Nah, that doesn't work." X rejected my suggestion. "Something else. A special joke?"

Nah. X had just reminded me of the joke from a couple of weeks ago. "I got it!" I declared. "Tell Dad that Jo Ann Nah will join you."

"Who's that?" X asked, looking doubtful that my idea would work.

"Me; it's an inside joke. Only my parents would know that."

"Good enough." X typed something into the tablet and slipped it back into the slot next to him. "He'll answer soon.

I'm sure of it." He closed the box and pushed it under his chair again.

"Why are you so sure?"

"Because you're here." X pinched his lips together. "Some people will risk everything for love."

"Would you?" I asked.

X shook his head. "In my line of work, it's considered a liability."

"But you're putting yourself at risk for my dad," I observed. "So, you must care about him."

"Guess I am." X shrugged. "He's my Achilles' heel . . . the one tie to my past that I couldn't cut."

It felt like this was my chance. X and I had worked together to send my dad a coded message and now there was a crack in X's armor that I could exploit to get more information. I'd reveal the little bit we'd discovered in the hope of learning more.

"Are you also doing it because my dad was so dedicated to his experiment?" The question hung in the air. "I'm sure you know what I'm talking about," I added, hoping X would take the bait and tell me something new.

"Perhaps." X cocked his head to the side. "But what do you know about it?"

"I know enough." I thought about how many times my parents had put the blue liquid on one of my cuts. "You might say I have firsthand information."

X studied me. He was trying to determine how much I knew and understood. We were playing a game and I wasn't going to let him win.

"We can call it by name . . . Epsilon III Alpha," I said.

I waited for the slightest movement from X. A facial twitch or a shift in the shoulders . . . anything to tell me that I was on the right track. But what I saw was unexpected.

A flicker of sadness, or maybe guilt, briefly flashed across his eyes.

But it was gone almost as quickly as it had appeared.

"Your father had many projects," he responded. It was a very noncommittal answer. X was a master at speaking without really saying anything.

But I wasn't giving up. There was something there. I could tell by how hard he was trying to remain even-keeled. I'd been lying for too many years not to pick up on the subtlest cues.

"But that's the one that really mattered to him," I said, with a bit of snark from the pent-up frustration of having been put into this situation by my father's choices.

"That's not true." But his denial made me more convinced that it was at least partially true.

"Oh, right . . ." I folded my arms across my chest. "There were two experiments." I took a step closer to X, who was looking slightly uncomfortable. "But can you really tell me that my father didn't sacrifice everything, including his family, for those two projects?"

"What?" X's eyebrows scrunched together.

I had gone too far. I'd let my emotions get the better of me.

X shook his head and stood up. "You may have overheard some names over the years, but you don't have the vaguest idea about any of it." He walked away from me, then turned before going down the stairs. "And your father . . . he destroyed his lab, walked away from all his research, from everything . . . to protect you." Anger had replaced whatever other emotion X had been grappling with before. "You know nothing about sacrifice."

"Then tell me about it," I challenged him, angry in my own right. "Because this affects me as much as anyone else and no one wants to tell me anything!"

X took a long, deep breath and regained his composure. "There must be a good reason for that, don't you think?"

I silently seethed as X walked down to the kitchen. He wasn't going to tell me anything. The only information I was going to get was whatever I discovered on my own . . . just like always. It was no surprise that my parents were close with X—he was just like them.

"Um . . . what's going on?" Parker cautiously asked, coming up the stairs. "I heard you from my room."

"Nothing," I snapped, turning away from him to hide the tears of frustration that were welling up in my eyes.

"Hey . . ." He put a hand on my shoulder.

I shrugged him off. "Leave me alone," I ordered, wiping my eyes as I stormed to the very back of the boat. "You have as many secrets as everyone else."

My thoughts swirled as I stood by myself, staring at the crystal-blue water sparkling beneath me. I was tempted to dive in and disappear from everyone and everything.

The minutes passed, but I didn't seem to notice.

"Don't jump," Parker said from behind me.

"What?" I squinted as the sun beamed over his shoulder.

"You've been standing there staring at the water. I thought you might jump." He gave me a lopsided smile, the one he usually reserved for when he thought himself witty or funny. "Although it's not actually a bad idea . . . if you know how to swim."

"I know how to swim."

"Well, that makes one of us, 'cause I can barely doggy paddle." He cupped his hands and pretended to do little strokes and then sank down like he was drowning. "Woof, woof."

I could feel the weight of my anger lifting as I smiled.

"That's better," he said. "And I'm sorry about what I said last night. I've only known your dad a few weeks, but I can tell he loves you. He probably has a good reason for whatever he did . . . like you said."

I glanced down at my bare feet.

I wasn't sure about anything anymore. But it did seem like Parker was on my side. He was a good friend and I wasn't treating him like one.

"I'm sorry for saying you're like everyone else with your secrets," I said, keeping my head down. "You have a right to your privacy. It doesn't change how you've had my back during all of this."

"I don't mean to be secretive, it's just that I don't like talking about stuff that happened in the past." He sighed. "You already know my dad took off on me and my mom was an addict. There was nothing I could do to get her to stop . . . to help her." His voice cracked a little as he opened up to me.

"But you were just a kid," I replied, taking a long look at him.

"Yeah, I guess." He shrugged. "All I could do was get rid of some bills for her, so I did that. And as for the foster families I was sent to . . . none of them really cared about me. I've sort of gotten used to no one sticking around for very long, so I make it easy for them to get rid of me."

"I care," I said. "I'll stick around."

Parker tilted his head and furrowed his brow. "That may not be up to you."

I couldn't say anything because he was right. In the end, being together might not be a choice.

But being friends could be.

"Even if something happens and we eventually get split up, we'll always be friends. Deal?" I held up my pinkie. "I pinkie promise it."

Parker smiled and wrapped his finger around mine. "Fair enough." He glanced over his shoulder at the bridge and lowered his voice. "Now that we have that settled, did you find out anything from X?"

"No, not really. But he's using a tablet and something inside a tackle box that's under his seat to get messages to my dad. Do you know what that might be?"

"Probably some type of portable hot spot . . . maybe using a satellite." Parker scratched his head. "But if he only uses it for a minute or two, I won't be able to hack into it unless . . ."

"Unless what?" I could see Parker was coming up with a plan.

"Unless we steal it tonight and I set it up in my room. It'd be amazing." Parker was already relishing the thought of acting like some spymaster. "Can you imagine what he might have access to?"

"It's too risky and—"

The engines rumbled and the boat began to shake.

"What the—"

"It's the anchor," I said, hearing the chain being brought up beneath the deck. "Something must have happened. Maybe my dad responded."

Parker and I hurried back to the bridge and, as we opened the sliding glass door, I noticed the locked tackle box sitting on the captain's chair.

I pointed it out to Parker and he gave me a slight nod.

"Is it my dad?" I asked, my voice filled with hope. "Did he contact you?"

"He did," X replied. "Phase three of getting your family to safety is about to begin."

CHAPTER 19

RUSSIAN DOLLS

THE WAVES CRASHED AGAINST the boat as we headed to meet my father at a dockside restaurant near Palm Beach. He was already there waiting for us, so X had the engines going at full throttle—we didn't want him to have to wait any longer than necessary. Even at our current speed, with no bad weather, it would take us several hours.

I couldn't believe it.

Soon I'd have my parents back—and some answers. I couldn't imagine Dad not telling me the truth at this point, after everything that we'd been through and everything I'd found out on my own.

I was nervous but excited, too, for a new start where my family wasn't weighed down by the secrets of the past.

The hours on board dragged on, but they also gave me and Parker a unique opportunity. X was too busy navigating to pay attention to us, and that meant we could go back to trying to decipher the files in Parker's cabin.

"Put on a DVD or something," I suggested as we walked into Parker's big cabin. "In case he asks what we're doing."

"Good idea, but hold on." Parker stepped back into the lounge area.

He was gone for less than a minute but came back with two sodas and a mischievous grin.

"What did you do?" I asked, holding DVDs on the rain forest, marine life, and space exploration in my hands.

"There has to be a reason why we'd be watching it here and not on the main TV in the lounge, right?" He set the cans on the night table by the bed and shrugged innocently. "Too bad the DVD player out there is broken."

I lifted a single eyebrow. "Yeah, it's a shame." I held out the DVDs. "Which one?"

"Doesn't matter." He glanced at the titles and pointed to the top one. "Start with the space one and we'll go from there."

"Sure. And let's look at everything you decoded again." I popped in the DVD as Parker pulled his laptop from under the mattress. "Maybe we missed something the first time."

As the TV talked about the wonders of space and alien life, we stared at the document with all the experiment names and scientific information. It might have well been written in an alien language because none of it made sense. No more than when we first read it.

"Go to the one with the financial transactions or the photograph," I said. "Maybe we can find a clue there."

"I was actually thinking about that picture this morning,"

Parker said as he typed something into the computer. "Why is it included in these files? Maybe the reason your dad stole the liquid has to do with you being in the hospital."

"What do you mean?" There was a knot in my stomach. I didn't like to think of my dad's motivation too much anymore for fear that the truth might shatter whatever notion I still had of him being a good person.

"I know I said people do things for money, but they also do crazy things for the people they care about."

I stared at the picture of me sleeping in the hospital bed. "Hmm, now you sound like X."

"He said that? About your dad?" Parker squinted as he stared at the picture.

I sighed. "Sort of."

Parker hit a few other keys and enlarged the photo. "Then there's got to be something about this that makes it important."

"The code at the bottom!" I pointed to where it said *EIIIA exp.* before the date. "That could stand for Epsilon III Alpha experiment."

"Maybe they were trying to save you by using it." Parker made the picture bigger and zeroed in on the machines. "Because . . . um . . . I don't know how to say this . . ."

Parker pulled away from the computer and stared at me.

"What?" I looked at the picture but couldn't see what was freaking him out so much.

My eyes met his.

"Just tell me what you're thinking," I said, bracing myself for whatever he was about to say.

His lips twitched nervously. "I . . . um . . . I think you died."

I didn't know whether to laugh or not. The idea seemed far-fetched. Wouldn't I know if I'd died?

The TV was now droning on, talking about the possibility of extraterrestrial life-forms visiting Earth, but the only life-form I was thinking about was me.

"You're kidding, right?" was all I managed to say.

"No." He pointed to the machines next to my bed. The picture was grainy, but you could see that there was a flat line on one of them. "When my mom died, I was in the hospital room with her. She had a machine hooked up to her, too. I remember how it beeped when the line went flat." He paused to catch his breath.

I reached over and touched his arm.

He slowly exhaled. "Everyone came rushing inside and kicked me out, but I'll never forget the machine—it looked just like that."

I wasn't going to argue with his memory, especially considering I had none of my own, but there could be other explanations.

"Maybe there's another reason, even if it is the same type of machine," I suggested. "It could have just been unplugged. Or it was a glitch."

"Anything is possible," Parker mused. "But what would

you store on a super-top-secret file—a picture of a glitch or a picture of someone who comes back from the dead?"

I stayed silent. He was right.

"Look, I'm not saying you stayed dead," Parker explained. "But maybe that experiment, the blue liquid that heals anything, saved your life."

"That's not how it works. The blue liquid only speeds up healing; it doesn't magically cure you in an instant, and it definitely doesn't bring someone back to life."

"How can you be sure? Maybe it does all sorts of things." He arched one eyebrow. "The cross-purposing stuff, remember?"

I shook my head. "That doesn't make sense, because why would my dad take it if it could help people? There has to be another explanation."

Every answer seemed to bring more questions.

It was like the Russian nesting dolls my mom had once bought me. She had said they reminded her of the ones her father had bought for her when she was little, but I just loved them because every time I opened one, there was another one hidden inside.

But at that very moment, I really didn't love the Russian nesting dolls that had become my life.

CHAPTER 20

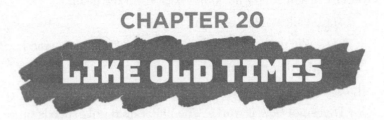

LIKE OLD TIMES

THE SUN DIPPED BELOW the horizon as we approached the coastline. Behind us to the east, there was the ever-growing darkness of night, and up ahead I could see dock lights next to a restaurant.

X had said that we wouldn't be there long. That we'd pick up my dad and head back to sea . . . back to safety. We'd then figure out a way to rescue Mom.

"You two need to get below deck," X instructed. "I don't want anyone seeing you."

"But . . ." I wanted to see my dad.

"That wasn't a request," he stated, turning the boat toward the shore. "Go . . . now."

Parker pulled me by my hand and led me downstairs. "We can peek through the windows in my room. You'll see him as soon as he gets close to the boat."

My chest felt like it was full of butterflies. Excited and nervous ones all clashing together, wanting to escape. It made breathing a little more difficult.

We could hear the engines shut off and X shouting to

someone on the dock. At first, I thought it might be my dad, but it was someone from the restaurant who was helping tie us to the dock. We could do nothing now except wait.

Luckily the wait wasn't long.

Peeking through the curtains of the cabin, I spotted my father the second he walked under a streetlight. He had a hat pulled low over his eyes, but there was no mistaking him. I knew him too well.

"He's here!" I exclaimed, barely able to contain my excitement.

It felt like finally everything would be all right.

X said something about a rope, and I could see my dad walk by our window to go to where the boat was tied.

The yacht's engines cranked up.

My heart beat faster. I just wanted my dad to climb aboard and for all of us to be somewhere safe so we could figure out how to get Mom back.

Because Dad would know what to do next.

He always knew what to do.

I turned away from the window. "I'm going to wait for him upstairs. I'll stay out of sight."

"Mm-hmm." Parker nodded, but he wasn't really listening. "Did you see that bush shake over there? I could've sworn something inside it caught the light and glistened."

"No, and we'll be off in a few seconds." I headed to the stairs. "It's probably nothing."

The boat shifted as we pulled away from the dock.

I heard the sliding glass door on the bridge open up.

"B!" X exclaimed. "Good to see you!"

That was all I needed to hear. I ran up the stairs and tackled my father, who was still standing in the doorway.

His arms quickly enveloped me. The sea breeze blew my newly blond hair into my face. No matter my name or my hair color, I would always be my father's daughter.

"My precious, precious girl." Dad's voice cracked as he hugged me even tighter. "I—"

"WATCH OUT!" Parker screamed from the cabin.

But it was too late.

A man, dressed all in black and wearing a ski mask, had jumped onto the yacht. He was already leaping toward the open door where Dad and I were standing when I saw the gleam of a gun's barrel in his hand.

X spun around just as my father shielded me, knocking me to the floor.

As the gunman pulled the trigger, X threw a kick worthy of any karate instructor, forcing the unknown man to stumble back toward the outdoor sundeck, his gun firing into the roof before spinning out of his hand and across the deck. X chased him out onto the deck.

"Hide!" Dad shouted as he pushed me toward the stairs, but Parker was blocking my path. He was frozen in place, staring at X fighting the gunman.

But before I could tell him to move, Parker snapped to attention, grabbed the wheel, and pointed to the open sea.

"There may be more of them back there!" He pushed the throttle to increase our speed. "We've got to get out of here."

I looked through the glass door as X narrowly dodged a dagger that the unknown man thrust toward him.

We needed to help X, or at the very least be able to defend ourselves.

"I'll get us some weapons," I yelled, racing down to the kitchen and grabbing a couple of steak knives. I ran back up and passed one to Dad, who was standing by the door, waiting to defend us, as X continued the fight outside.

The boat began to bounce as we hit open water at full speed and the wind made the ocean swell.

X seemed to be stumbling around more than the other man.

"We have to help him!" I said.

"Stay here," Dad ordered as he gripped the knife tighter and opened the glass door.

The ski-masked man glanced at my father just as the boat hit a large wave. X took the momentary distraction to gather up all his strength and do a roundhouse kick, hitting the man squarely in the chest, causing him to fall over the side of the yacht.

"YES!" I yelled over the sound of the crashing waves.

"What happened?!" Parker asked from the captain's helm as I chased after my father, who was leaning over the edge, looking into the water.

There was only the dark ocean and the trail of white foam left behind from our engines.

Dad grabbed me and hugged me tight. "I'm so sorry," he whispered. "For everything." He stroked my blond hair.

I nodded as X stumbled past us.

"Who was that guy?" Parker asked as Dad and I walked back inside. X was back at the helm, slowing the yacht down. "Does he work for Sterling?"

"Probably not, but he's definitely one of the bad guys," X mumbled. "There are plenty of people who have become aware of the . . . um . . . the circumstances. Let's just hope he was the only one who followed your dad."

"I thought I'd been careful," Dad said. "I don't know how he tracked me."

"They're pros and . . ." X slumped into the captain's chair. His left hand slowly reached down to his stomach and, when he pulled it back, his palm was full of blood.

"X!" I shrieked. "You're hurt!"

"Oh man." Parker looked away.

Dad rushed over and lifted X's shirt. "It's a deep knife wound," he said, inspecting X's abdomen. "We need to make sure there isn't organ damage."

"I'll be fine. I've had worse." X slowly pulled down his shirt. "We need to figure things out. Sterling knows . . . or at least suspects that . . ." X grimaced and seemed to be having a hard time talking. "He'll figure out that you're with me. We have to explain . . ."

"We'll come up with something." Dad put his arm around

X to help him stand up. "But let's get you to the sofa first, 'cause you're losing a lot of blood."

"In a minute." X tried to push Dad away but couldn't. "We need a plan for your family to be safe."

"Dude." Parker took over steering the yacht. "You aren't looking so good. You should listen to Mr. Davis."

"Thanks," X muttered as he stumbled on his own to the sofa. "Just put the boat on autopilot for now and look out for other ships."

I could see that Dad was worried about him, but X was acting like it was no big deal.

"Seems like old times, huh, B?" X tried smiling, but it was more of a grimace. "Bandaging me up like when we were kids."

Dad shook his head as he took another look at the wound. "Billy Peterson never stuck you with a dagger." He took X's hand and placed it on top of his stomach. "Keep pressure on it." Dad turned to me. "Katrina, go find me a first-aid kit."

"I have a full medical bag in the bottom drawer of the galley," X said, closing his eyes.

I flew down the stairs and grabbed the large red bag from the kitchen.

"And get some clean towels!" Dad shouted as I was about to come back up the steps.

I spun around and ran to my cabin, taking two white hand towels from one of the shelves.

That's when I saw my backpack in the corner.

I had my own medical kit inside with the blue cure-all liquid. The experiment my dad had stolen from the lab. It would speed up X's healing because, if the man in the ski mask was any indication of what we'd be facing, we'd need X at full strength to get Mom back.

I opened up my backpack, took the bottle with the blue liquid, and put it in my pocket.

I ran up the stairs, then handed Dad the red medical bag and towels. "Is he going to be okay?" I asked, noticing how pale X had become.

Dad gave X a towel to hold against his stomach. "We just need to stop the bleeding," he said as he rummaged through the medical bag, taking out purple latex gloves, a bottle, and a syringe.

It was time for the truth.

"I think I have something better than what's in there," I announced. "The experiment. It'll heal him faster."

"Katrina!" Parker widened his eyes at me. "Are you sure?"

"We need him to get better fast," I countered. "Plus, Dad is already here."

But my father just looked confused.

"I have the magic mermaid potion," I explained, smiling at Dad and taking the vial of blue liquid from my pocket. "Mom put it in my bag . . ." I turned to Parker. "We can use it on X and then trade whatever is left for Mom."

I expected several reactions . . . shock, surprise, grati-
tude, but never the one X gave me.

He stared at me, my hand trembling a little as I clenched
the bottle, and then I saw it.

His eyes were full of pity.

CHAPTER 21

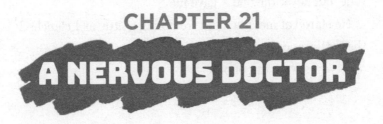

A NERVOUS DOCTOR

X'S REACTION LEFT ME stunned.

"Oh, little one," he said, shaking his head. "You . . . you . . . think that whatever is in that bottle can heal me?" X gazed at Dad. "B, she needs to know. You need to tell her. It's not fair."

"Tell me what?" I could feel tears welling up. Years of pent-up anger and frustration were bubbling over.

Dad pinched his lips together and nodded. "I know, and I will." He looked at me. "I'll explain everything to you . . . I promise. Just as soon as we take care of X."

X winced as Dad lifted the blood-soaked towel.

"That wound is really deep," Dad said, putting on the pair of latex gloves. He probed the wound. "You need more than a few stitches." Still, he didn't even reach for the blue liquid, the one that had always healed my every cut or bruise.

"I've been through worse," X replied with a half-hearted smile. "Even stitched myself up a couple of times."

I looked at the blue bottle in my hand. "So, this won't help him at all?" I asked. "It only helps me?"

"It's complicated," Dad answered while filling up a syringe with whatever was in the small glass bottle. He turned X's arm over and began looking for a vein. "I'm going to give you a sedative because I'm going to have to go in pretty deep."

"I don't need it." X pushed away Dad's bloody gloved fingers.

"But I do," Dad said as he held on to X's arm. "I'm nervous enough without thinking that you might twitch or that you're in pain."

"A nervous doctor," X mocked as Dad injected him with something. "Just what the patient wants to hear." X looked over at Parker. "Keep the boat heading east at a slow pace. I'll take over as soon as . . ."

His words trailed off as the sedative kicked in.

"Is he okay?" Parker asked, going back to the captain's chair.

"He'll be out for a bit." Dad spread the other white towel out on the table and began removing more supplies from the medical bag. "But I can't waste time. I didn't give him that much."

The bridge was turning into an operating room. There was a slight earthy smell in the air that I could only imagine was from the blood. It made me feel a little light-headed.

"Katrina," Dad called out to me. "Katrina!"

I shook off the sensation and focused back on Dad. "Yeah?"

"I need you to bring me some filtered water and a flashlight," he instructed. "I'll need you to shine it on him while I . . . um . . . while I fix him up, okay?"

I nodded and went below deck to get the items.

The entire process of "fixing him up" was something I didn't want to do. I'd never thought of myself as squeamish, but I'd never seen so much blood either.

When I returned, Dad had everything laid out on the towel. It seemed that besides being a scientist, Dad also had some medical training. It was another secret being revealed.

"Point it right over him," Dad said as he wet the gauze and began cleaning the wound.

I did as he asked, but turned my head so I wouldn't have to see anything else. Instead, I concentrated on the night sky and the churned water that we were leaving as the boat made its way back to the Bahamas.

We didn't speak again until Dad was done and said he was going to wash up downstairs.

Parker had opened the sliding glass door to let fresh air filter through the cabin, but X was still out of it. I walked over and took a seat in the first mate's chair next to Parker. It felt like we hadn't had much time to process anything that had happened.

"You doing okay?" he asked me.

I shrugged. It was the best answer I could give. I wasn't sure about anything anymore. "I really thought that the blue medicine was the experiment, but obviously it only works on me."

"I bet it's somehow connected to your life being saved,"

Parker mused, his eyes still on the dark, barely perceptible horizon. "Maybe you need it to stay alive or something. It could counteract some side effect of whatever they originally gave you."

"Maybe. Anything's possible at this point." I sighed, staring out at the water. "I just need answers. I feel like I'm somehow being dragged along . . . like a dinghy tied up to a bigger boat, and I'm just bouncing along over the waves."

"We've got waves up ahead?" Dad asked, climbing back up from below deck.

"No," I said curtly. I didn't want any chitchat. I only wanted answers.

"Oh." Dad took a deep breath as if summoning his courage. "Why don't we go to one of the cabins and talk."

For some reason, I hesitated.

I knew there'd be no going back from this. And what would happen if having answers didn't make things any better? What if it only doomed me to being trapped in a world where I'd have to carry my family's secrets . . . forever?

I had to accept a singular fact.

The truth might not set me free.

"Go on," Parker urged. "You can do this. I'll keep an eye on things up here."

Dad took a couple of steps down toward the galley.

"No," I said.

"No?" Dad looked back at me. He was confused. "I thought you wanted—"

"I mean I'm not going downstairs," I clarified. "Whatever you're going to tell me needs to be said up here."

Dad glanced at Parker and scowled. "He isn't part of this," he said, rejoining us on the bridge.

"He is. Parker became part of it the moment he risked everything to help me. He's owed the truth as much as I am." I smiled at Parker. "Plus, he's my friend. I trust him."

Dad shook his head. "But I don't."

Parker stared defiantly at my dad but didn't say a word.

Inside I was furious, but I tried my best to remain calm. "Parker's life is in as much jeopardy as ours is," I answered, crossing my arms and waiting for Dad's next move. "And Sterling BioGenysis will already assume he knows the truth."

"You know about Sterling BioGenysis?" The shock on Dad's face meant that I'd caught him completely off guard.

"Yeah, we do." I spat out the words with all the spite that had been bottled up for years. "Just like I know my name was Eva before you decided to take *that* away from me."

The silence stretched out until—

"Fine," Dad relented. "I'll tell you both . . . everything."

CHAPTER 22

ALONE AGAIN

PARKER SLOWED THE BOAT down to a crawl as we both waited for Dad to tell me what he had been concealing for so long. I could hear the hum of the engines as my ears strained to capture every word that was about to be said.

Dad took my hand in his. He looked me in the eyes. "Before I tell you what I did, you have to understand that all I wanted to do was help people. I was never in it for the money or the prestige. I was looking for something that would make people stronger . . . make them live longer."

I pulled my hand away. "Just tell me."

Dad rubbed his head like he always did when he was stressed. "It started years ago. Before you were born. I wanted to make a scientific impact." He began to pace around the bridge. "I was doing research at BioGenysis on how to improve immunity to certain viruses. Help the world avoid future pandemics. I was toying with DNA mutations and there were some small incremental advances, but nothing too significant."

"Uh-huh." I waited for him to continue.

"I was working with CRISPR technology and—"

Parker and I exchanged a quick look. We had seen information on CRISPR in the files from X's flash drive.

"Wait," I said. "I don't know what that is exactly."

"Right, not many people do, really. Let me see if I can explain . . ." He stopped pacing and turned to look at us. "CRISPR is actually called CRISPR-Cas9, and that's because Cas9 is an enzyme that works . . ." He paused as if he were trying to translate words from one language to another. "I guess you can say it works like a pair of scissors. It cuts specialized strands of DNA that we call CRISPRs, but that really stands for 'clusters of regularly interspaced short palindromic repeats.'" Dad's voice had picked up speed as he spoke. "It's a specialized region of DNA with two distinct characteristics: the presence of nucleotide repeats and spacers. Now those—"

"I'm lost," Parker muttered.

"Yeah, me too," I said, surprised and impressed by this new side of my father. "Dad, you're getting too scientific on us."

"Oh, right. Right." Dad bit his lip. "Okay. The simplest explanation is that it's a way to edit genes. Scientists can find a specific bit of DNA to be altered and use CRISPR technology to change the genome sequence. Make sense?"

Parker and I stayed quiet.

My thoughts were starting to race, but Dad kept talking.

"CRISPR technology has been used to develop better plants, for example, and used for thousands of medical research projects. That's what I was doing, research on human immunities, when the unexpected happened."

"The unexpected?" I repeated.

Dad nodded and started to pace again. "You have to believe me, I never thought there would be a continued progression when the cells began to develop, but once it started . . . I felt like I had to continue the research. It was an opportunity that I couldn't pass up. Nothing like that had ever happened before, nor did it happen after. My desire to see if I *could* continue blinded me to whether I *should* continue."

"Cells? Are you talking human cells?" Parker asked, his face showing he was still struggling to understand what my dad was saying.

Dad nodded.

"So are there human cells in the blue liquid or something?" I couldn't believe my own father had turned me into a human guinea pig. "Were you just trying it out on me to see if your experiment worked?"

"No, no. The experiment . . ." Dad studied my face for a second as if taking a mental snapshot before continuing. "It was never the liquid. You were the experiment."

My chest felt like someone had squeezed all the air out of it.

"I knew it!" Parker exclaimed, slapping the side of his

leg. "You gave her something to bring her back to life!" He looked over at me, smiling, as I tried to just keep breathing. "Didn't I tell you that's what it was, Katrina?"

"What?" Dad looked shocked. "Bring her back to life? No. No one can do that."

"But I'm guessing this does have something to do with me almost dying and you injecting me with whatever you were working on, right? Those human cells you were working on."

"What?" Dad's eyebrows scrunched together as if he was genuinely confused. "I don't know what you're—"

"After the accident. In the hospital." I was getting tired of Dad's delays and denials. "We saw the picture."

"I seriously don't know what you're talking about. There was never any . . ." Something clicked in his brain and his face grew somber. He knew what we meant. "Oh."

"Oh?" I repeated. "That's all we get?"

"There's a lot you're not understanding." Dad took a deep breath and slowly let it out. "The experiment I was working on wasn't something that I injected into you. It was you from the beginning." He stood up and leaned against the ship's console and stared into the dark ocean water. "Like I told you before, I was working with modifying DNA cells for years. Then, this one time, the cells continued to develop and divide. Beyond what I ever expected. They became viable embryos. I knew that it violated all sorts of ethics and governmental laws, but I was fascinated by the science of it all. It was a breakthrough moment. I got caught up in the excitement of the discovery and couldn't pass up the opportunity to continue the research to see the evolution of something new. Your mother agreed to be a surrogate and carry you and—"

"Wait. Something new?" Shock and a little fear filtered through my voice. "Are you saying that I'm not . . . *human*?"

"Whoa . . ." Parker's eyes widened.

"No." Dad seemed frazzled. "I mean, yes. Of course you are." He reached out to touch my cheek, but I quickly backed away. "That didn't come out right. I've thought about how to tell you this for years and I'm making a mess of things." He gathered his thoughts. "You're actually a better version of us. A step up in evolution." He tried to smile. "Think of yourself as human 2.0."

Everything around me felt like it was spinning. It was one thing not to know *who* I was, but it was something very different to not know *what* I was.

"Is that why she heals so quickly?" Parker asked. "Like that cut on her arm. Is that what makes her different from everyone else?"

"One of the things that makes her *unique*," Dad corrected him.

"Hold on." Another realization hit me like a sledgehammer. "If I was developed in a lab from some cells . . . then you and Mom . . . are you even my parents?" I saw the flicker of pain in my father's eyes. "You're not, are you? You're just some random scientist who grew me in a test tube or something."

Dad reacted as if my words had been a physical blow.

"No, no." He shook his head, desperately trying to convince me. "I'm your father in every way that matters."

"But not biologically," Parker clarified.

Dad glared at Parker, but Parker was immune to any type of stare-down from my father at this point. The two of us had gone through too much in the last couple of days to be intimidated anymore.

"So, I *am* just a lab creation?" I said, my initial shock and fear being replaced with anger.

"No!" Dad countered. "Your mother carried you. I saw you be *born*. Once you were with us, I realized how much I loved you. But . . ."

"But what?" I inched closer.

Dad bit his lip and paused. "But not everyone saw you like we did."

"The people at Sterling BioGenysis," Parker said.

Dad nodded. "At first we thought they were going to help us protect you. Because we knew if anyone learned what we'd done . . . well, we could be arrested and they'd certainly take you away. They convinced us that with them we'd all be safe. That it only meant that they'd observe you and do some mild testing. I had already refused to repeat the . . . um . . . um . . ."

"The experiment," I said with scorn. "Call me what I am."

Dad ignored my comment and continued. "I explained

that I wasn't quite sure how it had all happened nor what the future ramifications might be. That we needed time to evaluate you and your sister."

"My sister!" I exclaimed, not sure I had heard him correctly. It was almost too much to absorb. "I have a sister?"

Dad nodded. "A twin. That's who you saw in the picture." He sighed. "Her name was Ellla."

"A sister," I repeated, realizing the significance of my memory-like dreams. It wasn't my subconscious telling me to trust myself. Ellla had been the one hiding in the closet with me. She had been the one I'd seen holding my mother's hand. *She* was the person I trusted more than anyone.

I wasn't alone. There was someone else just like me.

"Wait, you said her name *was* Ellla?" Parker questioned.

Dad looked out to the horizon. "She died a few years ago," he said, his voice quivering. "I wasn't able to protect her."

She was gone?

It felt like I'd been punched in the stomach. The pain of losing a sister was only magnified by realizing that I had barely any memory of her even existing.

The few seconds of feeling that there was someone who could truly understand who I was had been stripped away. There was no one like me anymore. I was alone again.

Dad turned to look at me, his eyes full of tears. "It was then that I realized that I couldn't let the same thing happen to you. I knew I had to get you out no matter what."

"I was just an experiment that you didn't want to leave behind," I mumbled, feeling like my entire world was crumbling apart.

"No! Not at all!" Dad stepped toward me, but I put my hand up to keep him away. "Please, you have to understand," he begged. "I tried for the two of you to have as normal a childhood as possible. I thought it would only be small tests, but nothing you would notice."

"What kind of tests?" Parker asked.

Dad spun around and pointed to the wheel. "Um . . . shouldn't you be a little more focused on navigating the boat?"

"Nope." Parker crossed his arms. "It's on autopilot. What kind of tests did Katrina have to do?"

"I'd like to know, too," I said, trying to keep my emotions in check.

Dad relented. He was going to have to fully disclose anything and everything we wanted to know. "At first it was small things. Social-emotional assessments . . . Regular developmental testing . . . in which you both exceeded all expectations. Then when you were about two, you scraped your knee. It healed within the hour. More physical testing started at that point, but your body always repaired itself. You were even impervious to viruses. You had an immunity like no other."

My stomach turned, and it wasn't because of the ocean

waves. It was the deep sense of betrayal that was making me queasy. "You tried to make me sick? On purpose?"

Dad's head dropped a little, but I refused to believe it was shame, because if it was, it was too little too late. "I never wanted you to get sick and you never did," he said. "I always made sure to test blood samples in the lab beforehand to see how you both might react to any virus. There was barely a risk. But eventually, even that wasn't enough. They took me off your case and assigned Dr. Olga—"

"Porchencko," Parker and I said in unison.

Dad cocked his head to the side. "How in the world do you know her name?" He turned to look at X, who was still sleeping off the sedative. "Did he tell you?"

"No, but we've discovered a lot in the last couple of days." I scoffed, realizing how little we had actually known. "But obviously we didn't know *that* much."

"I just figured something out. The experiment names . . . Epsilon 3 Alpha and Epsilon 5 Alpha," Parker mused. "Those were their names, right? E, Roman numeral III, and A looks like Ellla; and E, Roman numeral V, and A spells—"

"Eva," I said, my voice coming out as soft as a whisper. My original name, the thing that I'd thought was truly mine, wasn't anything more than an abbreviation for my experiment classification.

"Yes," Dad responded simply, without trying to make any justifications.

I didn't know what to say or do at this point. Nothing felt real anymore. I stared at my hands. Were they even really human?

"Um, I think we have a problem." Parker interrupted my thoughts. "There's a blip on this radar that's approaching us real fast." Parker pointed to a screen on the console. "Do we make a run for it? Because I don't think X was expecting company."

I looked out the window and, in the distance, I could see boat lights getting closer. Dad was already next to Parker, pushing the throttle forward to increase our speed.

I shook X's shoulder. "Wake up!" I ordered, but he wasn't responding.

"They're gaining on us!" Parker shouted.

I stared as the boat lights got closer and closer. A strong searchlight flooded the dark ocean and was almost close enough to light up the back of our boat.

The speedboat was going to intercept us no matter what. There was no way to outrun it.

Dad slowed the boat down.

"You two hide down below," Dad said. "Let me handle this."

"I don't think so," I answered, still feeling spiteful for everything he'd done. Plus, I didn't trust him anymore.

"We can take care of ourselves," Parker added, taking a stance next to me.

But the truth was, there wasn't much we could do at this

point. It was just a matter of seconds before we'd be caught. We were in the middle of the ocean, far from everyone and everything.

It was the perfect place where no one would hear from us again . . . even if we screamed.

CHAPTER 23

FULL DISCLOSURE

THE BRIGHT SPOTLIGHT BLINDED me as the mystery boat pulled up behind us. The three of us were on the back deck waiting. I shielded my eyes but still couldn't see much.

"US Coast Guard," a voice declared over a speaker. "Who is the captain of your boat?"

I heard Parker breathe a sigh of relief, but I wasn't convinced. "Remember that Sterling had people impersonating feds when they took my mom," I whispered to him. "We have to be careful."

Dad stepped forward onto the deck, but I instantly realized that he had no clue about our entire cover story. I had to act quick.

"Our dad is," I shouted, pulling my dad back and stepping into the light. "Henry Garcia." I smiled and pointed toward X. "But he's sort of passed out right now."

Parker stepped forward next to me. "Yeah . . . but this is our . . . uncle. We're going to the Bahamas to see our grandmother." He gave a weak smile. "Do you need our passports? I can go get them."

I clenched my teeth. Parker was offering too much information. The less said, the better.

"Hold on," the voice replied. "Do you all have life jackets on board?"

"Right here." Parker rushed over and pulled out a couple from under the outside bench, then dropped them to lift up a couple of others. "Plus, there are more of them inside. I can get those, too."

Dad put a hand on Parker's shoulder as a way to control his overeagerness.

"Officers, I'm not sure if this is an issue, but we just saw a speedboat headed toward Miami without any lights about twenty minutes ago. It zipped by us."

"No lights, huh?" the Coast Guard repeated.

All three of us nodded.

A couple of seconds passed and I could feel a trickle of sweat run down my side.

"All right. Your boat checks out." The Coast Guard cutter turned off its spotlight and pulled back. "Just make sure to keep a safe speed out there!"

"Yes, sir." Parker gave them a small salute as they pulled back and turned away from us.

None of us said a word until we got back inside the bridge and closed the glass door.

"Whew!" Parker threw his head back. "That was close!"

"Um, yeah." I sat on the edge of the sofa, my insides still shaking. "But remind me to give you some pointers on lying."

I looked over to my dad. "Or you can ask the master over there. He seems to have a lie for everything."

"Ughhh." X stirred and his eyes fluttered open.

"He's waking up." I hopped out of my seat to check on him.

"I wouldn't be moving just yet," Dad cautioned as X pushed himself up onto one elbow.

"You wouldn't, but I would." X still sounded a little groggy, but he managed to sit up and look down at the bandage covering his wound. "So . . . what did I miss?"

"The Coast Guard just left. Other than that, not much," Parker deadpanned.

"What?" X rubbed his eyes. "The Coast Guard stopped us?"

"We took care of it," I added.

"And I told the kids." Dad had a resigned look on his face. "About everything . . . even about Ellla."

"Almost everything," I corrected him. "You haven't told us what exactly happened to my sister."

"I did. I couldn't save her." Dad shook his head. "The day Sterling took you girls away from me and your mother, I contacted X. We were willing to risk anything to get you two back, but it was going to take time. We thought about going to the government for help, turning ourselves in even if it meant jail time for some of the decisions we'd made at the lab, but we couldn't be sure you'd be safe without us. A few months later, X discovered that Porchencko was planning to run some experiments involving brain surgery." His voice quivered. "Her disastrous surgeries resulted in accidentally wiping out most of your memory, and your sister . . ." He rubbed his forehead. "She wasn't as lucky. That's why we had to risk everything and get you out right away, because Porchencko would keep going until it was too late for you, too."

"And I got you out within hours," X added. "Had to move up our timeline, but it worked."

Dad gazed at X with a sense of appreciation. "I'm not even sure how X has managed all these years to have Sterling believe he was working for him."

"Yeah, about that . . . there's something you should know because, well, I think our current predicament calls for full disclosure." X took a deep breath. "In order to keep my promise to protect her"—he pointed at me—"I had to make certain trade-offs. Things that you won't be happy about. But I had to do it."

Dad tensed up. "What did you do?"

"Sterling BioGenysis has never questioned my loyalty because . . ." X pulled back, away from my father. "Because they know that I've continued helping them with furthering their research."

"How?" Dad's fists were clenched. It looked like he was about to throw a punch. "How did you help them with the research?"

"Avoiding governmental oversights. Finding them a new lab. Something out of reach of most governments." X stared at Dad as if he was reevaluating what he was about to say. "I set them up to do research in a remote mountainous area in Turkistan. I thought they had figured out how to replicate your research . . . I didn't see a reason to tell you."

"Uh-huh. But what else are you still not telling me?" Dad asked, gritting his teeth.

"About a year ago I learned that they were still struggling to do what you did on a cellular level." He paused. "But yet there had been ongoing research and development." X's eyes darted over to me and Parker before landing squarely back on Dad. "I think you know, B. There's only one way Sterling would be able to do that."

"No." Dad slowly shook his head, refusing to accept whatever X was saying. "It can't be. You're wrong."

"What is it?" I asked, but Dad wasn't listening to me anymore.

"I wasn't sure either, but I got confirmation about five months ago," X explained. "I didn't tell you because you'd probably do something irrational, which would just expose everyone. I had to keep my cover and wait for the right time."

"No! I had a right to know!" Dad yelled. "I thought I could trust you. That there weren't secrets between us."

"There are always secrets, B. Always." X struggled to sit up straight and leaned on the table for support. "It's what we choose to share that's important."

"Knock off that wise secret agent crap," Dad said, his face flushed with emotion. "How could you do that to her?"

I got between Dad and X. "Who?" I asked again, insisting on being made a part of the conversation.

Neither of them spoke.

The only sound I could hear was the soft voice in my head telling me what neither X nor Dad wanted to say.

"It's Ellla, isn't it?" Parker said, breaking the silence and confirming what I was already thinking. "She's alive."

CHAPTER 24

NO ONE'S DAUGHTER

IT WAS ALMOST TOO much to absorb. Discovering the truth about who . . . or what . . . I was and then finding out that I had a sister being held captive somewhere. I had to force myself not to run away and scream.

"Say it." Dad grabbed X by his shirt collar and pulled him close. "I want to hear you say the words."

X peeled Dad's fingers away. "Yes. She's alive."

Dad's arms dropped by his sides as if he was completely defeated. "You had no right to keep this from me," he muttered. "I could have done something."

"No, you couldn't." X closed his eyes, and when he reopened them, I could almost see a hint of regret. "I've tried to get close, but Sterling had her under tight security. I had to be careful because one wrong move and it would have put"—he pointed at me again—"her at risk. You made me swear to protect her at all costs."

"But that's because I thought Ellla was DEAD! I would've had you rescue both of them. Protect both of them!" Dad squeezed the sides of his head as if he was trying to squeeze out the pain of his thoughts. "Who knows what they've been doing to her for the past three years."

"If it's any consolation, Porchencko got taken off the case about two years ago. She works exclusively in the cellular lab trying to reproduce your research," X said. "And, from what I've gathered, Sterling treats Ellla well. She's managed to become his prized possession . . . a daughter of sorts, from my understanding. He rarely leaves her behind even when he travels."

"She shouldn't be there," Dad mumbled.

X nodded. "I know, but first—"

"But first nothing!" I slammed my hands down on the table. "We have to rescue her!"

"Obviously," X answered, unfazed at my outburst. "And now that we've been placed in this situation, we can use it to our advantage and try to lure Sterling to bring her to us."

"But why not just tell the cops, the feds, the president, or whoever and get them to help us," Parker suggested. "Have them send in a rescue team."

"You really think things work like that? Several government officials already know, and their motives to help may not be pure." X held his stomach, his hand supporting his wound, as he leaned back to make himself more comfortable.

"How do they know?" Dad asked. "Sterling would never have let it leak."

"With enough time, nothing stays completely secret." X's jaw tightened. "And I may have had to divulge a few things in exchange for some favors. Create a little bit of strategic positioning in case things went sideways . . . like they are now."

"People know and they still won't help?" I couldn't believe that we were in this by ourselves.

"Some people know," X clarified. "And they'll help . . . help themselves to the research for their own use and make sure the world doesn't know you exist." He sighed and shook his head. "It's like a nuclear arms race . . . the human kind, but it's all kept under wraps. Can you imagine having soldiers that can heal themselves in battle? What some people would do to have exclusive use of that kind of biological warfare?"

Biological warfare. I wrapped my arms tightly around my own waist. I couldn't believe that it was me they were talking about.

"Then we blow the lid off all of it!" Parker declared. "We go to the media. Tell the world what BioGenysis did. Force them to help us."

"We could, but it would take time for anyone to corroborate what we're alleging, and by then we'd lose our leverage on Sterling. He'd have no incentive to keep L alive. That can only be done after we rescue both of them." X gazed out the window to the starry night. "Also, once you go public, you can kiss goodbye to any chance of living a semi-normal life."

"Then what can we do?" I asked, my eyes starting to well up. Not from sadness or fear, but from feeling completely overwhelmed.

"Oh, honey." Dad held me in his arms as tears streamed down my cheeks. "We'll figure something out," he whispered into my hair.

For a split second I felt safe. Dad's hugs had always made me feel like everything was okay. But then I remembered how he had lied. How I wasn't really his daughter. I was no one's daughter.

I pulled away and wiped my own tears.

"X," I said softly. "Do you have a plan to rescue them? Please tell me you've come up with something."

"I have." He looked over at Dad. "It starts with getting Sterling to agree to a deal. You will return to work at BioGenysis if they promise that the four of you will live in safety under Sterling's care."

"What?" Parker exclaimed. "You can't do that. They'll make people to be supersoldiers or something."

"Of course we're not going to really do that." X smirked. "It's part of a plan to lure Sterling into bringing L and Ellla to us. I'll tell Sterling that I was only able to capture B and that he has his daughter stashed away somewhere. That he'll only tell us where she is after he sees his wife and Ellla."

"He won't believe any of that," Dad argued. "Sterling would just kill me and L and hunt down Katri—I mean, Eva."

"I'm still Katrina," I said, refusing to be known by my experiment name. "And that really doesn't sound like a very good plan, X."

"First of all, you'd be surprised what smart people are

willing to believe when it coincides with their own thinking. We know that Sterling believes that the advance of science justifies any action, so he might think that you feel the same. Second, we don't need him to believe it. This is where we hold the advantage." X raised a single eyebrow. "If he chooses to double-cross you, he will turn to the guy who hunted you down in the first place. Someone he believes has no scruples . . . me."

Dad began to walk around the bridge in figure eights. "I might be able to convince him. I do know how he thinks . . ."

"We just need to pick a place to meet up that will be to our advantage, but will seem like a benefit to Sterling." X fiddled with his fake mustache. "I could suggest his ship since we have a boat of our own. He'd believe himself to have the upper hand since his yacht has state-of-the-art security and navigation software."

"Software, huh?" Parker asked, giving me a nudge. "Real high-tech stuff?"

X nodded. "He has it that way so there are less people required to be on board. Which is another reason why that might be the best place to make our rescue attempt. We just need an exit strategy once we have L and Ellla."

"I think I can cover that." Parker had a twinkle in his eye. "If you get me access to one of their computers, I can hack in and disrupt their navigation systems, disable their security protocols and stuff. Give us a chance to escape."

X chuckled. "Kid, I read your file and I know you think

you're some computer genius," he said dismissively. "But trust me, you're not *that* good."

"You're wrong," Parker insisted. "I *am* that good. I have my computer with me and, if I can find a way into their system, then I'm pretty sure I can disable it at least for a little while."

"Wait, what?" X shot upright and grimaced with pain, his hand clutching the area around his wound. He took a deep breath. "You have a computer? Here? Have you been trying to use it?" His eyes narrowed. "Because you know that they have software that can trace your IP address."

"Nah. I have camouflage software that bounces the location around the world. Not even the Pentagon could find me. I know what I'm doing."

"That story was true?" I whispered.

Parker shrugged.

"This isn't a game, son," Dad chimed in. "Lives are at stake."

"Yeah . . . I know." Parker was defiant. "*My* life included." He looked at X. "Listen, you said you read my file. Then you think you know all about me, but you only know about the stuff I got *caught* doing. I can do this."

"Hold on . . . so, I was right about you?" Dad studied Parker. "You have been in trouble with the law."

"Just some computer-related stuff," Parker mumbled.

"But that's how Sterling found us, isn't it?" Dad tossed out the accusation. "You were prying into our family and—"

"No. It wasn't him," I said, defending Parker. "It was me.

I messed up and didn't tell you about a picture of my elbow that got posted on the internet."

"Your *elbow*?" Dad squawked.

"I didn't know that you were in the background," I admitted.

Dad stayed quiet. Parker was the only innocent person here and he was up to his neck in trouble . . . because of me. Everything that had happened stemmed from my being *created*. Whoever came into contact with me was put in danger.

I was just a weird experiment that had gone horribly wrong . . . for everyone.

CHAPTER 25

HASH MARKS

WE SPENT THE NEXT hour talking about the plan and I still wasn't convinced it would actually work. There were too many ifs.

If Sterling believed Dad and agreed to bring Mom and Ellla to the meetup. *If* Parker was able to disable Sterling's security and navigation controls. *If* X could create a distraction to be able to rescue Mom and Ellla.

It was a long shot.

"Shouldn't we have a backup plan?" I insisted. "What if you and Dad get on the ship and can't get back? Or Parker can't disable the computer system? Or someone finds us hiding on the boat? Or—"

"Adapt and improvise," X replied. "That's the key. You can't plan for all contingencies."

"But we haven't planned for *any*!" I argued. There was still so much that we hadn't discussed or prepared.

"Katrina has a point. We should have a more detailed plan," Dad said. "I know this is how you've lived your life, but you usually work alone . . . this time it's a team effort."

"Fine, think of the plan as having hash marks."

"Hash marks?" Parker repeated. "Like in football?"

"Yes, like in football. In order for our team to get to the end zone . . . meaning everyone is back here and we escape without them following us . . . we each need to move the ball to a hash mark." X glanced at me. "A hash mark is a certain spot on the field."

"I know what a hash mark is," I said. "Just because I'm a girl doesn't mean I don't know football."

X shrugged. "There aren't details because it doesn't really matter what you do or say to get to your hash mark . . . you just need to make sure you get there. B, your job is to make Sterling believe that you will take him to Eva—"

"Katrina," I corrected him.

"Yes, fine. That you will take him to Katrina after you speak to L and Ellla. While we are doing this, Parker's hash mark will be to disable the ship's computer system. My hash mark is to take care of everything else that is required for us to escape with L and Ellla."

"Wait, what about me?" I asked. "What's my hash mark?"

"Yours is to . . . stay out of sight. I have a secret compartment under the bed in your room. You and Parker can hide in there until we board Sterling's ship . . . just in case they search this boat."

"So, I'm doing nothing?"

"You're staying safe," Dad answered. "That's the most important thing. We'll take care of the other stuff."

Just like everything else in my life . . . I had no say, no input.

"So, when's the first play of the game happening?" Parker asked.

"In a few minutes," X said. "I'll place the call to Sterling letting him know that I have B and that he wants to make a deal. Katrina's location and B's return to work in exchange for everyone's safety."

"And if he doesn't go for it?" Parker asked.

"He will." X looked at Dad. "But first I need to talk to you about a couple of things . . . in private."

I laughed in his face. "A private conversation . . . are you serious? After all the secrets that have been kept from me, you want to start your plan with another secret?" I shook my head. "Uh-uh. No way. Say whatever it is with me here."

"You've got spunk, little one, but you don't give the orders." He yawned, stressing the point that he was in no hurry. "I'll only make that call *after* you and the boy go downstairs. The plan won't start until I discuss a couple of things with B . . . and only B."

"Come on." Parker pulled on my arm. "Let's get some food."

"But . . ." I didn't want to go. It was wrong for them to discuss anything without me.

"It's not worth it." Parker headed down the stairs. "Just leave them."

"Ugh!" I exclaimed, storming down the stairs.

Parker opened the refrigerator and pulled out some ham

and cheese to make himself a sandwich. "You hungry?" he asked, grabbing the mustard.

"No." I plopped down on the bench.

All my thoughts felt jumbled. My mind was bouncing from one thing to another and landing on all things simultaneously.

I'm some sort of modified humanoid experiment.

I have a twin sister.

I'm part of a rescue attempt where failure likely means my parents and Parker get killed and I'm basically trapped by Sterling forever.

Oh, and my parents aren't even my parents because . . . once again, I'm some sort of freak humanoid experiment.

"Hey . . . you doing okay?" Parker asked as he took a bite of his sandwich.

"How can you eat?" I asked, not even remotely hungry. "After everything that's happened?"

He shrugged. "We need to fuel up." He eyed me carefully. "Is that something you can control? The need for food. Is it like the self-healing thing?"

"Of course not." I stood up. "I need to eat like everyone else . . . even if I'm not like everyone else!" I stormed off to my cabin, slamming the door behind me.

I couldn't believe he had asked me that.

How much of a weirdo did he think I was?

Five seconds hadn't even passed when there was a light knock on the door, followed by a stronger one.

"Katrina?" It was Parker. "Can I come in? Please."

I didn't want to talk to him or to anyone. All I wanted was to stay in the cabin and never come out.

"I'm an idiot," Parker declared. "But I really didn't mean anything bad by my question."

I thought about Parker standing there feeling guilty. He was the only one who had, for the most part, been honest with me. I should be the one apologizing to him for ruining his life.

I got up and opened the door. "I'm sorry, Parker," I said. "I overreacted."

"Meh." Parker looked at me with a sheepish grin. "It's a lot to take in, you know?"

"Tell me about it," I said. "Not exactly what I expected to find out when I asked for your help in doing some research." I walked back to the galley and started making my own sandwich. "And I'm extra sorry for ever getting you involved. I didn't know it would lead to this."

"It's okay. It's not your fault." Parker took a seat at the small table where he'd left his plate.

I put up a fake smile. "Who knew you'd be trying to help some freak experiment escape from a lab," I said, trying to be funny.

"Hey, don't talk about yourself like that," Parker scolded as I came to the table.

"But it's the truth," I insisted. "I'm this weird genetically manipulated thing."

"Stop," Parker said. "You're not a thing."

"No one really knows what I am, Parker. I don't even know what I am exactly."

"I know what you are." He smiled. "You're my friend. And it's like your dad said . . . you just have an upgrade to what the rest of us are born with. Human 2.0."

"Okay. Sure."

"Seriously. Think about it . . . it's kind of cool," he said. "Scientists messing around with DNA to make superhumans . . . it sounds like you're one of those comic book heroes."

"Well, this is definitely real and I'm really not super-anything."

"Ah . . ." Parker held up a finger. "But you could be. And I could be your sidekick. Your very smart, good-looking sidekick."

He struck a pose by turning to the side, arching a single eyebrow, and flexing his bicep.

I laughed.

"See . . . now that's better." Parker smiled and took a big bite of his sandwich.

It felt nice to have someone know the truth about me and not seem to care. It gave me hope that maybe things wouldn't always be horrible.

"You know, I was thinking . . ."

"Not more superhero stuff, right?" I teased. "'Cause I'm not wearing tights and a cape. I'm more of a flannel and jeans kind of girl."

"No." Parker's voice took on a serious tone. "About what happens after we get away? What do we do then?"

Parker had posed one of the questions that had been nagging at me this whole time. There was no long-term solution for me or my family. This wasn't a movie and I wasn't a superhero. There was no predictable happily ever after. No one was going to simply let us go. We'd have to return to life on the run.

"I'm guessing we'll have to go into hiding again," I said. "It worked for the last few years; it'll have to work again."

"But what about me? I have some family in the DR. I may not know them very well, but I don't want to just disappear."

I didn't know how to answer him, so I stared down at the table. Saving my mom and sister would not be the end of our problems . . . in fact, it could be the beginning of a bigger set of them.

"Maybe you could go live with them," I suggested. "X obviously has access to money. He could give you enough to get there."

Parker squished up his face. "And be worried that someone is going to come after us because I know your secret? I don't want to live like that." His face softened. "You shouldn't have to live like that either. We should both be free."

I sighed. "That's never been an option for me," I said, realizing that there would always be people wanting to put me under a microscope. Whether it was Sterling or someone else, I'd never really be free. But I could get Parker his freedom.

An idea took root.

This wasn't about me anymore . . . it was about Parker. He deserved to live his life on his own terms, even if I never could. "What if . . ." I mumbled.

"What if what?" he asked, carrying his plate to the galley sink.

"What if there was no secret to keep? If I told the world that I'm . . . I'm . . ." I searched for the right word, but could only come up with Parker's description. "I'm this human 2.0 . . . then it wouldn't matter if you knew about me or not. And X could get us a security team like Sterling's to protect us."

"Some bodyguards won't be enough when there are governments who want you, but . . ." Parker's eyes lit up. "If you had hundreds of millions protecting you"—he smiled—"then maybe it could work."

"Um, I don't think we can build our own worldwide army." I scoffed. "Even X doesn't have access to resources like that."

"He doesn't, but I do," Parker replied.

"What?" Parker was being cryptic on purpose.

"It's what you said. By telling the world, then there would be no need to hide and we could use the world as your bodyguard."

"I'm not following."

"Exactly. You're not following . . . yet." Parker paced quickly around the kitchen, obviously excited about the idea. "But the rest of the world will be."

"Again, you're talking in riddles."

"Followers on social media. We create a site where everyone finds out about you and they become invested in your life. You might not be a superhero, but you could be a superstar. You can do a daily check-in or podcast and if anyone tries something weird with you . . . well, your worldwide army will find out."

"I don't know about that. It seems . . ."

"Brilliant!" Parker declared. "I can hack into the top sites . . . distribute the proof we have from BioGenysis. People will go crazy over all of it. It's a reality show that's never existed because no one like you—"

"Has ever existed," I said, finishing his sentence. "But even if it works, I don't think my parents will go for it."

"Do we have to tell them?" Parker asked.

"Tell us what?" Dad came down the stairs but stopped on the next to last step.

Parker widened his eyes, waiting for me to answer.

"Nothing," I said, choosing to keep our idea quiet for now.

"Really?" Dad stared at me like he used to do when I was younger. "Because it seemed like I interrupted something important."

"Guess you and X aren't the only ones who get to have private conversations," I tossed back, staring right at him.

A few days earlier, a remark like that might have gotten me in trouble, but now Dad didn't know how to respond.

Parker broke our silent standoff. "Um . . . is X making the call yet?"

Dad blinked and looked away. "Yes. I was coming down to tell you both."

"Okay, we should go listen, then," Parker suggested, walking past Dad and going up to the bridge.

"Don't hate me." Dad blocked me as I tried to pass him on the stairs. "I love you, Eva." He sighed. "Wow, I've missed calling you by your name."

"That's the experiment's name," I said, brushing by him. "My name is Katrina."

I rushed up the stairs so he couldn't see the tears starting to prick my eyes.

"I told you that I'd take care of things," X was saying into the phone when I approached. He had the tackle box open and a bunch of equipment strewn around. "I have him with me . . . but he wants to make a deal before giving up the location of the girl. He says he's willing to return to BioGenysis, if he's assured that his wife and the two girls will be safe and placed directly under his care."

X paused for a moment to listen, giving us a slight nod as he did so.

"Well, he seems sincere," X said. "But he insists on speaking to his wife and other daughter first. Having them understand his decision." X shrugged, completely immersed in his role. "Up to you, of course. But I can rendezvous with your ship by tomorrow if you want." He paused.

I held my breath as the time dragged on. Everything

depended on Sterling agreeing to this, and it seemed like Sterling had a lot to say.

"I understand. I can take care of that, but that brings up another issue." X paused dramatically. "I had a run-in with one of your henchmen as I was luring Fisher to me. I took care of him, but it made me realize that perhaps we need a new . . . *arrangement*."

X pursed his lips as Sterling said something.

"Well, if he wasn't yours . . . then it means others know more about this situation than you imagined. I now realize the true value of what's at stake, and that has a price."

I didn't understand what X was doing. How was this part of the plan?

"I want twenty million. Half wire-transferred to my Caymans account tonight . . . as a sign of good faith. The rest can be sent after I deliver the girl."

X smiled as an agitated Sterling could be heard protesting.

"I don't care if it's not the original agreement," X interrupted in a completely calm voice. "This assignment was more complicated than anticipated. I burned myself with the agency and other partners in order to get this done. If you are now my exclusive client, that has a higher price . . . and you know I'm worth it. Plus, I've taken certain precautions to assure my safety and your compliance . . . just in case you get any ideas about my usefulness. Or I can seek out another interested party. Your choice."

"What is he doing?" I silently mouthed to my father, wondering if X might have only been in this for the money. Maybe we were wrong in trusting him.

"He's throwing Sterling a curveball," Dad whispered in my ear. "Keeps him thinking that money is the motivation. And by having to negotiate on that, Sterling will have less of a chance to worry about the other terms like bringing your mom and sister."

There was a little more back and forth between X and Sterling, then X nodded and gave us a wink.

"That's what I thought," he said, sounding victorious. "I'll send you the coordinates for a cay in the Bahamas where we can meet and I can make the delivery." He gave us a thumbs-up and my heart skipped a beat. "How long for you to get there?" He nodded as if approving whatever was being said. "That works. I'll deliver Fisher to you at noon tomorrow."

I glanced at Parker, realizing that in less than twelve hours my family would either be rescued or be held captive.

Then X's lips tightened as Sterling told him something else. "Of course. When we find the girl, I'll make sure to take care of the boy that's with her," X responded, looking directly at me and Parker. "You know that I never leave loose ends."

CHAPTER 26

HIGH DIVE AT THE OLYMPICS

I TOSSED AND TURNED all night. I kept thinking about everything I'd been told. The whole idea of having modified DNA freaked me out. I imagined the cells throughout my body holding some sort of weird code that made me different. And if the way my body healed itself was different, maybe other things were, too. I'd always thought I was an average girl, but I wasn't even an average human. I wasn't even human . . . at least not in the typical way.

And then my thoughts turned to Ellla. I concentrated on those two recent flashbacks where I'd thought I was seeing myself, but it was actually her, my twin. She would understand me. But what if she didn't have any memory of me either?

It was with that thought that I finally fell asleep.

Soon a sleepless night turned into a restless morning.

I was growing more anxious by the hour, and nothing seemed to quiet the voice inside my head that kept declaring that we were headed for disaster. Not the clear blue sky, not the soft Caribbean breeze that gently swayed the boat, and definitely not Dad's feeble attempts to mask his own fears with idle chatter.

I had come up to get some fresh air and clear my head before having to go into hiding in X's secret bunker under my bed. Now it was just a matter of hoping X was as good as Dad believed he was.

"Hey." Parker stepped out from the bridge and joined me on the deck. "It's almost time." He took a deep breath and looked up at a few of the white, puffy clouds floating along in the sky. "X says Sterling might send drones to scout the area ahead of his arrival, so we should get downstairs and be ready."

"Yeah, let's go." I took one more mental snapshot of the sparkling crystal waters around us and inhaled the fresh ocean air. It was like filling up my lungs before taking a deep dive.

"You two ready for this?" Dad asked as Parker and I walked down the steps into the galley. "You need anything?"

"Nope," I said, trying to keep my conversations with him short and impersonal. "Don't need a thing from you."

"Um, I think we have everything," Parker offered, trying to defuse the tension in the air. "We're just going to stay out of sight from this point on."

"Smart," Dad muttered.

"Yep." I pulled Parker by his shirt and headed toward the main cabin. "We are. Let us know if X needs us for anything."

Parker followed me into the room and sat on the floor next to the bed, which was already raised on hydraulic lifts, revealing the steps to the safe room below deck. He shook his head as he opened his laptop. "Man, you're tough."

"What does that mean?"

"Just that you're not cutting your dad any slack."

"Why should I? He's lied to me for my whole life."

Parker shrugged as he typed something. "I think he was trying to protect you. It's good to have people who care for you like that . . . whether or not they're blood."

"Humph," I muttered because Parker just didn't understand. This wasn't about whether or not someone cared about me, this was about Dad lying about who, or what, I was. There was no one who knew what I was feeling.

Well, there was one person.

Ellla.

She'd understand because we were more than sisters, more than twins . . . we were the only two of our kind.

"Anyway, I want to show you something I've been working on now that we have a secure internet connection." Parker turned the laptop around. "Check this out."

I sat down next to him and noticed that the screen had a list of social media accounts with strings of letters and numbers next to each one. "What is all this?"

Parker glanced at the door and lowered his voice. "It's the top accounts worldwide." He pointed to the codes. "These are access points to temporarily take over each account. Once we're ready, I'll hijack them and direct traffic to a new site that will tell everyone what's been going on and who you are."

I bit my lip, unsure if this was the right move. "But then everyone will know about Ellla, too. It's not just my secret to share anymore."

Parker sighed. "I thought you wanted to do this. Take back some level of control."

"Maybe. I don't know." It didn't seem right to make a decision that would change Ellla's life without even talking to her about it. "Let's not do anything until we rescue my mom and sister, okay?"

"Sure, but we—"

Dad knocked on the door even though it was wide open. "They're coming," he said, his voice full of angst.

Parker closed his laptop. "You sure it's them?"

"Yes," Dad answered.

I peeked through the closed curtains of the cabin. My heartbeat picked up speed as I saw a large yacht, five or six times the size of ours, getting closer and closer.

"Time to go," X announced, joining Dad in the doorway. "You two ready?"

"You really think they won't find us here?" Parker asked.

"At this point, you can't go anywhere else," X replied.

"You'll be fine," Dad added.

It wasn't enough to reassure Parker. He still looked worried as he stared at the raised bed. He didn't like the idea of being trapped in a small space.

I touched his shoulder. "It'll be okay," I said.

"Let's go." X hurried us along. "We don't have much time. They'll be sending a small boat to take us to Sterling's ship soon. You two can watch and listen to what happens on the bridge through the closed-circuit TV that's down there."

Parker stood over the stairs to the safe room and looked down as if he was about to do a high dive at the Olympics. A second later he disappeared.

"Good luck," I said, and started to follow Parker when Dad grabbed my arm.

"Katrina."

The way he said my name put a lump in my throat.

I turned to see tears in his eyes.

"No matter what happens, always know that I love you and that I'm so sorry for all the pain I've caused." He took a deep breath. "That no matter how mad or disappointed in me you are right now, I won't stop trying to earn back your love."

I wanted to stay angry. Say something spiteful that would make him feel lost and unmoored like I did, but I couldn't.

He was my dad. The only one I'd ever known and the only one I wanted to have.

And he was about to go off and risk his life to save our family.

"I may not like what you've done, but I still love you." It was the only thing I could say, but it seemed to be enough.

He nodded and stepped toward me to give me a hug, but I recoiled. I couldn't help it.

"That's okay. We'll talk more when I bring your mom and sister back," he said with all the false confidence he could muster. "This plan will work."

Another lie. He didn't know if it would work or not, but it was a lie we both needed to believe.

CHAPTER 27
EASY TRANSPORT

THE SECURITY CAMERA WAS hidden inside the bridge and gave us a bit of a view of the outside deck, where X was speaking to a man dressed in a white polo and white pants. The safe room had been equipped with a closed-circuit computer screen and a set of headphones that Parker and I were sharing. So far, we hadn't been able to hear anything because the glass door to the bridge was closed, but now all three men were approaching the bridge area.

"Go ahead and look around," X said as he opened the door. "But be quick about it, because Sterling doesn't like to be kept waiting."

Parker and I looked at each other, knowing that the slightest movement might give us away.

I could hear the clunky sound of shoes coming down the stairs, and on the computer monitor I could see Dad nervously wiping his hands on his pants. Then the footsteps got closer as Sterling's man walked into the cabin where we were hiding.

Parker and I sat motionless, trying not to make a single sound.

"Satisfied?" X asked from above our heads.

"Need to check the cargo hold, too," Sterling's man replied.

"Fine," X agreed. "But . . . what's your name again . . . Frederick?" I could hear X's voice growing more distant. "Just don't touch any of my equipment."

Parker let out a little puff of air. Both of us had been holding our breath.

A few more seconds passed and then Dad called out from the bridge. "Almost done?"

"We are," X replied, popping up on the camera once again with Sterling's man, Frederick, behind him. "I told you." X smiled at Frederick. "The man is eager to be turned in and I'm certainly eager to get paid."

Frederick chuckled. "Yes, Mr. Sterling did mention that this would be an easy transport . . . but that I still needed to check the boat."

"I just want to see my wife and daughter," Dad said sternly. "You said Sterling agreed to my terms."

"That he did," X replied, but his eyes stayed on Frederick.

"Boat is secure," Frederick announced into a cell phone that had been clipped to his belt. "Mr. Sterling can head to the ship with his guests."

"He isn't there?" Dad sounded alarmed.

"He will be." Frederick smirked and peered out the glass door, into the sky.

X followed his gaze. "A helicopter," he mused aloud . . . probably for our benefit, so that we would know what was happening. "How dramatic to land on his own ship's helipad."

"Mr. Sterling needed to be sure you weren't trying to set him up," Frederick stated. "Now we can go." He opened the bridge door and motioned for X and Dad to follow him.

We were now on the clock.

Although X had repeatedly warned us that it would be nearly impossible to hack into Sterling's computer system, Parker insisted that he could break into anything . . . given enough time.

"Anything yet?" I asked after what felt like an eternity of Parker typing furiously on his laptop.

"It's been like ten minutes since they left," he said. "It's not that easy. I was able to scramble their security feed, but the navigation system is much more complex."

The safe room was beginning to feel claustrophobic. It had been built for one person and wasn't much bigger than the space under the stairs in our old apartment in Oakland.

I stared at the screen showing the empty bridge. Everyone had left our boat and we were alone, with no idea what was going on outside. Not even where Sterling's ship was anchored.

"I'm going to scout the area," I announced, pulling on the lever to raise the bed. "We need to see what's going on outside."

"Just stay out of sight," Parker warned as the bed lifted above us.

I climbed out of our little bunker and peeked out the nearby window. I could see Sterling's massive ship anchored in the distance with the helicopter parked on the long deck.

But it was something else in the water that made me panic.

A small dinghy with X and two men, each dressed in white polos and pants, was headed back to our boat.

"Parker! Parker!" I yelled, glancing back at the lifted bed. "They're coming—"

The sound of gunshots stopped me cold.

I spun back to look out the window. The dinghy circled around the same area; X was no longer inside. Sterling's men let off another round of shots into the water.

Parker jumped out of the safe room, his laptop under his arm, and ran up next to me. "What's happening?" I could hear the fear in his voice. "Who are they shooting at?"

"X," I muttered. "Something must have gone wrong."

"What do we do now?" He looked around the room. "We'll be sitting ducks if we hide down there."

"We fight," I said, realizing that we were now on our own. "We can try to catch them off guard."

Parker nodded. "Okay. We need weapons."

I grabbed the screwdriver from underneath my pillow as Parker ran out of the room. Now it seemed small and worthless. I tossed it aside and went to search for something better in the kitchen.

"Here." Parker scampered out from the hatch that led to the engine room. He had a crowbar in one hand and a hammer in the other. "I spotted some tools down there earlier when X set up the Wi-Fi."

I took the hammer. "Hide somewhere," I suggested, my voice only a whisper, as the sound of the dinghy's motor could be heard outside.

Parker nodded and disappeared behind his cabin door.

I took refuge in the small bathroom by the kitchen, leaving the door only slightly open so I could see anyone approaching.

It didn't take long to hear two voices entering the bridge above us.

"Are you sure you got him?" a man's voice asked.

"He didn't come back up, did he?" a deeper, more gruff voice answered. "But check out this boat . . . it seems a shame to sink it." I could see the two men coming down the steps. "This thing is worth a pretty penny."

"Not our call. Boss said he wanted to see it go down without any visible smoke or explosion."

I watched as they bent over the open hatch that led to the cargo hold and engines.

"Well, it'll take a while to flood the—"

"Aaarrrgh!" Parker yelled, swinging the crowbar like a bat against the backside of one of the men.

He hit him so hard that the man went flying through the open hatch and fell into the cargo hold below.

"What the . . . ?" The other man grabbed the end of the crowbar before Parker could swing it again. They were locked in a life-or-death tug-of-war. "Oh, you little—" he sneered.

It was my turn to join the fight.

I thrust open the door and raised the hammer. But before I could get close, he yanked the crowbar out of Parker's hands, spun around, and used it to knock away my hammer.

I was about to run and try to get another weapon when I heard a noise behind me. Before I could react, something hit me on the side of my head and I could feel my legs crumple beneath me as I fell to the floor.

The last thing I saw was Parker's horrified face as black spots flickered in front of my eyes and I passed out.

‸

The next thing I knew, I was outside and my body was jostling back and forth.

"You really shouldn't have whacked her so hard," a voice said. "We could've tied her up like the boy."

My eyes fluttered open, hoping to see Parker, but all I saw was the bright sun overhead and Sterling's two men sitting across from me.

"She's waking up." One of the men hovered over me. "Told you it'd all be fine."

I sat up and looked around. I had been lying on the floor

of the fast-moving dinghy and we were heading away from X's boat . . . without Parker.

"Where . . . where's Parker?" I demanded of the two men, one who was steering and the other who had a gun pointed at me. "What did you do to him?"

"Relax. He's not hurt," the man steering the dinghy replied calmly. "Mr. Sterling told us to leave him on the ship. Apparently, he wasn't too surprised when we told him we'd found two kids on board, but he only wanted you to come back with us."

"So, you're just letting Parker go?" This didn't seem to make sense.

"Well, I guess that's one way to frame it," the other man snickered. "We *are* letting him go . . ." He paused for dramatic effect. "To the bottom of the sea on a sinking ship."

"No!" I stood up and almost fell overboard.

"SIT DOWN!" they both yelled in unison as I regained my balance.

This couldn't be happening. I had to come up with a plan. Something that would get me out of this mess and save Parker.

But I had nothing.

No plan, no rescue, no hope.

CHAPTER 28

FAMILY REUNION

MY HANDS WERE SHAKING so much that I shoved them into my jeans. I needed to remain calm, but it felt like the trembling was something I couldn't control. We had boarded Sterling's megayacht and, up close, it was even bigger than it had appeared in the distance. It was almost like a mini cruise ship with the helicopter parked on top and a small swimming pool on the main deck.

I tried to focus on making a mental map in case there was a chance to escape. We'd taken an elevator to a mammoth room that had a baby grand piano in the corner, and through the windows I could see a couple of people patrolling the deck's perimeter. They were dressed in what seemed to be Sterling's henchman uniform of white polos and white pants . . . just like the two men on either side of me.

"Excuse us, sir," the man to my right called out.

A slightly heavyset man in a blue suit jacket with khaki pants turned to face me. "And there she is!" he exclaimed, raising both hands in the air. "Welcome!"

It was Sterling.

A few feet behind him I could see Mom slumped over on a couch with Dad standing next to her.

"Mom!" I darted toward her, but Sterling's men held me back.

"M'ija?" Mom muttered, but her eyes couldn't seem to focus.

"Uh-uh-uh," Sterling chided. "No family reunion. Not yet. There are still things to discuss." Sterling pointed to a large wingback chair in the corner. "Jackson," he said to the man holding my left arm, "have our guest take a seat."

I fought Jackson off and stood my ground. "What about Parker? You can't just leave him out there."

"Parker?" Sterling questioned. "Oh, the boy on the boat. Not much I can do about him." He looked down at his watch. "The boat and he will be underwater in an hour or two, but your mother . . ." He raised his eyes to look at me. "That's a different story."

Jackson forced me to the chair, where I could see that Mom could barely stay awake.

"What did you do to her?" I asked, the concern resonating in my voice.

"Nothing permanent," Sterling responded. "She'll be fine once we finalize the parameters of our arrangement." He looked at my father. "Isn't that right, Bennet?"

Dad's jaw tightened.

"Bennet?" Sterling repeated. "You have a choice. My way, or you can follow Eduardo's path . . . straight to the bottom of the ocean."

Eduardo? Was he referring to X's alias of Eduardo Krajewski?

"I'll do what you ask," Dad muttered. "Just leave them alone."

Sterling smiled and cupped a hand around his ear. "A little louder so we can all hear you clearly."

"I'll do whatever you want," Dad declared. "You win."

What about our hash marks . . . our plan? Without our boat, there was no way to get Mom and Ellla and make a getaway. I looked around trying to come up with a new plan.

Sterling caught me scanning the room. "If you're thinking that Eduardo . . . or whatever you called him . . . might help you, forget about it. My men took care of him before disabling his boat." He smiled. "It was a lucky break that we found you when we did, though. Would've hated to lose you."

"I already know that you killed him." I spat out the words with as much venom as I could muster.

"Me?" Sterling pretended to be shocked at the accusation. "I'm a pacifist. A man of science. I don't like violence. Now my men here can be quite creative with . . ."

The elevator bell chimed as the doors opened.

"You sent for me, Father?"

I stared at the girl walking toward us. It was like looking in a mirror. The only difference was our hair. She still had our natural brown hair color and it was cut much shorter than mine. But there was no denying that we were twins.

"Eva." Sterling waved me over. "Come here."

I glanced at Dad, who gave me a slight nod.

My feet felt like they were plodding through sludge as I crossed the room.

Sterling smiled as he put an arm around Ellla's shoulders. "Isn't it great to have your sister back, Ellla?"

"It is," she answered with a big smile. "Thank you, Father."

"Father?" I stepped back, confused. "He's not our father."

Ellla raised an eyebrow and glanced at Dad. "Neither is he."

"Now, Ellla," Sterling reprimanded her. "I warned you that it might take her some time to accept the truth. She may not have the benefit of her memories like you do."

Memories. So Ellla had them?

"Do you remember?" Ellla asked, her eyes full of compassion and pity. "Life before you were stolen?"

"Stolen? I was rescued," I said, clarifying what had actually happened to me.

"Ha!" Ellla rolled her eyes.

"Ellla, it's obvious that she doesn't remember," Sterling said. "You'll have to explain to her how Bennet abandoned you and how I was the one who fought to have the two of you be together again." He gave Ellla's shoulders a squeeze. "How I saved you."

I shook my head. I didn't want to believe any of it. And a few days earlier it wouldn't have made any sense, but now anything was possible.

"Don't listen to him!" Dad shouted, and lunged forward, but one of Sterling's men blocked his path and pushed him back onto the sofa.

"It's true," Ellla answered. "I can only imagine what you've had to go through all these years. The moving around, believing all the lies, and never knowing who you really are. I've been so worried about you."

"Wait, you've been worried about me?" I was confused as I searched my sister's face for answers. "You were the one being tortured."

Ellla laughed, but it sounded hollow. "Look around. Does it look like I live a tortured life? I have everything a girl could want. That man"—she gestured at Dad—"took you to get back at Father. And didn't think twice about separating us . . . about leaving me." She tilted her head as she studied my reaction. "I know all about who we really are. Do you?"

Tears welled up in my eyes. I was confused. Of course I believed my own father—but hadn't he lied to me throughout my entire life? Hadn't all my buried memories, my deepest instincts, told me to trust my sister over anyone else?

"Ellla, I don't know what you've been told, but I thought . . . the reason I left was . . . they told me you had died," Dad said.

"Sure," Sterling scoffed.

"It's true," Dad insisted. "I would never have left you behind if I thought you were alive."

"No." She glared at Dad. "You left me because you knew I had my memories and could tell Eva what you'd done."

"No, no." Dad was despondent. "That's not what happened. But I should have looked for you anyway. I'm so sorry."

Sterling had his arms crossed in front of his chest and he looked pleased with himself. This was what he wanted. To tear my family apart. And while it was happening, Parker was out there . . . tied up on a sinking boat. I had to do something.

Adapt and improvise.

X's words came back to me.

I had been trained for the past few years to be able to tell lies. I had to shift strategies and figure out a way to rescue Parker—and that meant getting out from Sterling's watchful eyes.

"I don't feel well." I placed a hand over my stomach to stress the point. "I think I'm going to be sick." Which wasn't necessarily a lie, as part of me had felt like throwing up ever since X hatched the plan.

"It's a lot to absorb," Sterling said. "Ellla, why don't you take Eva back to your cabin. She can lie down and you two can continue to get reacquainted."

Ellla smiled and leaned closer to me. "You'll like my room. It's not as big as I'd like, but it's good enough."

I nodded and followed her to the elevator as one of Sterling's men hovered right behind us. We might be twins, but it was very clear that the last few years had changed us. Not only did we now consider different men to be our fathers, we also had very different personalities. Would I be able to convince her to help me escape, or at the very least rescue Parker?

The elevator doors opened and Ellla got in. "Come on, Eva. Things will be fine. Pinkie promise."

Pinkie promise. It was what we used to say when we were little. I remembered that from the memory of us hiding in the closet. We trusted each other back then . . . and we'd have to find a way to trust each other now.

CHAPTER 29
FLUSHED

ELLLA LED ME DOWN a small hallway where pictures of yachts and sailboats hung on the walls. There was a nautical theme everywhere you looked except when we entered Ellla's cabin. It was three times as big as the one I'd had on X's boat and it was decorated in pink and gold tones. Fresh flowers had been placed in a glass vase next to her bed.

"That'll be all," Ellla told Sterling's guard, who stood in the doorway. "And close the door behind you."

"Yes, Miss Sterling," he replied with deference. "But I'll be right outside . . . your father's orders."

"Whatever." Ellla waved him off as he closed the door, and then she paraded around the room. "Soooo, this is my cabin," she said, smiling. "I designed it myself."

"Uh-huh." I scanned the room. There were windows with a view to the deck outside, where I could see one of Sterling's men walking by just as Ellla closed the curtains. "It's nice." I smiled, unsure of how I was going to escape.

"Thanks." Ellla paused as if trying to come up with some neutral topic of conversation. "Um, since you weren't feeling well, you might want to splash some water on your face in the bathroom that's through there." She pointed to a door next to the night table.

"Nah, I'm okay." I sat on the bed and tried to get a read on my sister. It was eerie to watch her—the nuances in her voice and mannerisms were the same ones I had. Having spent years telling lies had made me pretty good at picking up subtle cues when other people lied, but everything with Ellla seemed perfect.

That was the problem. It was too perfect.

Of course: Like me, she was an accomplished liar. She was covering, just the way I did. It was subtle, but something was definitely going on. She was hiding something.

"You sure?" she asked.

"Yeah, I'm already feeling better," I said. "I think I just needed to step away from them for a little bit."

She nodded, her eyes darting over to the built-in bookshelves in the corner of the room. "I get that." She sat across from me on the bed, her legs crossed and a satin pillow tucked under her arms. I could see her searching my face as I did the same to her. It was about what we weren't saying. About the things that had happened while we were apart and our shared past that I no longer remembered.

"You really don't remember anything?" she asked, peering into my eyes. "I mean, Father said that was part of the reason Fisher took you instead of me. That you were a fresh start that he could mold."

"Dad didn't even know you were alive," I answered. "He freaked out when X told him and it made him want to come here even more."

"Come here? To work for Father?" Ellla questioned. I didn't know how to answer her because I wasn't sure if I could trust her yet or if she would trust me.

"Yes. Make sure you're okay." I smiled, trying to put her at ease. "He'd work for Sterling, but have you with him. We'd be a family."

"A family, huh?" She looked away. "Here?"

Instinctively I reached out for her hand, but my touch made her flinch and so I let go.

"Sorry," she said, grabbing my hand in hers. "A lot has happened."

"Were you lying before? Were you tortured by Sterling?" I said in a low voice. "Made to live through experiments?"

Ellla laughed, but her eyes were expressionless. "Father is the most generous man I know. Look at how I get to live."

It was not the answer I expected.

"The man you call your father, that man is the reason we got separated," she continued. "He let them do all sorts of crazy things to us when we were younger and eventually he got bored and walked away from us, leaving us in the hands of Dr. Porchencko."

"I remember her . . . a little bit," I said.

"Then you know what I'm saying is true." Ellla took a slow, deep breath. "Do you remember all the horrible things that woman did to us? The experiments where she'd hurt us just to see how fast we'd heal. Make us swear not to tell Mom. We'd hide . . ."

"In a closet sometimes?" I ventured.

"Exactly." Ellla nodded vigorously. "You do remember. We were on our own. No one was there to protect us. And eventually they just left us with her." There was anger in her voice. "Did you know that even the memory loss was because of one of her weird operations that went wrong?"

I shook my head. Everything she was saying explained a lot of the missing pieces in my memory.

"Well, Father made her keep working with me until she was finally able to restore my memories. Then he got rid of her," Ellla continued. "Since then he promised to never let anyone else touch me. We've grown a lot closer in the last couple of years. I've even told him I want to take over BioGenysis one day."

"You've been brainwashed—"

"Ha! Look who's talking," she mocked. "You're the one being lied to. But you'll understand once you get your memories. I'm sure Father will take care of you just like he did with me. You'll see."

This was not going well. I was starting to doubt everything and everyone.

We sat together in awkward silence for about a minute.

"Listen, we'll sort through all of this stuff later," Ellla said. "For now, why don't you go wash up a little and I can bring you some fresh clothes to wear. I've missed having a sister."

There were life-and-death issues surrounding us—Parker was sinking as we spoke—and she wanted me to freshen up?

But maybe there was a window in the bathroom that I could use to escape. I needed to somehow find a way to help Parker because he was running out of time. If I couldn't get to him, I realized, then maybe I could radio the Coast Guard.

"Eva?" Ellla was staring at me. "You okay?"

"Yeah." I got up and headed to the bathroom. "Clean clothes sound nice."

I closed the door behind me and looked around. It was a large bathroom with white marble everywhere, but there was no window. My heart sank.

Parker was counting on me because there was no one else left. X was dead, my parents were out of commission, and Ellla . . . well, she didn't seem like she'd be willing to help.

I stuck my tongue out at my reflection.

It had been stupid to think the person in the mirror with bad bleached-blond hair, ill-fitting clothes, and no memory was going to convince Ellla to leave her princess life behind. And I hadn't even told her the part about telling the world what we really were. She'd really hate that part of it.

No, I had to face the fact that Ellla was not going to be on my side in saving Parker.

Ellla knocked on the bathroom door. "Hey, can I come in? I have some clothes for you."

"Sure," I answered, opening the door wide.

"Oh, I have an even better idea. Why don't you shower and use my shampoo? It'll do wonders on your hair." She stepped into the bathroom and closed the door behind her before I could even answer.

"No." I shook my head. "That's okay, I—"

She stopped me before I could say anything else. She held a finger to her lips and went over to the shower to turn it on full blast.

"There won't be cameras or microphones in here," she whispered beneath the sound of the rushing water. "I've checked. They're only in the bedroom."

My mouth gaped open. It was as though a warped mirror had suddenly come into focus and I could see my real sister.

"Ignore everything I've said so far," Ellla continued. "That was all an act. You can't trust anything Sterling says."

"What do you mean?" I asked, not sure if she was being sincere or not.

"I don't have much time to explain because . . . well, it would be weird for me to be in here while you shower." She glanced at the closed door. "I've convinced Sterling to treat me like his daughter, but I know the truth. He thinks that by making sure I appear well-adjusted and normal, he can get a higher price for the research . . . if someone could figure out how to replicate it. I'm the sample product."

The water from the shower drowned out the momentary silence as I struggled to find words.

Ellla grabbed my hands and pulled me closer. "We can't let that happen. They'll turn us into lab rats again." I could see the real fear in her face, and I knew for certain that my father had saved me from a horrible existence.

Before I could reply, she turned and opened the door.

"I'll get you another outfit that you might like more!" she called out as she walked into the bedroom. "Something that goes better with that blond hair. Interesting choice, by the way."

I stayed still.

A feeling of guilt crept into my gut. While I was out there complaining about not knowing my real identity, she had been forced to play a role just to survive.

"I've got three for you to choose from!" Ellla sounded bright and cheery as she reentered the bathroom.

"I'm really sorry for everything you've had to go through," I said the moment she closed the door. "We'll get you out of here. I promise."

"That's the problem. Getting out isn't easy. Sterling is powerful and he's got his men around . . . all the time." She grabbed my hands as the ship began to rumble and then fell silent again. "We have to make a run for it. First chance we get. Together we can do it. Go into hiding like you did."

"But even if we escape, it'll never work because someone will eventually find us. Sterling or someone else . . . they'll hunt us down."

"No!" She vehemently shook her head. "I can't stay here

any longer. Being hunted is better than being trapped. I'd rather die trying to escape."

I pulled her close and wrapped my arms around her. "I know, but I have an idea where we won't be hunted and, well . . . we'll still be watched, but we'd be in control. But first you have to help rescue a friend of mine who Sterling left to die on our boat. I have to get back to him right away."

Ellla's eyebrows scrunched together just like mine did when I was both confused and intrigued. "I'll help your friend, but what do you mean we'd be in control?"

I smiled. "I have a plan. Do you trust me?"

Ellla nodded. "You're the only one I trust."

A wave of excitement and adrenaline washed over me. I wasn't alone anymore. Together we'd figure out a way to escape and save Parker.

"Okay, so first thing is saving Parker back on the boat," I said. "We can get back to him on that dinghy that brought me over . . . do you know how to get to it?"

"You mean the yacht tender," she clarified in a way that reminded me that she'd led a much worldlier existence the last couple of years. "And yeah, it should be tied up on the bottom deck."

"Perfect." I nodded, already improvising my own rescue mission. "You think you can convince the guard outside to leave?"

"He won't go against Sterling's orders, but . . ." She chewed on a perfectly manicured nail. "Maybe we can trap him."

"How?" I thought of how easily Parker and I had been overpowered when we had tried to attack Sterling's men. "He won't go down easy."

"If we can get him to come in here, then we can lock him inside by jamming my desk chair under the doorknob." Her eyes were twinkling with excitement. "I've seen it done in the movies."

I nodded, thinking that this idea could work. It was at least worth a try. "We can clog the toilet . . . make it overflow. Pretend to panic and he'll run in."

Ellla continued biting another nail. "I'll blow my cover of being the 'good daughter' because the room cameras will pick up what we're doing, but it's worth it to get out of here and get to your boat."

"But the cameras won't see you," I said, stuffing the toilet with a washcloth and a roll of toilet paper. "My friend Parker shut down the security system. The cameras are probably off."

I flushed and the toilet water began to rise and pour over the edge.

"Then let's do this!" Ellla opened the bathroom door. "Help!" she yelled out. "Help!"

Sterling's guard flung the bedroom door open and rushed inside. "What's wrong?" he asked, his eyes darting around the room.

I pointed to the bathroom. "The toilet!"

Ellla pulled him by his arm. "The water is going to flood

everything! You've got to stop it," she said. "It's so gross!"

"Um, yeah. Sure." He didn't look pleased, but he went into the bathroom and knelt down next to the toilet, trying to stop the flooding.

"Ugh! I'm closing the door before that nasty water gets into my room," Ellla declared.

I was already looking out into the empty hallway as Ellla grabbed her desk chair. I gave her a thumbs-up that we were all clear. She lifted a finger to her lips for me to be quiet.

"And I'm going to get some more help," Ellla announced. "I don't want everything ruined."

"No. You stay put," the guard ordered.

Ellla jammed the chair under the doorknob and motioned for us to go.

"Hey, what's going on?" he yelled, twisting the doorknob in vain as we raced out of the room.

We were free . . . for now.

CHAPTER 30
A SINKING FEELING

"THIS WAY." ELLLA RACED down the carpeted stairs and I followed her like a blond shadow. "It's just one more flight down."

As we rounded the corner, she stopped abruptly, causing me to almost crash into her. She pointed down below. It was another one of Sterling's guards.

"Follow my lead," she whispered, slowly sauntering down the remaining steps.

I wasn't sure what she was planning, but I was ready for anything.

"And you'll just love going to the out islands," she said, looking back at me, but speaking loud enough for the guard to hear.

We were making our presence known, which seemed to defeat the purpose of trying to escape.

"Stop!" The guard held up his hand as we approached the bottom of the stairs. He was larger and more muscular than the others and he seemed slightly confused upon seeing me.

"I'm sorry, miss, but you can't be here. You'll have to return to your cabin," he said with a heavy accent.

"Excuse me?" She put her hands on her hips, and I could see her transform into the other Ellla again. "You're new here, so you may not know, but I'm free to move around this ship as I please. I'm Mr. Sterling's daughter."

"Yes, but it is for your own safety," he answered, glancing over Ellla's shoulder to me standing right behind her. "Mr. Sterling said no one comes down here."

"Really? Because Father said for me to give a full tour to my long-lost sister." Ellla was speaking with an air of entitlement. "And I do believe this is part of the ship." She pushed him aside and dismissively tossed her hair over her shoulder. "Call my father if you wish."

She walked around the edge of what appeared to be a huge garage with the ocean as its floor in the middle.

"I can't. The communication links are—" The guard followed her. "Miss . . . please go back."

I was beginning to worry. This guard could force us back to the room as soon as he lost patience with Ellla. We needed a new strategy.

I spotted a fire extinguisher and pulled it off the wall.

Ellla spun around. "And where is the yacht tender?" she asked as I approached the guard from behind. "I wanted to show it to my sister."

"It's—"

I swung the fire extinguisher with all my might, hitting

the guard squarely across the back of the head. He collapsed onto the floor.

"Seriously?" Ellla widened her eyes and I thought she might be upset at my having hit the guard.

Then she smiled. "Took you long enough to figure something out. I was getting tired of making small talk." She grabbed his gun and threw it into the water.

"Had to find something strong enough to knock him out." I looked around. "But the dinghy . . . yacht tender . . . it's gone."

"Yeah, but we have that." Ellla pointed to the corner where a bright blue Jet Ski was perched on a ramp that led to the water.

I held on tight to Ellla, my arms wrapped around her waist as she sped across the smooth water toward our boat anchored in the distance. As we got closer, I could see that our boat was sitting very low in the water, but it wasn't as bad as I'd imagined. There was still hope.

"Parker!" I called out as I swung my leg over the Jet Ski and jumped onto the back of our boat. "PARKER!"

I ran up the steps to the main deck as the glass door to the bridge opened. For a split second I allowed the unbridled joy of seeing Parker, standing there with his goofy smile, wash over me. Then I raced over, tackling him with the biggest hug I could muster. "You're okay!" I exclaimed, squeezing him tight. "They didn't hurt you, did they?"

He pulled back and shook his head. "I'm fine; they only tied me up." He stared incredulously at me. "But I can't believe you came back for me."

"*We* came back for you," Ellla said, joining us on the deck. "I'm Ellla, by the way."

"Um . . . thanks. And I'm Parker," he replied, giving her an awkward wave. "Katrina's friend."

"Katrina?" Ellla looked over at me for an explanation.

"It's just the name I was using when I met Parker," I explained quickly.

Parker cocked his head to the side. "Wait, I thought you wanted to keep that name because . . ."

I widened my eyes to try to get him to be quiet. This was not the time or place to be having this conversation. Eva was the name of the person who Ellla remembered, and I'd use that name if it meant developing a closer bond between us.

Ellla caught on to what was happening right away.

"Hey, if you want to be called something else, that's fine." She seemed unconcerned. "Doesn't change that you're my sister. A lot has happened to both of us in the last few years. I get not wanting to be reminded that your name comes from an experiment classification."

"You sure?" I asked her.

"Yeah." She smiled. "Who knows, maybe I'll change mine, too. I've actually always liked the name Grace, and—"

Ellla's eyes suddenly grew bigger as she stared at something behind us.

I spun around and was shocked to see . . .

"X!" I exclaimed. "You're not dead!" I took a step forward,

wanting to hug him, but stopped, knowing that we didn't have that kind of relationship.

"Takes more than a couple of those guys to keep me down," he said, giving me a wink. "That plus having a pocket-size rebreather with me."

"A what?" I asked.

"Never mind," X said, brushing off my question.

"I thought it was game over until X showed up," Parker added. "Water was coming in fast, but we've managed to slow it down."

"It's only delaying the inevitable," X explained. "We're still sinking."

"Sinking?" Ellla repeated. She narrowed her gaze as she looked at me. "You brought me to a boat that's *sinking*?"

"To rescue Parker," I said. "You knew that."

"You didn't tell me the boat was sinking!" She was becoming visibly upset. "I thought we'd get away on this thing. That this was part of your plan." She threw back her head. "I probably would've been better off staying on the yacht and planning my own escape."

"Relax," X said. "I'm coming up with something."

"I don't even know who you are," Ellla complained.

"He's on our side," I explained. "He's a secret agent . . . of sorts."

Ellla was not impressed and crossed her arms. "This sucks," she muttered.

Parker raised an eyebrow, clearly annoyed by her attitude. "Well, even if we weren't sinking, did you really think we'd outrun Sterling when he has a helicopter?"

"The helicopter," X mused. "That's what we're going to use to get away." He pointed to the back of the boat. "How'd you two get here? The tender?"

"No, a Jet Ski," I answered, looking out toward the yacht.

"Hmm, that'll only get me to the helicopter." X rubbed his forehead. "I need to sneak us all over there."

"Maybe the key isn't sneaking us over," I said, thinking of how Ellla had handled our run-in with the guard. Instead of trying to slip by him, she'd distracted him by making our presence known. We could do that on a bigger scale. "What if we use this boat to ram into the yacht? Sink both ships while we get to the helicopter."

"It won't work," Ellla said. "Sterling's men will be waiting for us. They must've seen us come over."

"They'll be waiting for some kids . . . they won't be waiting for me," X replied, then smiled as he looked over at me. "Nice improvising, kid. But for it to work, I'll need a few things." He turned and went into the bridge with the three of us following.

We watched in silence as X started the engine. The floor beneath us began to shake as the engines rumbled to life, and the anchor chain clanked as it rose from the ocean floor. X then pushed a couple of buttons on the underside of the console, causing a panel beneath the wheel to pop open.

"One of you go get me an empty backpack," he ordered as he pulled out a couple of guns, ammunition, grenades, and at least a half dozen syringes, setting everything on the floor next to him.

"I'll get mine," Parker said, racing down the stairs.

"What is that?" Ellla pointed to a large vial that X was now using to fill up each syringe.

"None of your concern," he replied.

"I beg your pardon?" she said, surprised at his response. She glanced over at me. "I thought you said he was on our side?"

"X, please . . . just tell us," I said, wanting Ellla to trust us.

He let out an exasperated sigh. "It's a fast-acting knockout drug." X continued preparing the syringes. "Not everyone on board is part of Sterling's armed security, but some of them may need to be temporarily neutralized."

"Here." Parker returned, holding his backpack open for X to put things inside.

As X took the backpack, he shook it. "I said I wanted it empty. What's in here?"

"My laptop," Parker said. "It's in the back pocket. It could be useful if I have to scramble some of their software again."

"Fine." X put the ammunition, guns, and syringes inside. "Whatever." He zipped up the backpack and put it over his shoulders. He put the guns in his waistband.

We were going to do this.

"What should we do?" I asked X. "Besides hold on as we crash into the ship?"

"You take cover and wait for my signal," X said. "I'll clear the area."

"This just doesn't feel like a good plan," Ellla reiterated.

"Well, it's the only one we've got," Parker replied. "But you can take off on the Jet Ski if you don't want to come along."

I scrunched my eyebrows at Parker and motioned for him to cut it out. He didn't need to add to the tension.

X glanced at Ellla to see her reaction.

I could see her weighing her options, deciding if she should trust people she'd never met.

"Ellla?" I prodded.

She remained motionless for another second, then quickly nodded. "Yeah, I'll stay . . . for now."

"Okay." X gave me a little nod. "Let's go rescue your parents and sink that battleship."

"Um, it's a huge yacht, not a battleship," Parker said, correcting him.

"Yeah, I know. It's a play off a line from an old board game that . . ." He shook his head. "Ugh . . . never mind," he muttered, and turned the wheel to head toward Sterling's ship. "I hate kids."

I shrugged, but I knew the real game . . . the game of our lives had just gone into overtime.

CHAPTER 31

FENCING MATCH

IT WAS ABOUT TO happen. Our boat was barreling toward Sterling's yacht at full speed, and I could hear the distant yells from across the water.

Ellla and I had decided to brace ourselves for impact beneath the fixed table inside the bridge, while Parker had sought refuge under the captain's chair. Our job was to survive the impact and keep our heads down until X gave us the all clear.

It was easier said than done, as I desperately wanted to poke my head up to get a peek.

X was crouched against the glass door, guns in each hand. "Here we go!" he called out. "Brace yourselves!"

The impact was harder and more violent than I had imagined. The sound of metal cracking and ripping apart was followed by the boom of an explosion. "Stay close behind me!"

We jumped from our boat onto the lowest of Sterling's

outside decks and ran alongside the bent railings toward a door that led to the interior deck.

The moment we stepped inside, X was attacked by a skinny man dressed in white. X ducked as the man's fist flew through the air. Then, in one quick move, X swung the backpack off his shoulder, grabbed the man by the arm, and twisted it behind his back until he collapsed onto his knees.

"Please!" Sterling's man begged as X thrust him facedown to the ground. "I'm only following orders. I usually just work in the kitchen."

"Wait!" I grabbed a syringe from the backpack. "Use this," I said, holding it out for X to grab.

X hesitated for a moment, then snatched it and jammed it into the man's neck. Almost instantly, the man's eyes rolled back and I saw his body go limp.

"Whoa," Parker mumbled.

"Helipad?" X asked.

Ellla pointed to a carpeted staircase on the other side of the dining room. "That'll take us to the upper deck, and then there's a spiral staircase that goes up to the sundeck."

"Fine, let's go," X said. "We can't waste time."

I glanced around the empty room.

"What about my parents?" I asked. "I'm not leaving without them."

"I'm not planning to either, but we have to keep moving," X said. "They could be on any of these decks. Just be on the lookout for them."

I felt like I could trust X. He had risked everything for my parents; he wouldn't abandon them now.

"Come on." Ellla waved us over to the stairs.

We sprinted up two flights of stairs, but before we could cross the upper deck, we heard voices shouting from the deck above us.

X grimaced as he looked at the three of us. "I can't do this and take care of three kids." His eyes darted around the room. "You need to hide somewhere."

"But we can help," Parker offered.

"I know some of the guards, they might listen to me," Ellla added.

"We can be lookouts or—"

"No way." X cut me off. "Best thing you can do is stay safe somewhere while I take care of things."

"There's a supply closet down there." Ellla pointed to a louvered door a few feet away.

"Perfect," he said, taking the last of the grenades from the backpack and several more syringes. "You keep this," he said, handing the backpack to Parker. "I think it's time to release the kraken."

"What?" Parker turned to me for an explanation, but I shrugged, not knowing what X was talking about.

X sighed and shook his head. "Your plan. The one you told me about when we were on the boat. The social media thing." X looked at me. "You should do it now . . . just in case things don't work out for us here."

"You told him?" I said, not sure why Parker would reveal our plan to X.

"I had to," Parker said, slipping the backpack over his shoulder. "I didn't know if I'd see you again."

"No more chitchat." X pushed us toward the closet. "Go."

We hurried down the hallway and watched as X disappeared around the corner.

Inside the closet, it was a tight squeeze. The three of us could barely move and we were standing side to side, pressed against one another with mops, buckets, vacuum cleaners, and brooms surrounding us.

"So what's this plan you're all talking about?" Ellla whispered.

"We have a copy of a bunch of documents that prove what Sterling and BioGenysis were doing with the research on us." I took a deep breath to try to get the fluttering in my chest under control. "The plan is to release them and then be protected through millions of social media followers."

"You think that would work?" Elllla asked. "I mean, I do like the idea of being famous."

"Well, it removes the risk of you disappearing into a lab somewhere," Parker responded. "Which is why I talked to X about it before I put it on a timed release. He's old-school and still thinks I have to hit the send button or something."

"Wait, you did what?" I asked. "What if Elllla and I had decided that we didn't want the world to know about us?"

"I can cancel it," Parker explained. "But at the time we were sinking and I didn't want the information to sink with us. I also copied—"

"I'll check up here!" a voice shouted from down the hall.

"Aw man," Parker whispered. "This feels like déjà vu, and it didn't work out for us on the boat last time either."

"Fine," someone else answered. "I'll go down and check the cabins. But if you find the girls, take them to the piano room where we have the other two."

My heart skipped a beat.

The other two had to be my parents. They were still where I'd last seen them. This meant that I could go get them, before heading to the helicopter. But nothing could happen unless we avoided being captured.

I tugged on Parker's backpack. "Check what's in there," I said. "Maybe X has something we could use to defend ourselves."

"Don't think so." Parker dropped the bag for both Ellla and me to go through as he reached behind me to grab the broom. "X took most of his stuff with him."

A quick survey proved Parker right. Inside the bag was Parker's laptop, a rope, zip ties, and two syringes.

"No good." Ellla turned and grabbed a mop. "Maybe we can catch him off guard."

She was right. I looked around, but only the vacuum and a couple of buckets were left. Nothing seemed like it could be used in a fight.

I grabbed one of the syringes. It meant that I'd have to get close, but it would likely do the trick.

"He's coming," Ellla whispered as the sound of heavy footsteps drew closer. "Get ready."

I held my breath as the pulsating sound of my heartbeat resonated in my ears. It was like the countdown clock on a bomb about to go off.

The footsteps paused in front of our door. Through the door's louvered slats, I could see someone's silhouette.

This was it.

We each grasped our weapon of choice tightly as the door was flung open.

One of Sterling's men, with a shaved head and tattoos covering both arms, stood there staring at us.

Ellla was the first to attack. She plowed the mop head straight into his chest, knocking him off balance for a moment and causing him to stumble back.

Parker came flying out behind her, swinging the broom stick over his shoulder, and smacked the man across his head. It was a hard whack, breaking the stick in half, but Sterling's man had been trained for moments like this. He shook off the hit and kicked Parker so hard in the stomach that he went flying back into the supply closet, landing with a thud against the buckets and cans.

Ellla grasped her mop tighter, as if daring Sterling's man to a fencing match. He chuckled, flipped the broken broomstick over, and with one broad swing knocked the mop out of her hand.

He grabbed Ellla by the arm and twisted it behind her back. "Ow!" she yelled. "You're hurting me!"

I stood frozen.

"And you?" he sneered. "You going to try funny business?"

I looked over at Parker, who was wheezing in a crumpled heap on the floor, having had all the air knocked out of him.

"We give up," I said, trying to hide the syringe like a magician hiding a quarter. "Go ahead and take us back."

I took a couple of steps forward, my head down.

Timing was going to be everything because I'd only get one shot.

I tried to act like I was completely defeated and hoped Ellla picked up on what I was doing.

"Now!" Ellla said, pulling down on her arm even though I was sure she was probably dislocating her shoulder.

It was enough to startle Sterling's guy and give me a chance to slam his tattooed arm with the syringe.

He instantly let go of Ellla, jerked out the syringe, and turned on me, grabbing me by the throat and slamming me against the wall.

I had both my hands around his fingers as he squeezed tighter and tighter, trying to choke me. My legs flailed as I tried kicking him, but it wasn't making a difference.

Black spots floated in front of my eyes. I was going to pass out, and whatever was in the syringe didn't seem to work on him.

"AAARRRGH!" Parker yelled, tackling Sterling's man from behind and forcing him off me.

I slid down the wall, gasping for air.

Parker took a defensive stance, fists up high, but Sterling's man didn't budge from the floor.

Whatever knockout drug X had put in the syringe had finally taken effect.

Parker dropped his arms, turned, and knelt down next to me. "You okay?" he asked.

I nodded. "Where's Ellla?" I croaked.

"Right here," she said, running back from the end of the hallway. "There are two more coming this way. We'll be cornered and outnumbered, but I have an idea. I'll get them to go down to the yacht tender and you can make a run for the helicopter."

"What?" I stood up. "No."

"Yes," Ellla insisted. "I can convince them that you forced me to go with you and that I managed to escape. They'll think I'm still on their side."

"Um, that's not a good idea," Parker muttered.

"We're not leaving you." I reached out to take her hand, but she took a few steps back and shook her head.

"It's the only way," she insisted. "I'll meet you up there if I can, but splitting up now gives us a chance. Worst case I'll pretend to be Sterling's good little daughter again until you can break me out. I know you'll come back for me, just like you did with Parker. I have to do it."

"No." I was adamant. I didn't want to lose my sister when I'd only just found her. "We have to stay together."

"They're going to come this way." She glanced down the hall. "If we stay together, we'll get caught, and then we're all doomed." I recognized the tone in her voice. It was the way I sounded when I was certain of something. "Trust me."

She had trusted me earlier; it was my turn to trust her, even if I didn't like the idea.

"Be careful," I whispered.

"Always."

She turned and ran down the hall, but before rounding the corner, she looked back at us. Then I saw her look forward and yell, "Hey, they're headed to the tender. Hurry! Follow me!"

CHAPTER 32

LOOSE ENDS

"NOW WHAT?" PARKER ASKED as soon as Ellla led Sterling's men away. We could both hear gunfire coming from the helipad. "We can't go up there."

I only had one thought in mind. "I'm going to save my parents."

Parker glanced at the closet door behind us. "Do you even know where they are? Maybe we should just hide here in the closet until X gets your parents, like he said."

"They're on the main deck where the piano is," I said, listening to more shots being fired from above. "But you should stay here. I can heal in ways you can't." Fear shot through me. I had no idea what my body was capable of doing. "You can tell X where I went."

"Hey." Parker raised a finger as if scolding me while simultaneously giving me his lopsided grin. "Don't go pulling that superpower stuff on me. We're in this together." He stepped into the closet and grabbed his backpack. "I'm with you to the end. The superhero's ever-faithful sidekick."

I nodded. "But you're my partner . . . not sidekick," I corrected him.

Without making a sound, we made our way down the flight of stairs to the main deck. It seemed that Ellla's plan had worked, because there was no one in the hallway or the stairwell. We entered the lounge area where I'd seen the grand piano earlier, but as I snuck in, I noticed an eerie stillness to the room. I began to worry that my parents had been taken somewhere else or something bad had already happened to them.

Then a muted groan caught my attention.

That's when I saw them.

Mom and Dad . . . on the floor next to the couches.

Dad was facedown, his hands and feet tied behind his back with an electrical cord, and Mom was curled up as if she were asleep.

I rushed over to them, my footsteps muffled by the large area rugs. "Mom! Dad!" I exclaimed in a low whisper, the words escaping my mouth even though I'd been trying to be quiet.

Parker shook Mom's shoulder, but she muttered something and drifted back into unconsciousness. I turned to Dad, whose eyes were flickering open.

I sat him up and he groaned once again as his eyes regained focus.

"Dad, are you okay?" I whispered as Parker untied him.

"Yeah," he muttered. "They bonked me on the head pretty good, though, after the boats crashed." He looked around. "Where's Ellla?"

"We'll meet her and X by the helicopter," Parker said as he finished untying him. "But we have to hurry."

"X . . . is alive?" Dad asked. He looked around. "Hold up . . . where is he? Why is he leaving you on your own?"

"We got separated," I explained, trying to pull Mom up. "He's taking care of Sterling's men, but we have to get Mom up there."

"What about Ellla?" Dad asked, picking up Mom and propping her on the sofa. "You said she's meeting us there, too? Did you explain that I never meant to leave her?"

"Yes, yes," I said. "She was only pretending to be that way with Sterling in order to survive. She knows the truth."

"Okay. Good." Dad was now trying to get Mom more alert by tapping her cheeks. "Come on, L. You need to wake up." He pulled her forward by her arms so she was sitting somewhat on her own. "Lydia. Wake. Up."

Mom opened her eyes and gave him a drunken smile. "Hi there, B," she said, slurring her words. "But remember, you're not supposed to say my name." Her gaze shifted to me. "Aw, sweetie. You have blond hair." She reached out to touch the strands around my face.

"L, you need to be quiet." He put his shoulder under her arm and had her stand. "We're going to get out of here. Parker, help me out."

"Here? Where's here?" she asked, stumbling as she took her first steps.

Parker gave me his backpack to hold and got on the other side of her. "Mrs. Davis, you really have to concentrate and not say a word."

Mom nodded. "Shhhh." She smiled, still not understanding the situation.

We made it up the stairs as quickly as we could considering Mom was dragging her feet. Once in the hallway, we stepped around the guy I had stabbed with the syringe and continued to the next set of stairs that led to the helipad.

"Let's first make sure the area is clear," I said as we all peeked through the glass to where the helicopter was parked on the deck.

"Looks like X took care of business," Parker remarked as he pointed to two of Sterling's men unconscious on the floor.

"The pilot, too," I whispered, noticing that someone had been dragged off the helicopter and lay next to it.

"Something feels off," Dad said. "X doesn't seem to be out there."

"Stay here," Parker said, ducking out from beneath my mom's arm and slowly pushing open the door. "I'll check it out."

"*We'll* check it out," I corrected him, walking a few inches behind him.

"Be care—"

Dad's words of warning never made it out as Parker was

yanked sideways away from the door and Sterling emerged from around the corner, holding a gun to his ribs. Ellla was standing calmly by his side.

"Nice of you to finally join us." Sterling stepped away, pulling Parker along with him.

"I told you they'd come here," Ellla said with a smug look on her face. "We didn't need to go looking for them. They're so predictable."

Dad moved, pushing Mom toward me.

"Uh-uh-uh," Sterling warned. "One inch closer and the boy dies."

Dad stayed still.

"Ellla . . ." I stared at her, not believing that she was actually helping Sterling. "Why are you—"

"Helping Father?" She laughed. "Did you think I was going to run away with a family that had no problem abandoning me? Spend my life in hiding? You really are naive."

"Ellla, you have to understand . . ." Dad tried explaining as he shifted Mom's weight back onto his shoulder.

"Oh, I understand everything," she said. "Including the fact that the four of you were headed to the helicopter without me. I'm always the first to be left behind."

"No," I argued. "We wouldn't have left you, but we had to get Mom."

My feelings of guilt flared up again. It would make sense if Ella was still angry and distrustful. We'd been living as a happy family of three while she . . . I watched her closely, trying to recognize my own tells, but I was having a hard time deciphering if she was playing a role or if she had simply played the role with us.

Mom seemed to come out of her stupor at the sound of her name. "What . . . what are we doing here?" she whispered to Dad, still in a fog from whatever drugs had been given to her.

"Well, I was never going to go with you anyway." Ellla shrugged as if anything I might say was irrelevant.

Parker glared at Ellla, but the gun pressed against him kept him quiet.

"Ellla, what you told me in the bathroom . . ." I wanted to hold out hope for my sister.

She shrugged. "I said whatever needed to be said to get you to tell me your plans." She paused and smiled. "I'd have been shot in the arm, if it meant you'd believe me. Just like Father asked me to do."

"And you did your job well, Ellla," Sterling praised her. "She even told me your little plan to reveal our secret to the world."

"What?" Dad glanced at me.

"It was the only way we could be free," I said. "If everyone knows, then no one can own us."

"But things aren't that simple," Dad said. "Don't you think I would've . . ."

"Oh, don't worry, Bennet." Sterling's lips curled into a patronizing sneer. "No one will disrupt our research or reveal our secret now. And just as soon as my men find X or my pilot wakes up, we'll be ready to resume where we left off a few years ago."

"But what about if they already set things up to go public?" Ellla asked Sterling. "We have to stop them." She stared at me intently as she spoke. "We need to knock out anything they may have prearranged."

I wasn't sure if Ellla had intended it or not, but she'd given me an idea. There was still one syringe with the knockout drug in the backpack. All I needed was a way to get close to Sterling.

"Ellla' s right," I said. "Parker made it so that if anything happens to us, then all the proof of who we are and what you've done gets released. It's all on his computer right here." I tapped the backpack. "So you better let us go."

"I doubt you have any of that," Sterling chuckled. "But nice try."

I wasn't sure if my plan was going to work, but I was all in at this point. "Don't believe me?" I crossed my arms and tried to not look at the gun pointed against Parker's rib cage. "How else would I know the names of the early experiments starting with Alpha I Alpha? They're all there. We even saw—"

"Stop!" Parker shouted. "Don't say anything else."

Sterling was studying me. I had to be very careful with my next move.

I slipped the bag off my shoulder. "I can show you the

documents, but you have to let Parker go." I slowly unzipped the bag.

"Hold on. Don't open that," Sterling ordered. "Ellla, you go check. I don't trust her."

My heart sank a little. My plan was to get close enough to Sterling to stab him with the syringe, but now it was Ellla who would be next to me.

"Good thinking, Father." Ellla took a couple of steps forward, then stopped. The wind blew her hair across her face and she pushed it behind one ear. "I actually don't trust her either. Slide the bag over to me," she said.

A lump formed in my throat. How could I have completely misread Ellla? She'd come with me to get Parker. But had that just been a trick?

My head was spinning.

"Slide it!" she ordered. "Now."

Anger at being betrayed welled up inside me as I kicked the bag across the deck. "How could you do this?" I spat out the words. "We're *sisters*."

"No." Ellla shook her head as she opened the bag and pulled out the laptop. "We're strangers. You don't even remember me."

Her words stung. "Well, I guess that's a good thing!" I retorted.

"Now, now, Eva," Sterling chided.

I cringed, hearing that name from him.

Ellla laughed and turned to Sterling. "Oh, I forgot to tell

you, Father. She doesn't even want to be called Eva anymore." She then glanced over her shoulder, her eyes locking with mine. "Her new name of choice is . . . *Grace*."

Grace? That was the name *she* liked. How could she confuse that—or was she trying to tell me something?

Parker shot me a look.

I still wasn't 100 percent sure if Ellla was on our side, but it felt like something had shifted. Parker gave me a slight nod to indicate that he sensed the difference, too.

Things were not as they appeared to be.

"You're going to kill me no matter what, aren't you?" Parker's voice had a little bit of a tremor to it.

"Probably," Sterling replied coldly. "But the timing depends on you."

"He's only a child," Dad pleaded. "There's no need. Let him go."

"In my world . . ." Sterling glared at Dad. "I decide what's needed or not. So, I suggest you remain cooperative since your wife isn't really needed either."

"Here it is." Ellla held the laptop in her hand as she sauntered back toward Sterling.

"Wait right there." Sterling smiled victoriously. "Toss it overboard."

"NO!" Parker yelled.

"You sure?" Ellla hesitated at the edge of the helipad. "You don't want to take a look at it first?"

"If the information is there, it'll disappear just like he

will," Sterling said. "If it's on a server somewhere, then the laptop is of no use anyway. Throw it."

"Of course." Ellla flung the laptop far over the side. Then she turned back around and smiled sweetly at Sterling. "But I was thinking . . . maybe you don't have to get rid of Parker. Didn't you say you wanted to try out some new experimental drugs that Dr. Porchencko was working on? He's better than hurting one of those cute monkeys that I like to play with."

I was confused once again. I'd thought Ellla was trying to send me a message, but maybe that was wishful thinking.

"Hmm." Sterling considered what she had suggested as she strolled toward him once again. He nodded, a proud grin on his face. "Ellla, you continue to surprise me. You may have exactly what it takes to one day be my heir."

"Aw . . . thank you, Father." She leaned in to give him a kiss on the cheek.

That's when it all happened.

Ellla plunged a syringe she'd been hiding in her hand straight into Sterling's neck.

"Wha—" Sterling stumbled and Parker spun out of his grasp, the gun firing aimlessly.

Ellla grabbed the hand still holding the gun and aimed it at the sky as Sterling's knees began to buckle and I tackled him at full strength.

Dad wrestled the gun out of Sterling's grip just as X came running from the far side of the deck.

"X!" Mom clapped happily, leaning against the doorway. "Nice to see you!"

"Good of you to finally show up," Dad said, pointing the gun at Sterling, who had crumpled to the floor, his eyes beginning to roll back in his head.

"I heard the gunshot," X said, his face bruised and bloodied with a gash under his swollen right eye. "I was busy searching for all of you downstairs and getting rid of a few more guards."

Dad's hand was shaking as he passed the gun to X. "We need to get out of here."

"Couldn't agree with you more," X said, nudging Sterling's unconscious body with his foot.

"Where to?" Parker asked.

"I know a place nearby where we can make a pit stop. Sort out some things. Ten million dollars can go a long way for you." X gave us a wink. The money he'd gotten from Sterling was for us. "Now grab L and get in the chopper. We can't waste any more time here."

Dad grabbed Mom and we all boarded the helicopter, but Ellla pulled me aside. "Hey, I'm sorry about all that stuff I said," she explained. "I had to have a backup plan in case I got stuck with Sterling, and I was also trying to buy time until we could get the syringe."

"I know," I said. "It just took me a little bit to figure it out, but I got it."

"So much for any type of twin psychic connection." She

smiled. "I was tossing out clues for you left and right. I said a shot in the arm, knockout, and finally had to use the Grace thing."

"Let's go," Parker shouted, interrupting us. "We can talk later."

Ellla and I boarded and a moment later X jumped into the pilot's seat.

As the helicopter rose, I looked out onto the empty deck a few feet below us. "He's gone!" I pointed to where Sterling's unconscious body had been only a few minutes earlier.

X shrugged. "Don't worry!" he shouted over the whirring sound of the helicopter blades as we flew out over the open water. "I always take care of loose ends!"

CHAPTER 33

BEACHSIDE HIDEAWAY

OUR HELICOPTER KICKED UP sand and dirt as it hovered inches over the grass of a perfectly manicured estate complete with a mansion, tennis court, and two gigantic pools. We were at the private island home of someone who X claimed owed him a couple of favors and would be able to help get us to our next destination. X had already radioed ahead for permission to land, and there were two men in dark suits wearing mirrored sunglasses waiting for us. A wheelchair was at their side.

"You all stay here while I take care of L." X's voice filtered through the headsets we were each wearing. "My 'associate' is very particular about not having guests see him or his place."

"You're just going to give L some IV fluids, right?" Dad asked as the helicopter touched the ground. "Flush her system with some saline to get rid of that drug Sterling gave her."

"That and get things going for the next stop in your

journey. My associate has connections in several countries where you can stay while we figure out any charges that may pop up once you all become internet famous." X glanced over at Dad. "Trust me. I've never let you down before."

Dad nodded and looked back at Mom, sleeping once again in her seat, and the three of us in the back row.

"This associate of yours," I said as the helicopter blades above us slowed to a full stop. "He won't wonder what's going on with us? Why we're running?"

"He operates on a need-to-know basis," X explained. "And he doesn't need to know anything about you."

We all remained quiet as the two suited men brought over the wheelchair and Dad helped put Mom into it. A woman had come out from the house and was waiting for X at the edge of the large patio, surrounded by fake Greek sculptures.

I slipped the headset off and looked at Ellla sitting to my right, staring out the window at the horizon. She hadn't said much since we got away.

So much had changed for both her and me.

Ellla's fingers twirled a strand of brown hair and I couldn't help but look at my own fingers. Comparing the identical shape between hers and mine . . . even if hers looked much prettier with her painted nails.

Parker tapped me on the shoulder. "What do you think of this place?" he whispered, pointing to the enormous mansion. "Drug lord hideaway? Mob boss beach house? Eccentric billionaire's secret lair?"

I raised my eyebrows. "I think we've had enough of eccentric billionaires."

Dad opened the door and got back into the copilot's chair as X wheeled Mom toward the house.

"I don't like waiting here for them to come back," Dad muttered.

"Tell me about it," Ellla said snidely, looking directly at our father. "Imagine when people don't care to come back for you at all."

"No, Ellla." Dad shook his head. "That's not what happened."

"And we did come back," I corrected her. "As soon as I found out about you, I knew—"

"Not everyone lost their memory," she said, cutting me off.

"Ellla, please let me explain again." Dad moved to take the seat in front of us, and I could hear the pain in his voice. I hoped Ellla could, too. "Your mother and I were devastated when we discovered that you'd died. I couldn't believe it, but we saw the picture and the medical reports. I knew that Porchencko was capable of extremes and I even confronted Sterling about it. His response was an offer for me to restart with new cells—as if you could be replaced!—but of course I couldn't . . ." His eyes became watery. "No one could ever replace you."

This made me want to ask my own questions about what had happened, but it felt like I was intruding in a private conversation between Ellla and my dad. This was their time . . . Parker and I just happened to be witnessing it.

Ellla's tough exterior seemed to crack a little. "So . . . when did you find out that I was alive?" She pointed a finger at him. "And don't lie because I'll know."

"Yesterday," Dad said, a single tear rolling down his cheek. "X told all of us."

Ellla glanced at me and Parker. We both nodded and confirmed what Dad was saying.

"So, that's it? Now we're supposed to all go off and be one happy family?" Ellla asked. "Because a lot of stuff has happened."

Dad reached over and held out his open hand. "I just want a chance to make it up to you." He looked at me and stretched out his other hand. "To both of you."

I reached over and took Dad's hand. Ellla hesitated, but then followed my lead, just as one of the suited men knocked on the helicopter door.

"Family in the making," I said, squeezing Dad's hand.

While Dad was being told that Mom was fine and that X would be back in about fifteen minutes, Parker leaned closer to me and Ellla. "Um, anyone in this 'family-in-the-making' interested in having a pseudo-brother?" He had his goofy, lopsided smile, but I knew there was something serious behind it. "Don't think I have any place to go and I'm pretty sure X doesn't want a partner."

Ellla smiled. "We'll figure something out."

"I think you're stuck with us for a while," I gave him a little nudge. "Plus, you have to help us with our online show."

"It'll be much nicer to be under the media's microscope rather than a real one," Ellla mused.

For a moment my thoughts drifted to what the world would soon discover . . . the secret of who or what Ellla and I were. I still wasn't completely sure if I even knew how to answer that question, but at least I wouldn't have to answer it alone.

I now had a sister and a best friend, and that was more than I'd ever had before.

CHAPTER 34

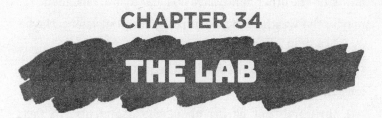

THE LAB

I STARED AT THE screen, waiting for the clock to hit ten and for the preprogrammed cameras to turn on. It had been a few weeks since a new kind of reality show had captured the attention of people all over the world. Ellla and I were the stars of a show about two girls growing up in a world that had never seen anyone or anything quite like them.

The news media had been given select documents that showed how we'd been created, and Sterling's involvement in all the experiments. There were reports that Sterling had gone into hiding, but I suspected that X had pushed him overboard. Either way, no one had seen or heard from him since we left in the helicopter.

"Two minutes until we go live," Parker announced.

"Do I look okay?" Ellla smoothed her recently highlighted hair. "Last time someone made a comment about wanting to know what I did to get it so shiny, so I'm going to talk about that today."

I rolled my eyes. "You look great . . . like always." I wasn't sure how identical twins could be so different. Here I was with my dyed hair growing out and no interest in fashion at all. "I, on the other hand, have no idea what to talk about . . . maybe the weather? It's been really nice out lately. Maybe people will like to hear about island life."

"And your comments will then be just as borrrring!" Ella teased.

I shrugged, not caring about the comments. In fact, Parker had been forced to set up filters and blocks to keep out a lot of the weird and hurtful remarks we'd gotten during those first few days. We'd seen everything ranging from people calling us some sort of superhumans who would save humankind to others who viewed us as medical freaks who would destroy all of humanity. But somehow, we'd now fallen into a space where most people just wanted to watch and see how we would "evolve." It all felt a little ridiculous, being under the world's microscope, but it was the only way we would be safe from the Sterling types who might want to hurt or use us. Our viewers kept us protected to a certain degree . . . the men X had hired did the rest.

"I have a better idea." Ella pointed her perfectly manicured nail from Parker to me. "You've got to give the people what they want. Tell them about you and Parker."

"Nothing to tell," I said for the thousandth time. "We're friends . . . that's it."

"Uh-huh."

"It's true," Parker said. "You just want to juice things up for the audience, but you don't need to. You have over ten million followers watching and promising to keep tabs on you two." He checked the feed on his brand-new laptop. "Plus, starting tomorrow, I'll be a loyal viewer, too."

Ellla gave him a big smile, having become friends with him over the last couple of weeks. "Well, you better still come and visit us. New Jersey isn't on the other side of the world."

The idea of Parker having to go back into foster care wasn't very appealing to any of us, but there weren't many other choices. Plus, X had pulled some strings to get him into a boarding school for computer whizzes in the fall.

"Yeah, I guess." Parker didn't sound convinced. "My dad's cousin seems pretty nice . . . on the phone, at least. She also likes that I come with my own bank account."

I pulled Parker aside. "You sure about leaving?" I whispered. "I can talk to my parents. They'd let you stay."

"I'm not in danger anymore," he said. "And as nice as this place is, I still want to be able to go out and do stuff." He sighed, realizing that wasn't an option for me . . . at least not yet. "Eventually, you'll get to do that, too. And by then I can show you all the best places in Newark."

"Sure," I answered, realizing he was now the one doing the cheering up instead of the other way around.

"Well, take this." I slipped him the pineapple flash drive. "There's still a lot on there that we don't know . . . that X may not want us to know. Information is the biggest weapon I have in all of this."

"Once I get out of here, I'll start working on it." He smiled. "A hacker's gotta hack, you know?"

"You better keep me posted on whatever you find," I said.

"We're starting!" Ellla said, fluffing up her hair in front of the camera.

I rushed to where she was standing in front of a tripod with a computer tablet pointed at us so we could see ourselves and the comments coming in. The light turned green, indicating that we were now streaming live around the world.

"Hi, everyone!" Ellla smiled at the camera. "Welcome to your daily check-in with your favorite, not-quite-normal friends who you're keeping safe just by tuning in. I'm Ellla Grace . . ."

I waved. "And I'm Katrina."

Then the two us got close together, and squeezed each other's hands like we'd done at the beginning of each show. "And this . . . is *The Lab*."

AUTHOR'S NOTE

As an author I'm often asked, *Where do you get your ideas?* The truth is that they can come from anywhere. Some of my stories have been inspired by historical events, art, movies, dreams, and, in the case of *Concealed*, science. The key is to be interested in learning more about the topic and want to discover more about it.

For this book, it all started when I stumbled upon a news story about a Chinese scientist who used CRISPR technology to modify human DNA, resulting in the birth of twin girls. I had always thought that altered DNA was the stuff of science fiction, and now I was curious to learn more about this real-world scientific breakthrough. I read about how CRISPR technology is effectively used in agricultural, medical, and diagnostic settings and how it still poses serious ethical concerns when it comes to altering human DNA. Everything I discovered added a new layer to the story that had begun to form in my imagination about a girl whose identity is unknown . . . even to herself.

And so, now that you know how I find my ideas, the question becomes *What will inspire* you *to discover and learn something new?*

ACKNOWLEDGMENTS

Thank you to my family and friends for always being supportive of me in all my endeavors . . . writing and otherwise. I am blessed to have you in my life.

I also count my lucky stars to have some of the very best in the publishing world in my corner. Talented writers and good friends Danielle Joseph and James Ponti provided feedback and brainstorming sessions that helped me develop this story. Jen Rofé, agent extraordinaire, championed the book from the inception and made sure I always stayed on track. My fabulous editors, Emily Seife and David Levithan, provided guidance and suggestions to take this story to new heights . . . even during the midst of a pandemic. The Scholastic dream teams in copyediting, design, marketing, fairs, clubs, and sales showcased why they are some of the best in the business and ensured that this book would reach readers. For this collaborative effort, I am greatly appreciative.

A big thank-you also goes to all the parents, teachers, librarians, and media specialists who use books to connect readers to one another. In my book, you are all rock stars!

Finally, to the readers . . . the biggest THANK YOU! Whoever you are, wherever you are, know that it is for you that I write these books.

ABOUT THE AUTHOR

Christina Diaz Gonzalez is the award-winning author of several books, including *The Red Umbrella*, *A Thunderous Whisper*, *Moving Target*, *Return Fire*, and *Stormspeaker* (part of the Spirit Animals: Fall of the Beasts series). She lives in Florida with her husband, her sons, and a dog that can open doors. Learn more at www.christinagonzalez.com.